CRUELTY HAS A HUMAN HEART

A DCI Will Blake Novel

J E Mayhew

Obolus Books

ISBN-13: 978-1-9998407-7-8

Cover design by: Meg Cowley

For Mike Wright

Although the story is set on the Wirral, the names of some establishments and roads have been fictionalised to protect the unloved and godless... but you can have fun guessing...

Cruelty has a Human Heart
And Jealousy a Human Face

WILLIAM BLAKE

CHAPTER 1

Sam Percival knew the moment to get out of this place had arrived when she saw that the paper knife was in just the right place. It looked expensive and sharp with its leather handle and thin silver blade and she'd been waiting for it to be left on her side of Doctor Gillespie's desk. It matched the office in which she sat, wood panelled, sound muffled by thick carpets and heavy curtains. The letter opener was just the sort she would expect Gillespie to own. The doctor was a small but very well-kept man in his sixties. He wore a green tweed suit, horn-rimmed glasses and had a thick head of hair that he spiked up. Sam was pretty sure it was dyed brown, too. He looked like a member of a geriatric eighties boy band. And who uses a paper knife, these days?

Gillespie leaned back in his chair and steepled his fingers over his chest. "So, tell me, Samantha, how have you been getting on?"

Sam tensed. She hated anyone using her full name; Paul did that, spitting out the syllables like they left a bad taste in his mouth. At that moment, she could have snatched up the letter opener and plunged it into Gillespie's smug face. He was such a condescending prick. Instead she wobbled her head from side to side. "Oh, you know, up and down," she said and noticed Gillespie's brow crease. "But much better. Certainly improved…"

"No more dark thoughts?" Gillespie said, leaning forward. "And how do you feel about your husband?"

Sam shrugged. "He only wants the best for me, I guess," she lied. "I'm not pretending it'll be easy, settling back in, but I know he did what he thought best for me." The words almost stuck in her throat, but she knew it was what Gillespie wanted to hear.

"Why won't it be easy?"

"Well, you know," Sam said, blinking at Doctor Gillespie. "Being locked up here for months, not seeing my daughter. I mean, it's hard to forget that he imposed these things on me…"

"Nobody is holding you here. You know you're perfectly at liberty to leave whenever you want, Samantha."

Sam craned her neck over Gillespie's shoulder to look out of the leaded window across the immaculate lawns. "So you'd give me a key to that big iron gate, a lift across miles of cold moorland to the station and tell me to be back in time for tea?"

Gillespie smirked. "If you felt strong enough to

leave then you would. You know nobody would stop you."

"Then I feel strong enough to leave, Doctor Gillespie," Sam said. "Can I go and pack my bags?"

The smirk disappeared. "Of course," he said, his face clouding over. "Let me just make a few phone calls first."

"Go ahead then," Sam said, folding her arms.

Gillespie paused, his hand hovering over the phone on his desk. "If you could just wait outside…"

"I'm sure you wouldn't say anything about me to my husband that you wouldn't say to my face."

"Now look, Samantha…" Gillespie began, leaning forward and splaying his hands out on the desk. Sam saw her chance. She snatched up the sharp, pointed letter opener and slammed it down on Gillespie's outstretched hand with all her might. The impact jarred her arm up to the shoulder and blood splattered on her cheek. Gillespie gasped, his mouth opening and closing in a silent scream, like a landed fish. He stared in stunned silence at the paper knife that now protruded from the back of his hand, pinning it to the desktop. Sam dashed around the other side of the desk and yanked his silk tie off. He groaned as she pulled his good arm behind his back and tied it to the chair. Then she rummaged in his jacket pocket pulling out his car keys.

"You never had any intention of letting me walk out of here, Gillespie," she hissed at him. "Your job is to keep me here for as long as you can."

Gillespie had slumped back in his seat, shocked and pale. "My hand..."

"It'll heal. Stop your whining," Sam snapped. "And don't worry, I'll look after your precious car, but I'm not stopping another second in this place. Be seeing you."

And with that, Sam Percival stalked out of the room, locking the office door behind her for good measure. She was free at last. Free to go back to the Wirral and see her darling daughter. Free to go and see Paul and finish things once and for all.

*****

He hovered near the playground. The empty swings rocked in the breeze. The children were at school. Thank goodness. He knew he really shouldn't have been there, but this was where she would be. This was where he'd seen her on the same day, same time every week for at least a month now. His heart thumped with excitement. He thought of the pictures he'd taken of her and shivered. It was a bad thing to do but he'd also managed to work out where she lived just from the background in some of the photographs of her. He'd spent a while hanging around her house, hoping to catch a glimpse of her, but then he'd thought that might be a bit creepy and he didn't want to spoil things. She was small, cute and more than he'd ever hoped for. He could hardly believe it. He could hardly wait, either.

A shiver of anticipation ran through him as he imagined how the morning might stretch out. Licking his lips in anticipation, he scanned the park. It wouldn't be long now and she would be his. All his.

CHAPTER 2

They were in big trouble. Aiden knew this before anything else happened. They should have been in school, answering to their names when the teacher called them out. Instead, they huddled from the soft November drizzle under a tree, passing a badly rolled joint between them. Birkenhead Park was quiet; the rain or the need to get to work having emptied it of dog walkers. This was a big park with a lake, a Japanese garden and acres of playing fields, trees and bushes; a great place to get lost. Someone had once told Aiden that New York's Central Park was modelled on it, but Aiden found that hard to believe. It looked so ordinary to him and dreary in the grey morning. He shivered at the cold and looked covetously at the smouldering spliff hogged by his mate, Olly.

They were going to be found out. Aiden could see that now; what seemed like a fool proof plan at first was now so full of holes that he couldn't see why he thought they'd ever get away with it. It was Olly, though, who always persuaded him. Olly with his look of incredulity at any suggestion of failure. His big round face set in a permanent state of bewilderment at the notion

6

that anyone should question where they were or what they were doing. The same look he wore every time they got caught. Aiden wondered why he fell for it so often.

"It'll be fine," Olly said, and took a long drag on the joint. He held the smoke in his lungs for a while then spoke as he let it out. "It's assembly, now. Mr Carter goes on for ages anyway. We'll just swear blind we were in there and Miss Donaldson didn't see us. She's blind as a bat anyway." Olly passed Aiden the joint and crossed his eyes. "Aiden Murphy, are you there?" he said in a terrible impression of a Scottish accent. "I know it was you who farted just then!"

Aiden gave a feeble smile and tried to get a final drag from the smouldering stump between his fingertips. The weed was making him jittery and anxious. He wondered why he smoked anyway. "And when they ask us what the assembly was about, what will we say?"

Olly shrugged. "Frogger will fill us in on what was said, stop worrying."

Aiden's phone buzzed and he swore at the screen. Several times. Loudly. "I don't think he will." He held up the phone to show Olly the text from Frogger.

Where R U? Fire alarm in middle of assembly. Yre fckd.

Olly's eyes widened and the blood drained

from his cheeks.

"What're we going to do?" Aiden said. "We'd better get back."

That was when they heard the man screaming. Aiden had heard kids in school yelling and shouts of anger and frustration at Tranmere Rovers matches, but never had a voice had so much fear and desperation in it. It sounded like a name being called over and over again; 'Flossy' or something like that. It was hard to tell as the voice was so guttural and loaded with emotion.

"What the f.." Olly muttered and crept from the cover of the trees. Aiden followed, hypnotised by the howls of anguish.

A man in a black duffle coat and jeans ran back and forth around a deserted playground bellowing the name again and again. He looked as if he kept changing his mind about what he should do or which direction he should run. Aiden flinched when the man looked in their direction.

"Lads! Have you seen a little girl?" the man said, hurrying towards them. "About three, wearing a red anorak, yellow dress and blue wellies?"

Aiden shrugged and Olly shook his head. "No, sorry, mate. She didn't come past here," Olly said.

The man's eyes were red and puffy, he smacked the palms of his hands to the side of his head.

"Where is she?"

"Do you think you should call the police?" Aiden said.

Olly dug him in the ribs. "Behave. He doesn't need the bizzies. Anyway, mister, we're late for school. Hope you find her..."

Aiden nodded, turned and walked straight into a police officer. "Probably worth sticking around lads," she said, with a smile.

CHAPTER 3

DCI Will Blake really needed to get to work but he had unfinished business in the shape of a large Persian cat called Serafina. He looked up at the top of the pine Welsh dresser, another throwback to the seventies, courtesy of his deceased mother. Blake veered between loving the old house and wanting to burn it to the ground. Or, more likely, sell it. Serafina was intimately entangled in this complex relationship. But, for once, it wasn't the cat he had a problem with, it was the reason she was balanced at the top of the dresser, threatening to send half a dozen dusty Country Heritage plates crashing to the ground.

The reason crouched at Blake's feet, wagging its tiny tail and yapping excitedly up at the indignant cat. "It's just for a week," Laura said, squeezing Blake's arm. "I wouldn't have agreed but she was in a proper fix."

"Who the hell gets a puppy and then goes away for a week's holiday?"

"She didn't realise that the cottage they hired had a no pets policy and besides Chelsea isn't really on holiday, she's visiting her sick mum."

"Sick mum?" Blake snorted. "She hired a cottage to go and visit her sick mum? You're a sucker, Laura Vexley, do you know that? The truth is your mate Chelsea thinks it's okay to just buy a little scrap like that and then beggar off, leaving her mates to clean up the mess."

Laura pulled a face. "That's a bit harsh." She scooped up the little Jack Russell puppy and nuzzled the back of its head. "Anyway, Charlie's cute, aren't you Charlie boy? Yus, yus, yus, you are!"

Blake rolled his eyes and shook his head. Charlie wriggled and squirmed in excitement until a yellow stream flew across the kitchen splattering at Blake's feet and almost sending him up to the top of the dresser with Serafina.

"That's it," Blake said. "I'm going to work. You're the animal expert. I want my cat purring happily on her armchair and not a hint of dog in this house when I come in tonight."

"Ooh, get you, Mr bossy boots," Laura said, trying to keep a straight face. "Don't panic. I'll work something out."

Blake looked up at Serafina who hissed at him. "Don't blame me," he said before stalking out of the house. She should know better, he thought. Bringing a puppy into the house with a psychotic cat like Serafina was irresponsible. Why was it that Laura seemed to run rings around him? She was good for him, there was no doubt but every now and then, she'd ride roughshod over him with barely a thought.

*****

Blake's first port of call was a short drive from his house but it was a call he wished he wasn't making. He scanned the green expanse of Birkenhead Park. In the distance, rooftops poked above the copper-leaved trees that fringed the edges of the space. Space. That was what troubled him at the moment. Space and distance. Something else darkened his mood but he wasn't going to think about that. It was in the past and he would keep it there for now. He ignored the swirling well of anxiety that sat in the pit of his stomach. He could deal with that later. Right now a little girl had gone missing and they needed to find her fast.

He turned to DC Kinnear "So where are the child's parents?"

"The father is away at a conference and I haven't quite got to the bottom of where the mother is. They have a nanny looking after the girl."

"Jeez, who has a nanny these days, Andrew? Especially round here."

Kinnear grinned. "I know, sir." He was a smaller man than Blake and struggling with his weight. His face was puckered into a mischievous-looking smirk which made him seem flippant, but Blake knew that the opposite was true. "The nanny is in the house." He indicated to the huge villa that stood behind them. "Apparently the girl was there one minute and gone the next."

Blake and Kinnear stood at the bottom of a long garden which accessed the park through a heavy gate. Some of the houses that edged the park were small, ordinary semis and modern detached properties. But some hailed from the grand days of the park when it first opened. Then the wealthy merchants of Liverpool wanted a little bit of paradise away from the clamour of the docklands and the city's seething streets. They built villas around the edge of the fashionable park so that they could take the air with their families. When the trade and wealth abandoned Liverpool, the houses fell into disrepair and the park became something of a no-go area. Since then, it had been reclaimed and was fashionable once again. Many of those grand villas had been split into flats and bedsits but a few remained intact; owned by wealthy individuals or passed on through inheritance.

"Come on," Blake said, leading the way through the well-kept back garden towards the house. "Let's go and see this nanny, then."

A conservatory with huge bi-fold doors sat at the back of the house. Inside, a young man huddled in an armchair, cradling a mug of coffee. He was slight, with a straggly beard and his long brown hair tied in a bun. He wore a denim shirt and faded brown chinos. DC Tasha Cook, family liaison officer, sat in a chair next to him. Blake stepped inside relishing the sudden explosion of warmth that this suntrap provided. He nodded to his colleague. "Hi, Tasha. I'm looking for the nanny?"

The young man looked up from his steaming mug. "That's me," he said. "I'm Brendan Dockley. I look after Flossy."

Blake raised an eyebrow. "I'm DCI Blake. I'm sorry, I'd just assumed..."

"That the nanny would be a woman," Dockley said. His eyes were rimmed with red and he sniffed heavily. "It's all right. I'm used to it. There aren't many men doing what I do. Has there been any news?"

Blake shook his head. "No, I'm sorry. We're assembling search teams already and notifying local media outlets. We need to contact immediate family, of course. Has there been any progress?"

Tasha pursed her lips and shook her head. "Florence's father has his mobile switched off. He told Brendan that he was at a conference in Peterborough but the hotel he was meant to be staying at knows nothing about him or the event. We've contacted her grandparents who live nearby and are coming round immediately."

"And the girl's mother?"

"She's in some kind of clinic up in Scotland," Dockley said. "The Pines, it's called. Rehab sort of thing, I think. She's been there a while. Paul, Florence's father, didn't say much about her. The only thing I was told was that she couldn't have unaccompanied access. That she was a danger to herself and to Flossy."

"We're contacting the clinic's manager to assess whether or not Mrs Percival has the capacity to receive the news," Tasha said.

Blake looked up at a photo portrait of two adults and a child. They made a handsome trio. The woman was slim and limber, with thick conker-coloured hair and deep brown eyes. The man was so well-groomed, he looked like a model. His square jawline added to the almost fabricated perfection. Blake wondered briefly if their flawless skin had been photoshopped. The little girl had dark hair, remarkably long and thick for one so young. She took after her mother and had a fierce smile that he took to be the best they could coax out of her.

"Is this them?" Blake muttered.

"Paul and Samantha Percival and Florence," Tasha said.

Blake nodded. "Right. Mr Dockley, can you go through the moment you realised she was missing for me. I know you've probably been through this several times, but it helps to clarify things in my mind."

Dockley sighed but nodded. "Paul, Florence's father, had left on Friday for the conference, or wherever he's gone. So I had Flossy all weekend. It was rotten weather and, to be honest, she was getting a bit bored of being in the house. So I promised her we'd go and feed the ducks this morning. I dressed her, she had breakfast. I brushed her teeth and we set off." Dockley blinked and his eyes glistened. "We stopped next to the trees by Ashville Road..."

"That's the road that cuts through the park..."

"Yes. I only took my eyes off her for a couple of seconds and when I looked up, she was gone. At first, I thought she was hiding in the bushes. I ran out onto the road, nearly got run over. But I couldn't see her anywhere."

"What was it that distracted you so much?"

Dockley reddened and looked down into his coffee. "My stupid, bloody phone. It was something and nothing, really. A video about... God, I don't know what. One of those crap things about someone getting bullied and then getting revenge years later. It wasn't even..." He looked up. "I feel so awful..."

Blake held his breath, trying to figure out if anything that came out of his mouth at that moment would be considered professional or non-judgemental.

16

"You're only human, Brendan," Tasha Cook said, glancing a warning shot at Blake. "Everyone has lapses in concentration from time to time. Blaming yourself won't help us find Florence, now, will it?"

Dockley nodded and scrubbed at his eyes with the back of his hand. "Yes, I'm sorry."

"So you were on the footpath by the gates or on Park Drive itself, Mr Dockley?" Blake said, deciding to keep to questioning rather than lapsing into a commentary about Dockley's fitness to care for small children. Park Drive was the road that ran around the edge of the park, defining its boundary. The footpaths crisscrossed the open spaces of the park.

"On the footpath, why?"

"It just seems quite far away from the gates for a small child to run. How old is Florence? Three?"

"She was three last month."

"She covered a lot of distance getting from the footpath, across the grass, onto Park Drive and out through the gate. For a small child, I mean."

Dockley shrugged and smiled, sadly. "She's a fast kid. Honestly, the number of times recently, she's seen something and took off…"

"And yet you still felt compelled to look at your phone." The words were out of Blake's mouth before he could stop them. Tasha Cook's jaw tightened.

Dockley looked as though Blake had slapped him in the face. "I'm sorry," he said, shrinking in his seat.

"We're going to have to search the house as well as the park," Blake said, brusquely. He was tired of pussyfooting around this young man already, tired of the uncertainty and the thought of the search that lay ahead and all it might unveil.

"Why do you have to search the house?" Dockley said, staring in shock at Blake.

Tasha Cook intervened again, smoothly. "Sometimes missing children have been known to find their own way home and have been found cheerfully playing in their bedrooms on their own while officers and parents are out in the streets hunting frantically."

"Adults have deliberately hidden children in their care for other reasons. You might remember the faked abduction of Shannon Matthews a few years back..." Dockley blinked and shook his head. Blake continued, "I don't suppose you would. You probably weren't much older than Shannon was when her mother told the world she'd gone missing when she hadn't."

"I'm not lying," Dockley said, staring at Blake in disbelief.

"DCI Blake isn't suggesting that," Tasha Cook said. "But we do have to check every possibility. I'm sure you understand…"

Blake jumped to his feet. "Right. I'm assuming a picture of Florence and a sample of her DNA have been obtained. Kinnear, we need to get that physical search of the park moving. Do you mind if I have a look round, Mr Dockley?"

Dockley looked around as though someone other than the officers might be listening in. "I don't know. I mean it's not really my house. Paul is quite private…"

"Private to the extent that he'd hamper the search for his missing daughter?" Blake snapped. Feelings from the past were closing in on him and fanning the flames of hostility towards the young nanny. "You can accompany me if you feel the need…"

"It's okay," Dockley said, waving his hand, feebly. "Have a look around if you think it'll help."

"Thank you," Blake began to say but Tasha Cook's phone rang.

She looked concerned as she listened. "That was the clinic. Apparently, Samantha Percival assaulted a senior psychiatrist there yesterday and left in a stolen car. They suspect she might be heading for the Wirral…"

"If she isn't already here," Blake said, turning to Dockley. "Just how much of a danger is she to Florence?"

CHAPTER 4

Jeffrey Blake stood in the gents' toilet and wondered why he was straightening his hair in front of the mirror. It wasn't like he had a hot date. He was visiting a psychopathic serial killer. Josh Gambles had been jailed for murdering and mutilating at least four people and kidnapping another. Or at least he was awaiting trial, such that it would be. The evidence against him was damning. His DNA was spread across all crime scenes and he'd more or less confessed to several police officers and witnesses. But there was something about Gambles, something slippery and scheming. Jeffrey told himself he was tidying himself up out of self-respect because that was better than fear. Jeffrey couldn't afford to fear him. If he feared Gambles, then he had won. Jeff had to watch him and be on his guard. That way he was less likely to let Gambles get under his skin. After all, this was the man who, if he hadn't killed her, had watched Jeff's mother die and then had stolen her body. He'd kept it in a cellar for two years. Jeff felt his anger towards the man building.

"Calm yourself, Jeffrey," he muttered to himself, assessing his reflection. Every inch the author: tweed jacket, brown cords, thick glasses, swept back silvery hair, a matching goatee. Although Jeff's inner critic hissed 'Geography teacher' at him. He knew he wasn't bad looking, but he took after his mother with her fine, delicate features. His brother Will's appearance owed more to their father's heavy, pugnacious frame. Someone had once made the unkind observation that Jeff was what Will would look like if he'd been starved as a child.

It didn't help that Gambles was obsessed with Jeff's brother. That was probably the only reason Jeff had been asked to write Gamble's biography. Gambles saw himself and Will as two sides of the same coin, good and evil. Will had washed his hands of Gambles but that didn't stop the psycho from trying to foul up Will's life even from behind bars. Working with Jeff meant that Gambles could be close to the Blake family and be a thorn in Will's side. Jeff knew he was a great writer but had never had the breaks. His work had never got the attention it deserved but this stunt would grab headlines for sure. The writer and criminal were linked. Jeff could mine that emotional well for years and make a fortune from it. Will would huff and puff about it but if Jeff didn't write the Gambles story, somebody else would.

He entered the visiting room and saw Gambles sitting at the table, waiting for him. He was a small, dark character with a scrawny black beard. It always disturbed Jeff that the man wasn't cuffed in any way. He couldn't escape the whole Hannibal Lecter vibe of the situation.

"Jeffrey," Gambles said. "So glad you could make it. What are we going to talk about today?"

"Morning Josh," Jeff said, sitting down, trying to be casual. "I thought we could focus on childhood memories." Gambles' face darkened but Jeff managed to add, "not family-related but other incidents or observations. When you first realised you were… different…" He knew that Gambles hated any mention of his parents, though writing any kind of biography without bringing them in was a difficult job. Secretly, Jeff fully intended to include as much detail about Gambles' early life as possible.

The killer's face brightened. "Of course. There were what you might call 'lightbulb moments' when I realised that I was superior to my peers. In school, I remember a young arsehole trying to bully me. I can't remember his name; he was a nobody. But for a while, he made my life intolerable. I knew I had to stop him."

"So what did you do?"

"I knew he was allergic to wasp stings. So I collected a jar full of wasps and let them loose in his PE Kit bag. Then I stole his Epipen. You know those devices that inject adrenaline to ward off

Anaphylaxis? It was joyous to see."

"And you managed to do all that without being seen or caught?"

"Don't you believe me Jeffrey? That is disappointing. It was in the local papers. I'm sure if you do a bit of crosschecking, you'll see. It caused a bit of a stir at the time. The boy nearly died, and his teacher got the sack. I didn't like her anyway. Win, win as far as I was concerned."

Jeff scribbled a few notes down. "Thanks, that'll be great if I can find a few news reports to give it context."

Gambles reached to the side of his chair and put a sheaf of papers on the table. "I've taken the liberty of writing a few notes down of other memories. The powers that be have scrutinised them and said it's okay for you to take them out. It's just some random thoughts, suggestions and maybe some openings for you to use. I mean, I know you're the writer. Just thought it might help..."

Jeff leafed through the papers and kept his face poker flat as he read the garbled sentences. "Thanks, Josh. This will be really handy. Kyle Quinlan. Who's he?"

Gambles raised his eyebrows. "You don't know?"

"No," Jeff said, wondering what Gambles was

up to. "Should I?"

"He's an old friend of mine. We were in prison a few times together. Thick as thieves we were, if you'll pardon the cliche." Gambles' face split into a malicious grin. "He's also the ex-husband of your brother's current squeeze, Laura Vexley."

"Really?" Jeff said. "She didn't mention it. Does Will know?"

"Of course he does. Hardly surprising that they don't mention it. Kyle's gone missing. Laura was the last person to see him. There's a police investigation. It'll probably get covered up. You know what these coppers are like; one rule for them and one for us."

"Right. So what do you want me to do with this information?"

"Find Kyle Quinlan or at least find out what happened to him. It'll make an interesting chapter or two."

"But the police…"

"The police won't find him. The case is on a back burner somewhere and, as I said, your brother will do his best to stop anything coming out. Besides, they've got much more to worry about than a missing criminal. But I reckon you could find him easily with a bit of focus."

"I'm not sure. I mean what does this have to do with you and your life?"

"Kyle Quinlan was a friend. He saved my skin in prison on several occasions. There are many stories from our times together that would make great material, Jeffrey. But we need to find out what became of him."

"Will's not going to like this…"

Gambles smiled. "Will needs to accept that our lives are enmeshed, however much he wants to pretend that he is separate from me. There are invisible threads pulling us together. Our pasts are so interconnected it's not funny. So find Kyle Quinlan. It'll make a great chapter in the book."

"I wouldn't know where to start…"

"There are names and addresses there in my notes. His sister might be a good place to start. She's expecting you. I spoke to her on the phone yesterday."

"Okay," Jeff said, cautiously. "But if this is just another way to wind Will up, I'll close it down, Josh. I'm prepared to write your biography because I think our family dynamic will make it a fascinating piece of work but I'm not playing any of your games."

Gambles held up his hands. "Absolutely. It's not a wild goose chase and, trust me, I'm sure Kyle Quinlan will add a whole new layer to this story."

*****

The house lay empty and silent apart from the yapping of Charlie, the puppy, and the rumbling growl of Serafina from the top of the Welsh Dresser. Laura shivered. She wasn't sure why she always gravitated to Will's house when she wasn't working. It was cold and, despite Will's recent efforts to make it more homely, it still felt like a memorial to his parents. The décor and furniture hadn't changed in at least twenty years and screamed 'elderly couple in the twilight of their lives.' Photographs of Will, Jeff and Rosie, their sister, still sat on the shelves. Who has a picture of themselves in year 11 on display?

Laura had tried to get him to redecorate. He'd got an estate agent in to value the property, but Blake threw himself into case after case and things hadn't progressed. She knew that Jeff was pushing for his share of the house since their missing mother's body had been found and she was confirmed as dead. Will seemed to alternate between sticking his head in the sand and wanting to sell up and move on.

Charlie snuffled around her feet and she picked him up. "Come on fella," she said. "Let's go in the garden." Laura wondered when she was going to break the news to him about Chelsea and Charlie. Probably not for a few days. There was plenty of room here and Serafina would get used to the little dog.

It was cold outside, and the sun struggled to penetrate the thick grey clouds that hung over the Mersey. She loved being on the side of the river with its views and the cry of gulls. The rain in the air had crystallised the view making it easy to pick out the detail of the houses and trees on the Liverpool side of the water. The dog did its business and Laura poured praise and rewards on him. Then she froze.

A black car rolled past the front of the garden and the driver leaned forward as if to get a better look at Laura. He was just a silhouette in the driver seat, but there was something familiar about him. Something that chilled Laura to her core. Snatching up Charlie and hugging him to her chest, she ran inside and slammed the door shut.

CHAPTER 5

Before Brendan Dockley could answer Blake's question, a commotion further inside the house distracted them all. The front door rattled and banged open and urgent footsteps clattered up the hall towards them.

A thin old man appeared in the conservatory. He was tall and well-kept; a mane of silver hair was combed back over his head, giving him a theatrical appearance. His black corduroy jacket and red chinos suggested to Blake a certain vanity. The man moved with the air of someone who was used to being paid attention to, stepping into the centre of the room as if he was about to give a speech.

"Where is she? Where's Flossy?"

"DCI Will Blake and you are?"

"Roland Percival, Flossy's grandfather. Have you found her?" His voice was plummy and melodramatic.

"Not yet, I'm afraid. We're organising a search…"

Red spots glowed on Percival's pale cheeks. "You should be out there now. Time's wasting!

She could be anywhere. God!" He threw himself into one of the armchairs and then stared up at Dockley. "And you. How could you lose her like that? Honestly, what does my son pay you for if it isn't to look after our little girl?" Roland Percival buried his face in his hands and wept.

Dockley reddened and shrank even more into his chair. Blake felt no pity for him, though. Percival was right. How could you let a poor little girl just wander off? He felt the weight of emotion returning and pulled himself back to the case. "Officers are gathering to search the immediate area as we speak, Mr Percival. We were just about to have a look around the house. Sometimes, children find their way home without the knowledge of their parents."

Percival scowled, suggesting he wondered why all these things hadn't been done already. "Very well."

Blake nodded to Tasha and Kinnear who slipped away into the house. "Can you tell me about Mrs Percival?" Blake asked the old man.

"My wife? What's she got to do with this?" Roland Percival said, looking confused. "She's at home. Very upset as you can imagine. The sooner we find Flossy, the better."

Blake pinched the bridge of his nose, trying to hide his frustration. "No, I'm sorry, I meant Samantha, Florence's mother. What is the nature of her illness?"

"What's that got to do with anything. She's safely locked away up in Scotland," Percival paused and searched Blake's face. "Isn't she?"

"She assaulted a member of staff and stole a car. We don't know where she is."

Percival's eyes widened. "Oh my goodness," he whispered. "That isn't good at all…"

"Mr Percival, I understand that you're anxious about your granddaughter right now, but we are doing all we can. A couple of hours ago, we had no knowledge of you or your family situation. We'll do our level best to get Florence back safe and sound. That I promise."

"Of course," Percival said, breathing out slowly. "Forgive me, I didn't mean to berate you. It's just that she's such a trusting little child. If anything happened, I'd never forgive myself."

"So, can you tell me a little about Samantha?"

"Yes. I was never sure quite how she snared Paul. I mean she was pretty enough, but she had none of the social graces that he had. She came from a different circle entirely…"

"A different circle?"

"Socially. Paul is a merchant banker, we sent him to a good school. Samantha's family are from the North End of Birkenhead, shop workers with no education. She only had to open her mouth at the golf club, and everyone knew she didn't belong there."

"I see," Blake said, suppressing his distaste at Percival's snobbery. "So Samantha never fitted in with Paul's friends?"

"There was something odd about her from the start but, we didn't find out until later."

"Find out what?"

"She had epilepsy, Mr Blake. She kept it quiet from Paul and all of us. I mean it was controlled by medication but to keep that quiet…"

Blake shrugged. Percival's lack of care towards his daughter-in-law was beginning to grate. "Some might say that it was none of your business, Mr Percival and how does that have any bearing on her personality?"

"Well, it didn't until she found out she was pregnant and came off her medication. The absence seizures became very apparent. She would stare off into space as if she was in another world. It was so embarrassing."

"Embarrassing? Forgive me, Mr Percival, but that strikes me as a harsh judgement. I'd imagine Samantha found it more distressing."

"She never realised until we told her later," Percival snorted. "She went back on the medication when Flossy was born but apparently these things are finely balanced and whatever caused her absences was hard to control."

"So she went to this clinic to get her seizures back under control?"

"Oh it got much worse than that, Mr Blake. We could put up with her condition, but she became moody and depressed. Couldn't handle the baby. Paul found her having an absence whilst bathing the poor mite. Florence could have drowned. We suspected that she was hurting Florence, too. There were bruises and cuts she couldn't explain."

"Did you contact Social Services?"

"No. Of course we didn't. Paul didn't want social workers traipsing in and out of the house telling him what to do. We tried a succession of nannies to assist Samantha, but she became obsessed with the idea that they were sleeping with Paul. There was no reasoning with her. She became hysterical. It became untenable. Finally, Paul persuaded her to check herself into The Pines Clinic."

"You didn't consult your local GP first?"

"The clinicians at The Pines are the best money can buy, Paul found the place himself." Roland Percival looked darkly at Blake. "Quite how she's got out, I don't know."

"Do you think she'll come back here?"

"She's a Wirral girl, Mr Blake. Where else would

she go? This is where her family are. And her child."

"And if Samantha has got Florence?"

"Then I genuinely fear for Flossy's safety. She's unhinged, God knows what she is capable of. Time is running out for her."

*****

He sat alone in the bedroom with his head in his hands. It had been even better than the last time. The real thing. Not one of his twisted fantasies. So why did he feel so guilty? It was perfectly natural. There are those who would say it was immoral, but they were trapped in the dark ages. It had been fun at first. They were both laughing and playing. But then it had all gone wrong.

Suddenly she hadn't liked it. Wanted it to stop but it was too late for that. He was already on his way, so to speak. Now she was gone. And she wasn't coming back.

Tears coursed down his cheeks, even as his heart thumped at the memory of what had just happened. What was he going to do?

CHAPTER 6

Bodies crammed the Major Incident Room. Blake felt the usual tumble of nerves in his gut. He could cope with most things, but a missing child was his worst nightmare. He wanted to find Flossy Percival right away. There were systems in place to make searches more efficient and likely to succeed but galvanising large groups into action felt like wading through treacle.

DC Andrew Kinnear sat in his usual seat alongside DI Kath Cryer. Kath was a large bubbly woman with a voice that set Blake's teeth on edge, but she had a sharp mind and Blake valued her incisive observations. DS Vikki Chinn leaned against a wall close by and DC Alex Manikas stood next to her, silent and watchful as ever. The rest of the group consisted of detectives and uniformed officers all chatting and checking through papers. This was a big operation and could go national if Samantha Percival had taken Florence out of the area. If it *was* the mother who had taken the little girl and not some random child abductor. Blake shuddered at the thought. He would need every officer on this case and time was against them.

"Okay people, listen up," Blake said, clapping his hands. As ever he immediately felt ridiculous doing that, as if he was a primary school teacher bringing a class to order. Nobody else seemed to worry and the room settled down. "Three-year-old Florence Percival went missing earlier this morning in Birkenhead Park. Her nanny, Brendan Dockley got a bit too involved with his phone and when he looked up, the girl had vanished."

"Any witnesses, sir?" DS Vikki Chinn asked.

"Two boys from Birkenhead Park School. Apparently, they were bunking off and saw Dockley running about screaming. Apart from that, nobody seems to have seen anything. Alex, can you and Vikki speak to the two boys, see what you can find out? Also, check any CCTV on Ashville Road and the surrounding area."

Manikas nodded. "Will do."

"We need to put out an appeal, too."

"Local media have been contacted, sir," Kinnear said.

"Are we putting any pressure on this Dockley character?" Kath Cryer asked. "Last one to see her. Just saying."

"Yes, that does merit further investigation, Kath. I think we need to question Dockley further and do a background check on him. We have a team searching the house but I don't think he realises he's a suspect yet. I'm still struggling with the fact that his phone held his attention more than the child did, even though he knew she was prone to running off."

"What about the father, sir?" Manikas said. "Isn't it a bit weird that he's gone off the radar? There's something going on there, surely."

"I know, Alex. I wouldn't normally put a public request for information out before parents are aware but as both of them are AWOL, I don't have any choice. Florence's grandparents are trying to get in touch with Paul Percival. Hopefully he'll surface somewhere soon."

"What about the mother, sir?"

"She assaulted her doctor and stole a white BMW 5 series saloon. The registration is distinctive, D0C 60. Guess who owned the car."

"Classy," Kath Cryer said, sniffing. "I never get personalised registration numbers."

"I think they're cool," Kinnear said.

Kath gave Kinnear a nudge. "You would, soft lad. Waste of money, I reckon." Blake allowed himself a smile. It always surprised him that those two got on, now. They'd been at each other's throats until Kath took a bullet for Kinnear. Since then, they seemed to have a secret code which meant that Cryer could needle Kinnear and give him a hard time or the other way around but nobody else could. Cryer had become quite protective of Kinnear. Apparently, Kath and her boyfriend had even been out on the town with Kinnear and his husband.

"We're searching for the car and Police Scotland are keen to have a word with Samantha about pinning the doctor's hand to a desk with a paper knife. I'm concerned that the mother has come down to Wirral and has taken Florence, but we need to keep an open mind, too. Apparently, she poses a threat to the little girl but so might other personalities in the area. Alex can you speak to the doctor at The Pines Clinic?"

Alex Manikas nodded and made a note.

"You want me to organise a check of known paedophiles in the area, boss?" Kath said. Blake could see the fire in her eyes and wondered for a moment whether it was wise to let her loose. Mind you, he couldn't think of anyone better to do the job thoroughly.

"Yes please, Kath. Tread carefully, though. If the public get wind of any suggestion that we're pulling-in known paedos there'll be a lynch mob."

Kath nodded. "Don't worry, I'll be discreet."

"We've got door-to-door going on and the park is being combed for any evidence. The press is going to be in on this and we want their help. I assume we have up-to-date photographs of Florence."

"All sorted, sir," Kinnear said, holding up a picture of the girl. "Roland Percival supplied this one. It was only taken last week after she had her hair cut."

"Great. We'll need one of the parents, too. We need to find them but remember, try not to give the impression that they are suspects. I'll be making a statement to go out as soon as possible. Right. Let's get going. We need to find this little girl as quickly as possible."

*****

Dr Gillespie sounded more than a little peeved to be talking to the police again. Alex Manikas heard the man's frustrated sigh and felt his heart sink a little. It was hard to get information out of a witness after the fourth or fifth retelling and often, all you got was a version of events that seemed rehearsed or learnt off by heart rather than a genuine account.

"I'm sorry to trouble you with this again, Dr Gillespie but we're concerned that Samantha Percival will be heading our way and we need all the information we can get. Could you tell me in your own words what happened?"

"I don't see why you can't read the local police reports, detective but if you insist, I'll do my best. Samantha has been with us for several months, almost a year, in fact and, whilst making some progress, she had relapsed recently..."

"What was the nature of her complaint?"

"Paranoia and delusion. She was convinced that we were holding her captive. All we were asking her to do was meet with the Percival family to discuss what was in her best interests before she made any decisions. She could have discharged herself at any time. There was no need to assault me and steal my car. I have nerve damage in my left hand now and I'm in great pain, not to mention the trauma of being attacked."

"What about her epilepsy?"

"We mainly treat mental illnesses, detective. Epilepsy isn't a mental illness. We worked with Samantha's own doctors and managed to control her absences. It was easier once she had a regular routine. Hormones, stress and broken sleep patterns can upset medication regimes, but Samantha's condition wasn't intractable."

"Was Samantha normally a violent woman?"

"I have a hole in my hand, detective," Gillespie said. Manikas tried not to let the man's tone grate on him. "You'd take that as a sign of a violent nature, would you not?"

"I mean was she in the habit of being violent? In circumstances that maybe didn't warrant it?"

"The Percival family did report that she was

apt to fly off the handle but we didn't see any major sign of that until the other day," Gillespie said, grudgingly. As an afterthought, he added, "of course there were the marks on the wee bairn..."

"Florence, her daughter? Was there evidence that Samantha had hurt the little girl?"

"I never met the child but there were reports of bruising and cuts. Paul Percival had saved the girl from drowning in the bath..."

"But that wasn't a violent outburst, was it? She was having an absence seizure, right?"

"Perhaps," Gillespie conceded. "But we saw moments of irritation, flashes of annoyance here, too."

"So, in your opinion, does Samantha Percival pose a risk to her daughter?"

"Without a doubt. If she's troubled enough to drive a paper knife through my hand, I would say she could easily harm her daughter, either intentionally or by accident. If she has taken Florence, then I would be deeply concerned."

"What about Samantha's family? Do you have any contact with them, at all?"

"Why would I speak with them?" the doctor sounded irritated. "It was the Percivals who paid for her care. As far as I know, Samantha's family had no interest in her. I don't really see what they would have contributed."

Alex concluded the phone call and stared thoughtfully at the file. A paperclip held a picture of Sam Percival to the inside cover alongside one of Florence. Samantha had her tobacco brown hair in tight ringlets in the picture, whereas Florence's was wrestled into two short pigtails. There was no denying the family resemblance. They had the same round face, the same frown line between the eyebrows and the same intense, dark eyes. "I wonder where you both are," Alex muttered, quietly.

CHAPTER 7

Of the five hundred or so sex offenders in the area, Kath Cryer had narrowed her list down to just ten men. Most of the people on the register had been charged with offences that didn't involve children, many were sexual assault or exposure or even couples up to shenanigans in local parks or the backs of cars. Of the offenders likely to be a risk to children, some were currently being held at her majesty's pleasure. Only three had attempted to abduct a child in the past. One of those had recently come out of prison and lived fairly local to the park.

Kath shivered. She had a particular dislike of this kind of offender. Many criminals were people who got caught up in wrongdoing. They made bad choices but didn't necessarily set out to be a thief or even a murderer. There was something particularly insidious about a predatory paedophile. In her book, they were people who deliberately chose to harm innocent children. They didn't stumble into it and it caused huge amounts of damage. She knew that from personal experience. People like that didn't deserve a quiet life or a second chance in her book. She'd pass some of the names onto the team but she wanted to eyeball this one who had just got out of the clink herself.

She printed off the list of names and addresses and stood up. "Right, I'm off to ruffle a few feathers," she said to Kinnear who sat at the next desk squinting at a computer screen. "Wish me luck."

"Have fun," Kinnear said.

"Oh, I will," she muttered and headed for the car park.

It was raining outside, a cold November drizzle. Liverpool buzzed with activity as people hurried to get their Christmas shopping. Kath hadn't even started hers. She pushed that thought away. It'd all get done somehow. Not that Theo, her partner would help much. He was a last-minute online shopper. Kath's present had arrived on January the fifth last time. It was a bread maker. Dozy bugger. She grinned. He could have got one of them from Argos and saved himself the earache she gave him. Not that she even wanted a bread maker. They'd passed it on to a friend as a wedding present three months later.

Kath looked at the name of the recently fledged jailbird. Leonard Hill. He had been in prison up until a few months ago and lived out on the Woodchurch Estate, just a few minutes' drive from Birkenhead. He was the suspect who lived nearest to the crime scene. In Kath's mind, it was just possible that he couldn't resist temptation on his doorstep. He was certainly worth checking out.

The traffic snaked its way out of town and Kath listened to the thump and squeak of her windscreen wipers rather than having any music on. She barely noticed the cars around her, stopping and starting automatically at lights and running on autopilot as her thoughts ran back to her past. Back to the Memorial Hall in Bebington when she was a girl. And Mr Freeman. Maybe that's why she was so eager to eyeball this man. A confrontation she never had but should have done.

The satnav declared that she had reached her destination and Kath shook herself from her daydream, cursing herself. It was a wonder she hadn't crashed. The Woodchurch estate was a huge development built in the 1940s. Its roads were wide with grass verges and green spaces. A few football flags fluttered out of bedroom windows here and there, declaring allegiance to Liverpool, Everton or Tranmere Rovers. When she was a little girl, the Woodchurch estate had quite a reputation for crime and depravation but it was quiet these days. It had its problems like anywhere else but nothing like the mid-eighties.

Linley Road lay on the Arrowe Park side of the estate where the housing was denser. The dwellings were more recent and had wooden fencing around their front gardens or low walls. Some were privately owned, others clearly rented and poorly maintained. The front gardens caught in a state of constant debate about who should weed them and clear the debris that the wind dumped behind the low walls. Hill's house looked innocuous and tidy, with grey blinds shielding the windows. It declared 'nothing to see here, move along please,' but Kath knew otherwise.

Kath parked the car a little higher up the road and climbed out. Her wrist ached a little and she tugged at the splint, a reminder of the shotgun blast that nearly killed her last year. Curtains began to twitch the moment she walked down the road towards Leonard Hill's house. She knocked on the door and waited. At last it creaked open a crack and Hill peered out.

He looked older than Kath had expected. According to HOLMES, Hill was a man in his thirties. The man in front of her was stooped and pot-bellied. A greying frizz of hair clung to the top of his head like candy floss. He had a hangdog look about him, deep jowls and droopy bags under his eyes. His face was tanned and he wore a red polo shirt and jeans. For a dangerous paedophile, he seemed rather a pathetic man. But then they always did.

"Mr Hill? My name's Detective Inspector Kath

Cryer of Merseyside Police. I'd like to ask you a few questions, can I come in?"

Hill didn't open the door any wider. "What about?"

Kath raised her voice. "I just want to clarify a few things about a current case I'm working on. It's a bit delicate, considering you've been banged up recently, and I wouldn't want the neighbours hearing..."

"For God's sake," Hill hissed and pulled back the door. "Come on in, then, if you must."

"Thank you, Mr Hill," Kath said, suppressing a smirk. "I won't take up too much of your time, I promise you." She stepped into the house.

*****

It was late afternoon and, once again, Blake stood at the back of the Percival house, staring out across the park. Rows of officers searched the ground in front of them. Mallachy O'Hare the Crime Scene Manager was already cursing over the number of dummies and children's toys they'd found. "For the love of God, Will, tell me she didn't use a dummy" he grumbled. "I don't want to be testing all of these unless it's absolutely necessary."

"I don't know, Mallachy," Blake said. "I'll check."

It was clutter, Blake agreed. Half the junk found

would belong to one of the hundreds of kids who passed through the park everyday. Door to door hadn't revealed much, either. Most people were too intent on getting to work and school or hadn't woken up when Florence vanished. Tasha Cook appeared beside him holding an e-cigarette. "Do you mind if I vape?"

Blake shrugged. "Go ahead." It always seemed odd to him. He'd never smoked and so didn't understand the appeal. He thought vaping would be preferable to smoke because it smelt more pleasant but somehow, he still found it unpleasant despite the scent of strawberries or menthol. Still, Tasha Cook had a difficult job and he could see she needed to unwind. "Any sign of Florence's dad?"

Tasha shook her head. "Do you think he might have something to do with her disappearance?"

"I don't know, Tasha. Seems unlikely but it's odd that he lied to Dockley about where he was going. I mean, what if the child fell ill or something? He'd never forgive himself. Believe me, I know what it's like to lose a child..."

"I know, Will," Tasha said, quietly.

"Sorry, Tasha," Will said, clearing his throat. "It just makes me mad. How could someone just stand there staring into a stupid bloody phone while a three-year-old wanders into the road? And where's this father?"

"What do you make of the house?" Tasha said, expertly guiding Blake onto safer territory.

"Too tidy by far," Blake said. "It's like a child never even lived there."

"In fairness lots of people like tidy kid free areas and confine toys to a playroom. There's one room full of building blocks and those wooden train sets. I don't know why but if you told me that Florence visited here every weekend, I'd believe you."

"It's a bit odd, Tasha. What do you make of Dockley?"

Tasha shrugged. "He seems genuinely upset. I don't suppose there's any problem with having a male nanny but..."

"But?"

"He doesn't strike me as nanny material. I'd expect him to be more... I dunno... homely and practical, Ordinary. I mean, he looks and dresses more like a drama student or an artist... that could just be my own prejudice kicking in."

"I know what you mean. But it's not his looks, it's his demeanour. It's something intangible and, as you say, something you can't quite put your finger on. Shall we have another chat with him?"

*****

Leonard Hill's house looked as innocuous as he

49

did; it was rental beige and oatmeal from floor to ceiling. Nothing stood out that gave away his character. The three-piece suite was unremarkable, even the pictures on the walls were washed out seascapes, simple black ink horizons with squiggles for seagulls. A small West Highland Terrier lay curled up in front of the gas fire.

Hill sat down in his armchair. He licked his thin lips. "So what d'you want? I haven't been nowhere. I haven't seen no one neither." His voice was shrill and cracked. It reminded Kath of her grandmother.

"You haven't been out today at all Leonard?" Kath said.

"No," he said, giving his dog a sidelong glance. "Only to take the dog down to the playing fields. He had a little run, I picked up his poo and we came home. That's it. I didn't even look at anyone else."

"I never said you did," Kath murmured. "You sound like you've got a guilty conscience, Leonard."

"I haven't got a guilty conscience. I haven't done nothing."

"No?" Kath said, darkly. "Never?"

"Are you here to ask me questions about something specific, Detective Cryer?"

"Where were you between the hours of six am

and nine this morning, Leonard?"

"I told you I was here, then I walked the dog and then I came home again. I've been sat on my arse ever since."

"Anyone who can verify that?"

Leonard shook his head. "No. You'll have to take my word for it. What's this all about, anyway? Has a kiddie gone missing?"

"What makes you say that, Leonard?"

"Why else would you be bothering me?" Hill said, bitterly. "Every time some little darling goes wandering off, I get a visit from the police. There's no apology when they turn up though, is there? No. I've only been here a few months and you lot haven't left me alone."

"What playing fields did you go to? Not near a school, I hope."

Leonard blinked. "You can't move for schools round here. I don't know why they put me in this house. And no, I went over on the parkland behind the hospital for that very reason."

"But nobody saw you."

Hill licked his lips again. "I-I told you. All I was doing was walking the dog. What do you want me to do? Shout my name out to random strangers as I pass them by?

"There's no need for that tone of voice," Kath

muttered.

"Isn't there?" Hill snapped. "This is beginning to feel like harassment. You're entitled to check my whereabouts, I get that. But this insinuation that I'm lying to you and your general manner aren't very professional, in my opinion."

"Yeah, well, you can always make a complaint can't you, Leonard?" Kath said, with a tight smile. "D'you own a car?"

"Yes," Hill said. Kath noticed his leg had started twitching. Either she was just agitating him or he was lying. It was hard to tell because he was right, she'd come into this interview on the bounce and put him on edge. "Why?"

"Just useful for a quick check, to see if you were in the vicinity of Birkenhead Park today. Could you tell me the make, model and reg number, please?"

"Yes, it's a white VW Polo. RG10 KLD. They're quite common. Lots of them about..." Hill looked pale and worried.

"That's a funny thing to say, Leonard," Kath said. "I generally find that registration numbers are quite unique, whatever the make of car."

"I-I just know how this works. Someone says they saw a white VW Polo in the area and then you lot pounce on me and I spend the next three days being grilled about something I didn't do."

Kath stood up. "Rest assured, Leonard. If I have even the slightest suspicion that you were down in Birkenhead Park this morning, I'll be bringing you in for further questioning. But I'll base my judgements on solid evidence, not hearsay. Goodbye. For now."

Hill watched her as she stalked back to her car. Kath's skin was crawling. How could a man like that sound so injured? After what he'd done. He was hiding something, though, Kath was certain of it. She didn't believe the story about walking the dog for one minute. If he was about in his car, an ANPR check would sort out just where he was this morning.

"Are you a bizzie?" a voice called, startling Kath.

She stopped to look at the man who had addressed her. He was rangy, and bony looking; all teeth and cheek bones with blond hair cropped to stubble length on his head. He wore grey tracksuit bottoms and matching hoodie.

"I don't see that it's any of your business who I am," Kath said and turned to walk on.

"Has Leonard been a bad boy?" the man said, shaking his head and tutting. "We've been keeping an eye on him."

"And who might 'we' be?"

The man shrugged. "Just some concerned citizens, that's all."

Kath's heart lurched. "Listen," she said in a low voice. "Just stay away from him. He hasn't done anything and even if he had you shouldn't do anything about it."

The man gave a sly grin and wiggled his eyebrows. "So you are a bizzie. I knew it. If he's done anything, we've got a right to know. There are kids round here who can't play out because of him."

"You don't have a right to know anything but for your information, he hasn't done a thing. I've just come to check up on him. So you've no need to worry."

He narrowed his eyes. "All the same, kind of odd isn't it? You dropping in on him like that. Have you got kids?"

Kath shook her head. "What's that got to do with anything?"

"If you did, you'd know how worried everyone is round here. A nonce like that living next to you. Eyeing up your kiddies. It's only a matter of time. He won't be here long."

"Well, if anything happens to him, you'll be the first person I'll look for," Kath said. "Now go about your business and leave him alone."

Kath watched the man pull his hood up and saunter down the road. On one level, she had some sympathy for the guy, but she had a nasty feeling that she was going to see more of him.

CHAPTER 8

After a few hours researching old newspapers in the Central Library, Jeff Blake decided that maybe it was worth his while to visit Kyle Quinlan's sister. He knew that in one way, Gambles was just antagonising Will, but Jeff couldn't deny that the whole Quinlan angle could make for interesting reading. The search for a lost friend, delving into the dark corners of the Merseyside underworld to find him with who knew what result. Jeff could see a Netflix true crime docudrama script forming in his head. Quite where Will fitted into this, he didn't know but Jeff had to make a living; he had a paying tenant in his London flat and that covered his living expenses up here but he had little spare cash. If Jeff could make this work, he'd be set for life.

He phoned the number on Gambles' scribbled notes and waited. After a few moments, a voice answered. "Hi Jeffrey, I've been expecting a call."

"Oh, is this Leslee Quinlan?"

"Of course. I expect you've been at the library doing some background checks so I'll see you in half an hour, yeah?"

Taken by surprise, Jeff glanced down at the address on the notes. Leslee lived in Oxton. "Erm... yes, that should be fine..."

"Good. I'll get the kettle on."

Jeff ended the call and leafed thoughtfully through Gambles' notes. Was he being taken for a ride in some way? Gambles was slippery and had a very high opinion of himself. If this was some weird plan to make the killer seem like some evil genius, then Jeff wasn't having it. He gathered up his papers, stuffed them in his satchel and hurried out to find a taxi.

Leslee Quinlan's house was quite breath-taking. It was a perfectly restored Victorian Villa on Shrewsbury Road, with immaculate gardens. Jeff marvelled at the stained-glass door and the clean engineering brick. It looked as though it had been built yesterday. He reached for the bell-pull but the door opened and a woman smiled at him. She was in her forties, maybe, slight and dark-haired, with fine features. Jeff wondered if she was married before he could block the thought.

"Jeffrey," Leslee Quinlan said. "Josh said you'd like to speak to me."

Jeff couldn't help but frown. She was talking about Gambles as if he was a family friend instead of a sadistic multiple murderer. "Yes. I hope I'm not intruding."

"God no. Come in. I'll make you a cup of tea.

Milk? Sugar?"

"Both please. Two spoons."

"And there's me thinking you were sweet enough," she said wrinkling her nose.

Jeff felt himself redden. He was usually the fount of all cheesy flirtatious comments. He followed her through the house, wondering whether he should have taken his shoes off as his feet sank into the plush, cream carpet. They passed polished panelled walls and taste- ful hangings. Here and there a plant stood sentry in a corner.

"The house is beautiful," Jeff said as they en- tered a large kitchen-diner.

"Yes, I have a property development business, it gives me the pick of the crop. I fell in love with this place a few years ago and kept it for myself."

"A big house for one person," Jeff said, wanting to kick himself the moment the words left his lips.

Leslee raised one sculpted eyebrow. "I'm rarely alone, Jeffrey," she said. "I have lots of friends. Maybe you could be one of them."

"That would be very nice," Jeff said, grinning, as she passed him a cup of tea. "So, how do you know Josh Gambles?"

"I think you know. He's a friend of my brother, Kyle Quinlan. Oh, I know what he's done. I wouldn't invite him round for tea and biscuits. Not without several bodyguards, but my brother had a lot of time for him and that counts for something."

"Josh Gambles seems to think that your brother has vanished."

Leslee hugged herself and shivered. "He just disappeared about six years ago. He was working for a guy called Harry Thorpe…"

"Doing what?"

"Ask no questions, Jeffrey," Leslee said, raising her eyebrows. "That's my motto, anyway. Let's just say it wasn't anything legal. He'd just separated from his wife at the time…"

"Laura…"

"I believe you've met her," Leslee said, her voice flat.

"You don't sound too impressed."

"He vanished and she moved out of their house. Nobody really knows where she went for those intervening years but suddenly, she's back on the scene and dating your brother. I've always thought she knew something about his disappearance."

"And what do you think has happened to your brother?"

"I suspect he's dead. I reported him missing, of

course but nobody did anything. They told me: 'He's a grown man, can look after himself. Maybe he started a new life somewhere else after his divorce...'"

"A lot of that is true," Jeff said. "People do just walk out of their lives and if you say he was tangled up in something illegal, then maybe he needed to leave town."

Leslee Quinlan pouted her pink lip. "Poor Jeffrey. You don't want to believe that your brother's favourite girl could be a killer."

"Having met her," Jeff said, with a smile, "it is hard to imagine."

"That's because the Laura Vexley you see now isn't the Laura Quinlan I knew. Let me educate you a little, Jeffrey Blake."

*****

Laura paced back and forth in the living room. She was sure it was him. But how was that possible? She looked at the phone and bit her lip. She should phone Will, let him know. But how would he react? Maybe she imagined it. Since his name had been raised again, Laura had been on edge. It brought back so many unhappy memories. Could she just be hallucinating? Or could it have been someone who just looked like him? I mean, she didn't see properly into the car, the windows were slightly tinted, and it was gloomy.

She ran her fingers through Charlie's fur. She needed to calm down. Quinlan was gone and the police had lost interest in him. Nobody needed to know any more. She could put the past behind her. She hoped.

CHAPTER 9

The November sky darkened and the noise of kids coming home from school and the nearby sixth form college filled the air. Brendan Dockley sat in the same seat as before and Blake sat opposite him. Around them, Crime Scene Investigators searched the house for anything that might give them a clue to Florence's whereabouts. Blake had persuaded Roland Percival that he should go back and look after his wife rather than watch the team turn over the house and, in the end, the old man agreed.

"I don't know what they think they're looking for," Dockley said. "Why aren't they out there looking for Florence?"

"We have several teams doing that, Mr Dockley. Can I ask, how did you come to be employed as the nanny here?"

"There was a job advertised and I applied for it, of course. Florence's grandparents specified a male nanny, so there wasn't a massive amount of competition."

"Her grandparents employed you?" Tasha said.

"Yeah, they interviewed me and everything. Apparently, Paul was mad busy and distracted

62

by Samantha's... problems... if you see what I mean."

Blake cut in. "Why do you think they wanted a male nanny? I mean, it's quite unusual. Not unheard of, but Mr Percival struck me as fairly old-fashioned. Seems a bit out there for them to employ a man to look after their granddaughter."

"I suppose," Dockley began and then paused, gathering his thoughts. "I heard that Samantha was the jealous type. She'd accused Paul of having affairs with previous women who had come in to help. I dunno, maybe they thought having a male as a nanny would short-circuit all that. It would stop her worrying."

"I see," Blake said, nodding. "Makes sense, I suppose. You said before that Florence has developed a habit of running off recently. Why do you think that is?"

"I dunno," Dockley said, guilt clearly plaguing him. "Look, maybe I'm not cut out for this job. I'm not all that attentive, if I'm honest. I'm more distractible than the kid. Maybe she did it to get my attention..."

"So where did you train as a nanny?" Tasha asked. "Surely you had some opportunity to decide whether this was the job for you."

Dockley pursed his lips and looked from Blake to Tasha. "You have to train?"

"You need childcare and first aid qualifications. You need to be registered with the local authority, too. Are you telling me that you aren't?"

"I didn't know. I just saw the job and applied! The Percivals didn't seem too bothered. They said they'd see how I got on and then help me with training later on."

"But you need insurance and a criminal background check," Blake said. Dockley almost flinched when he spoke. "Is there something else you want to tell us, Brendan?"

*****

Although Alex Manikas had served in uniform breaking up riots, Birkenhead Park School felt like a jungle to him. Huge gangs of school children seemed to roam the corridors, the noise bouncing off walls, floor and ceiling. A teacher would appear, stand firm against the tide of pupils and suddenly they fell into single file. Some of them even smiled and greeted the teacher with a wave or a 'awright Miss?" Alex looked at Vikki and widened his eyes. "I could never be a teacher," he said. "Not without pepper spray and a baton."

Vikki laughed. "I guess it might be fun. I don't suppose it's all crowd control and discipline."

They sat in the foyer of the school waiting for the chance to see the two boys who were in the park when Dockley lost the child. The school was a brick-built establishment built in the 1920s. Fifty years ago, it was a grammar school but had, since then catered for a full range of children from the local area. Alex thought it felt very much like the school he attended over in Liverpool.

A smart woman in a business suit strode up the corridor accompanied by two young lads. She looked about Alex's age with masses of curly red hair tied back in a bunch. Alex looked at the boys. They were chalk and cheese; one was a big lad with a short back and sides, the top long and greased down. He reminded Alex of Billy Bunter. The other was small and dark haired, with narrow, suspicious eyes. The teacher stopped and shook hands with Vikki and Alex. "I'm Miss Zander. This is Olly and Aiden," she said. "They're in isolation at the moment while we decide what to do with them. I've booked an interview room. Can I get either of you a tea or coffee?"

"No thanks, miss," Olly said, grinning at Aiden.

Miss Zander raised her eyebrows and Olly's grin fell. "Quite the comedian, Olly Jones," she said. "A bit of respect in front of our visitors, if you please. I think you've let the school down enough. Let's see if you can redeem yourself."

"No, thanks, anyway," Vikki said.

Olly stared down at his shoes. Miss Zander gave

Alex and Vikki a secret glance and Alex couldn't help but smile. She led them to a small room set out with a table that almost filled it. They squeezed into the chairs that sat around it.

"Okay, Olly, Aiden," Vikki said, "I'm Detective Sergeant Vikki Chinn and this is Detective Constable Alex Manikas. We understand that you were in Birkenhead Park when the little girl went missing…"

"We don't know nothing about it, honest," Olly said. "We were just hiding from school. We get bullied here. It's not our fault."

Aiden, the dark lad stared at Olly in disbelief. "Bloody hell, Olly. A little kid's gone missing. Some paedo's probably snatched her and you're making up stuff about getting bullied. Behave."

Miss Zander raised one eyebrow but was professional enough to know that Aiden had just given Olly a better telling off than she ever could. Olly reddened and swayed his head. "Sorry, mate," he said.

"We were in the woods by the gate," Aiden said. "We were bunking off. Couldn't be arsed… I mean, didn't want to go to assembly. We got a text from one of our mates saying there'd been a fire alarm and we were about to leg it to school. Then we heard all this screaming."

"And who was screaming?" Vikki said.

"That fella in the duffle coat. He said his little girl was missing. Then the policewoman came and grabbed us. That's all we saw. Honest."

"So you were in the trees by the gate to Ashville Road? Can you show me on a map?" Alex said, pulling one from his jacket. Aiden pointed to the place on the map. "And you're certain that's where you were?"

"Yeah," Olly said, glancing at Miss Zander. "We always hide there. It's kind of far enough away from school not to get caught but near enough to get back quick if we need to. See what I mean?"

Alex nodded. "Did you see the girl? Did she run past you?"

Both lads shrugged and shook their heads. "Didn't see nobody except the fella shouting his head off," Olly said.

"There was that bloke by the playground. By the swings," Aiden muttered.

"What bloke?" Vikki said, leaning forward.

"White-haired bloke," Aiden said. "Had a kind of saggy face. Wore a suit with a flower in his lapel. Looked like he was going to a wedding."

"Looked like a right nob head," Olly said and then bit his lip and glanced at Miss Zander.

"What was he doing?" Vikki asked.

"Just hanging around by the swings," Aiden

said. "He looked a bit dodgy if you ask me. There were no kids or anyone around then, just us but, you know, he looked like a paedo to me…"

"Aiden, I know you're in trouble with school about bunking off and we're grateful for your help, but we need to be certain that you're telling the truth. You don't have to give us false information just to get in our good books."

Aiden's eyes widened. "I'm not lying! Honest. There was this guy hanging around the swings. Tell 'em, Olly. You saw him, too, didn't you?"

"Yeah, I saw him, too," Olly said. "But we didn't hang around there, cos it's the first place teachers look. Like we'd be playing on the swings at our age!" He gave Miss Zander a look of reproach.

"Could you give us a detailed description of this man?"

"Too right," Aiden said.

"I saw him too," Olly added. "Do we have to go to the station?"

*****

Brendan Dockley sat with his head in his hands. Blake leaned forward in his chair and clasped his hands together. "You didn't seem to like my mention of a criminal background check, Brendan," he said. "Is there something you aren't telling us?"

"No," Brendan said. "I'm just tired. It's been a stressful day and I'm worried about Flossy. I know it sounds bad that I haven't got those qualifications, but the Percivals were happy with me, so what's the big deal?"

"There are employment laws and safeguarding rules that mean you have to have those qualifications, Brendan whether the Percivals like you or not. Anyway, as I said, I think there's more. All I have to do is make a phone call, Brendan and I can find out if you have a criminal record or not."

"Paul Percival will kill me…"

"Even if we find Florence safe and sound, which I pray to God we do, d'you think he's going to give you a pay rise? You'll be lucky if you ever work again! So. Come clean. What are you holding back?"

"I was just a kid. It wasn't my fault," Brendan said.

"What wasn't, Brendan?"

Brendan looked up, his face tear streaked. "I killed my best friend."

CHAPTER 10

Andrew Kinnear shook his head and absent-mindedly slid another biscuit from the plate as he stared at the CCTV footage from Ashville Road. It was grainy but he couldn't see any sign of Florence popping out of the gate into the road. The camera covered the gate perfectly. Even in black and white, her anorak, dress and wellies combo would have made her obvious along with the fact that she was alone. She would have stuck out like a sore thumb. It didn't make sense. He watched the small gangs of children walking along to school mixed with dog walkers and some mums and dads with pushchairs. There were no lone toddlers there at any point.

"What am I missing, here?" Kinnear muttered to himself. He ran the tape again and watched as the crowds thinned. He saw the two boys vanish into the woods, pushing and shoving each other in some kind of play fight. Then Dockley ran out of the park, shouting and waving his arms around. He ran out in front of a car, slamming his hands on the bonnet as it screeched to a halt. Then he stumbled back into the park. It was like watching a film. Then the street was calm again until a police officer hurried through the gate in response to Brendan Dockley's cries for help.

The phone rang and Kinnear picked it up. It was PC Guyler from Merseyside transport police. "We've found the BMW you put an alert out on earlier," said the officer. "It's in Broadgreen station carpark. Looks like it's been there a couple of days from CCTV footage."

"That's great," Kinnear said. "I'll get CSI to have a look as soon as possible. Can you keep an eye on it?" he hung up and quickly warned Blake that Samantha Percival was in the area.

"Right," Blake said. "She's got to be a possible suspect."

"Thing is, sir, I can't find any CCTV evidence of Florence being on Ashville Road this morning. Not where we'd expect her anyway."

"Okay. We can pull other coverage higher up the road, but she would have to have run like the clappers to be that far away."

Kinnear looked down at the file on Samantha. "Should I have a word with Samantha's parents, sir? It could cast some light on where she might be hiding."

"Good thinking, Kinnear. She may well have gone to ground there. Go and have a word but be careful. She's hurt someone already."

Kinnear made a note of the address and headed out of the office.

*****

"I was only ten," Brendan Dockley said. "I lived over in Tuebrook with my parents. My best friend was a lad called Stevie. We were thick as thieves, did everything together and were never apart. But we fell in with a gang of lads who were older than us. They were up to all kinds of stuff. Shoplifting, drugs, they'd do anything, really just for kicks. None of them needed money, it was almost like it was something to do. They used to take the piss out of us because we were much younger."

"So what happened?"

Dockley lowered his head. "They stole a car one night. An old Ford Fiesta. Blue it was. And we wanted to prove ourselves. Well, I say, 'we,' what I mean is I wanted to prove myself. Stevie didn't want to go near the car. He was getting fed up of chasing after these lads and almost getting caught when they left us behind. But I said I could drive the car."

"And could you?"

"I knew the basics. My dad had shown me on holiday once. I drove round a field with dad helping with the steering. I could hardly reach the pedals. Anyway, the lads dared us to drive the car across the park. Not this one another one over by my house…"

"It didn't go well, I take it."

"No. It was okay at first. A bit of a laugh. We

skidded round on the grass, tearing the ground up and roaring the engine but then I got cocky and went onto the road. I remember seeing the looks on the lads faces as we left them behind. I was laughing but Stevie was crying. He said he wanted to go home."

"But you didn't stop."

"I wish I had. We went along Townsend Lane. Do you know it? Stevie was just saying to stop and let him out but I just laughed. Then we came to Queens Drive and this mad junction and I didn't know what to do. I think I went through a red light and had to swerve round a bus and I lost control."

"Go on," Blake said.

"It was just a lamp post. It looked dead thin. When we hit it, I thought we'd just knock it over and carry on but we stopped. Dead. It was like being punched, only really hard in the chest. It was the seat belt. There was glass everywhere. It only had an airbag on the driver's side. I remember thinking that the car would explode. You know like in the films? But there was just this crunch and then a hissing sound. Stevie was all slumped on the dashboard. He was staring at me and I knew he was dead. There was a bit of blood on his cheek but his eyes were just... empty."

"That must have been hard," Tasha Cook said. "You were just a child, though..."

"It stays with you," Dockley said, giving a shuddering sigh. "As if the guilt and nightmares aren't enough. If the Percivals did a criminal record check then it would show up. It's happened to me before. I just can't get a job that requires one."

"So why did you even apply for this job?"

"I knew Roland and Xanthe Percival," Dockley said, with a shrug. "We were all in the Mersey Marigolds Amateur Dramatics together. They've known me since I was a kid. Since before Stevie…"

"And you thought they might overlook the whole car theft episode."

"They knew who I was and what I was like. I hoped they'd give me a chance. They did and didn't even tell their son about it. But now, I've blown it." Dockley buried his head in his hands.

"One thing that's troubling me. Brendan," Blake said. "DC Kinnear just called, and he can't find any sign of Florence on the CCTV footage for Ashville Road at the time you said she ran away."

Dockley looked up. "Really? But she must have run that way. It would be the most obvious exit and, as you said, she couldn't have got that far. Oh God, she was keen to see the ducks. Could she have run the other way, towards the lake?"

"You were some distance from the lake," Blake said. "Surely you would have seen her across the park."

"Unless someone snatched her and dragged her into the bushes," Dockley said. "Have you found her mother yet?"

"We've located the car," Blake said. "It looks very much like she is in the area but we don't know that she has taken Florence."

"There's something else," Dockley said, looking troubled. "It hadn't occurred to me but I've been thinking. There was a man…"

"A man? Where? When?"

"I've noticed him over the last couple of weeks, hanging around the park and the street outside our house. I didn't think much of it but maybe he was up to no good. God I hope not."

"What did he look like?"

Dockley shrugged. "White, frizzy hair, short, glasses. Had a sort of hang-dog face, if you know what I mean. He wore a blue walking jacket, one of them Goretex things."

"We'll need a fuller description," Blake said, barely disguising his frustration. "Why didn't you mention this character before?"

"Like I said, I didn't think much of it before. I just thought Flossy had run off on one of her missions."

"Let's just hope it turns out to be a false lead.

I'd rather find Florence wandering lost than in the clutches of some unfriendly stranger," Blake muttered.

CHAPTER 11

The contrast between Samantha's parents' house and Paul Percival's was stark. Andrew Kinnear wound his way through the council estate in Leasowe to Caveney Drive, a small cul-de-sac created by three blocks of terraced houses. Some had clipped privet hedges and tidy lawns, others had old fridges and armchairs thrown out into the front. Samantha's parents front was a square of concrete occupied by three motorbikes in various states of dismemberment. Kinnear picked his way through a maze of engine parts, tyres and cans of oil to get to the front door. The house itself looked in good repair. Kinnear knocked on the front door and waited. A dog barked inside. It sounded shrill and yappy. Finally a groggy-looking man opened the door. He towered over Kinnear and filled the doorway. His head was bald and a long, grey beard spread across his chest. He clutched a small Yorkshire terrier in the crook of his arm and it yapped at Kinnear.

"Yeah?" the man said, frowning through bleary eyes. He was dressed in a black t-shirt and jogging pants but he looked like he'd been asleep rather than exercising.

"Mr Hughes? I'm DC Kinnear from Merseyside Police..."

"Is it about Florence? Have you heard anything?"

"If I could come in, Mr Hughes, it might be more private."

Mr Hughes backed away and let Kinnear into the narrow hall. The house smelt of coffee and dogs which, Kinnear thought, wasn't too bad. Hughes led Kinnear into the small living room which was filled by a huge television and two giant lazy-boy armchairs. A large fish tank dominated one wall and Kinnear could see brightly coloured fish darting about in the green murk.

Mr Hughes plonked himself down in an armchair. "So, what's the news?" he said.

"I'm afraid we haven't found her yet, Mr Hughes but we're still searching. Do you mind if I ask you a few questions? About Samantha?"

"Our Sam?" Hughes looked perplexed. "Yeah, sure."

"You're aware that she ran away from the clinic up in Scotland after assaulting a member of staff? She stole a car too."

Mr Hughes scratched his beard with a huge hand. "I didn't know. That's not good is it? Why would she do something like that?"

"I'm not sure, Mr Hughes. I thought you might

have more of an insight into how Sam ticks, to be honest."

Mr Hughes looked up at Kinnear. "She's not a violent kid, I can't imagine her harming anyone unless she had to."

"When did you last see her?"

"Dunno. It was months ago. Before she went up to that clinic place. I don't even know why she agreed to go up there to be honest."

"What makes you say that?"

Hughes pulled a face. "All that scab-picking and wondering why you aren't happy. I'd be bloody miserable stuck in a house with that streak of piss."

"Sorry, who do you mean?"

"Paul. He's enough to put anyone on the happy pills. We told her to leave him and bring Flos with her but she wouldn't."

"So Paul and Sam weren't happy together?"

"Paul doesn't know what happiness is. He's a funny fella. Everything has to be in its place and he gets twitchy if it's not. Know what I mean. Have you met him?"

"We're having trouble locating him at the moment," Kinnear said. "Any idea where he might be?"

Hughes shrugged. "Haven't a clue. So you're

telling me that he's not around at a time like this?"

"As soon as we find him, we can let him know. I'm sure he'll be upset."

"Yeah, right. He's a cold fish, that one, trust me."

"But Sam did have mental health problems, yes?"

"Not until she met the bloomin' Percivals. They have a way of making you feel not good enough. It's not just looking down their noses at you but it's the little things they say, the snide remarks. And the wealth. They think money can solve every problem. Like I say, she'd be fine if she got clear of that lot."

"Sam had trouble with her epilepsy during and after the pregnancy, is that right? There were moments when Florence was in danger..."

"Yeah, so they say. But last we saw her, Sam said her absences were back under control. She's had them a long time and she knows what to do. Sam can tell when the seizures are going to happen, she gets a feeling, an aura, they call it. There's no way she'd hurt little Flos and that's a fact whatever anyone tells you about her 'mental health.' We spent years building her confidence and the bloody Percivals demolished it in a matter of months. A bright, pretty girl like that." Hughes was leaning forward in his chair, spots of angry red on his cheeks.

"So, if Sam had come back. Do you think she'd come to you for help?"

"I think she'd go straight for Flos and then come here."

"And has she?"

"No."

"Has she called you?"

"No. She mustn't have had a mobile in that stupid clinic or we'd have heard from her. We tried to ring but she was always asleep or 'in therapy.' I didn't even know she'd come away from there, did I? I'm telling you, that Paul Percival controls everything. If my daughter has got Flos, then the little kid is safe as houses. Sam wouldn't harm a hair on that kid's head and if she came to me for help, I'd give it. But I'm telling you, she's not here."

"So you wouldn't mind me having a look around?"

Mr Hughes shrugged. "You can for me," he said. "I've got nothing to hide."

The big man stood up and led Kinnear around the house. It didn't take long. There were only two bedrooms and a bathroom upstairs, a hall, kitchen and living room downstairs. Mr Hughes even pulled the loft ladder down and let Kinnear poke his head up into the roof space. "Do you see Florence much, Mr Hughes?" he asked at last when they stood at the bottom of the stairs.

Hughes grunted and smiled mirthlessly. "Nah. The Percivals think we're a bad influence. Bloody snobs. Good people live on this estate, Mr Kinnear. We might be a bit rough round the edges, but we look after our own. People like the Percivals just look out for themselves."

Kinnear shook Hughes' hand and opened the front door. "Thank you for letting me..." he began but stopped as he saw a taxi pull up outside the house. The car door opened, and a woman climbed out. A woman with curly brown hair. Samantha Percival looked up and saw Kinnear.

"He's a bizzie, luv," Hughes shouted, reached over Kinnear and slammed the door shut.

"Mr Hughes, you're obstructing me in my duty..."

"Sorry, Mr Kinnear," Hughes said, stepping back and holding his hands up. "Wasn't me, I think the wind blew the door shut."

Kinnear glared at the big man and wrestled the door open in time to see the taxi hurtling out of the cul-de-sac. Quickly, Kinnear pulled out his phone and took a picture of the vanishing taxi.

"I should arrest you for obstruction, Mr Hughes. Do you realise that?"

Hughes smiled for the first time. "I'm really sorry Mr Kinnear. If you feel you have to, then I won't stop you. Sam's my flesh and blood."

"I really needed to talk to her. She could be in serious trouble, Mr Hughes," Kinnear said, looking at the image of the car. He'd got the registration number. "At least I can track her down now. If she gets in touch, then let me know…"

"It didn't look like she had Flos with her, did it?"

"No," Kinnear admitted. "But that doesn't mean she hasn't taken her?"

Hughes shook his head. "How can a mother be in trouble for taking her own child? She hasn't been banned from looking after her daughter. There's no legal reason she couldn't have had Flos in the back of that car just then, is there?"

Kinnear paused. "No but she has assaulted someone and stolen a car. And if she's got nothing to hide, then why did she run away just now?" He walked towards his car. "You said yourself you haven't seen her for months. How could you know what state she's in? I hope you did the right thing just then, Mr Hughes because if you didn't, then it'll be on your head."

*****

The press conference buzzed with journalists and cameramen. National papers were represented, and a few TV cameras poked their lenses at Blake and Superintendent Martin. Martin was a hawkish man with a sharp tongue, but he was fair-minded and Blake respected him. Images of Florence and Samantha Percival were projected onto the screen behind them.

"We urgently need to talk to Florence's parents who we can't get in touch with. If anyone sees them or Florence, get in touch with us immediately," Martin concluded. "Are there any questions?"

"Do you suspect that Florence has been kidnapped by her mother?"

"We don't suspect anything at the moment," Blake said. "We are just working for the safe return of Florence to her home. We aren't sure if a crime has been committed but the little girl's safety is paramount."

"Is it true that Mrs Percival is wanted in connection with an assault and a car theft in Scotland?"

Martin leaned forward. "I'm sure Mrs Percival is as concerned about Florence's safety as we are and that is why we are keen to talk her."

"Where is the girl's father?"

"Our understanding was that he was away on business, but we haven't been able to contact him."

"DCI Blake. You seem to be brought in on these unusual cases. Is this because of your experience with the Searchlight programme?"

Blake tried to keep his best poker face but he felt Superintendent Martin flinch beside him. Searchlight was a television programme many years earlier. It was a vehicle for requesting help from the public by presenting dramatised re-enactments of unsolved crimes. Blake had a small part hosting the CCTV footage section of the show and asking the public to identify the offenders caught on camera. He'd been put forward by his senior officers at the time because he was a good-looking young officer. 'Easy on the eye' was one comment he remembered. 'One for the mums' was another. It had seemed like an exciting adventure when he started but, looking back, he would happily have foregone the whole experience for a host of reasons. It had been used as a stick to beat Blake with ever since he'd returned to full-time service and was often a source of great hilarity amongst his colleagues.

For some reason, Superintendent Martin had a real stone in his shoe about the programme. It was as if Martin suspected Blake of being a publicity hunter and it was true that Blake had investigated a host of bizarre and fascinating cases that understandably went national.

"Our detectives are allocated to cases based on their experience on investigations and nothing else," Martin said, waspishly. "Now, unless there are any more questions pertaining to the actual facts of the case, we need to crack on and find this little girl." He turned to Blake as they packed up their paperwork. "Let's get this sorted and closed down quickly, eh, Will?"

CHAPTER 12

It was late but Kinnear couldn't stop now. He'd phoned in the registration number of the taxi and knew that the quicker he found it, then the closer to Samantha Percival he would be. He pulled into the taxi rank outside Three Sevens Taxi Co. The car in question was right in front of him. The driver sat in the front reading a paper.

Kinnear leaned down and tapped the window, startling the driver. "Blimey, mate, you frightened me to death, then," he said.

"I'm DC Kinnear," he said, flashing his warrant card. "You took a fare to Caveney Drive, this afternoon. Remember it?"

"Yeah," the driver said. "It was weird, she just got out and then climbed back in. Told me to drive away quickly. I didn't ask any questions. Thought it might be trouble. I've been in scrapes like that before. Boyfriend and girlfriend fights, whole families involved sometimes. You can end up in hospital or the car gets damaged. Better to just get away."

"It was me she was running away from," Kinnear said. "You remember where you dropped her?"

The taxi driver nodded. "New Ferry. Lilac Avenue. Number eight."

"And did you see her go inside?"

"Yeah. A woman answered the door and let her in."

"Did your fare have a child with them?"

"Nope. It was just her. What's all this about?"

"Thanks," Kinnear said and jumped back into his car. The drive to New Ferry was a matter of ten minutes. Kinnear struggled for a while to find the road, especially in the dark. He'd been around these parts before but was used to the older part of the town, where red brick terraces huddled in straight lines. Kinnear remembered that Blake lived somewhere around here but his house was much bigger and older than these. His satnav had brought him down to the river's edge and a small estate of detached properties. Lilac Avenue was lined on each side with modern houses. They reminded him of his own house and for a moment, he wished he was back there with his husband, Chris. No doubt he would have something waiting for Kinnear in the oven. It'd be cremated by now.

The woman who answered the door to number eight reminded Kinnear of an Aardman animation. She was tall, with a mouth full of huge teeth and eyes that seemed to want to pop out of her head. A shock of white blonde hair exploded from her scalp. She leaned against the doorframe, wrapped in a pink dressing gown and sucking on a cigarette. "Can I help you?" she said.

"Detective Constable Andrew Kinnear. Are you the owner of the house?"

"No, I rent it," the woman said.

"You're the householder, though."

"I live here, yeah. Why?"

"I'm looking for Samantha Percival. Her daughter went missing this morning, you may have heard about it on the news."

"And?"

"I've reason to believe that a taxi dropped her off here today…"

"Yeah?"

Kinnear was beginning to dislike the woman. "So is Samantha Percival at this address now?"

The woman blinked slowly and drew a breath. "I dunno what you're talking about. Sorry." She made to close the door but Kinnear put his hand out to stop it. "Can I have your name, please?"

"What're you doing? That's against the law, that is…"

"Not if I'm in close pursuit of a criminal who has assaulted a member of the public and stolen a car," Kinnear said. He knew he was pushing his luck, but frustration got the better of him.

"What is against the law is not supplying me with your name if I ask it. Now, who are you and where is Sam Percival?"

"Okay, okay! My name's Holly Young and Sam isn't here. She came to see me this afternoon, but I don't know where she went after that."

"And why did she come to see you?"

The woman's shoulders slumped. "I dunno. We're old school mates aren't we? She said she was sorting something out and needed somewhere to stay. I told her I couldn't help." She nodded towards the ceiling. "I've got two of my own asleep upstairs right now. Couldn't fit any more in…"

"So she was talking about her and Florence needing somewhere to stay?"

"Yeah. Of course she was. She's her mum. Why? What's all the fuss? I know she broke out of that prison they'd locked her in but…"

"You haven't watched the news then?"

"I don't do mainstream media. It's all made up."

"Right well, her daughter has gone missing and we're desperately trying to find Sam and Florence. Did she have Florence with her?"

"No, she said she was going to pick her up but needed somewhere to stay first. Yeah, that's what she said. Somewhere where her psycho husband wouldn't find her."

"Did she say where she was stopping for now?"

"No. She never mentioned it."

"Look, this is really important," Kinnear said. "We just want to help Sam. But we need to know that Florence is okay. If she gets in touch again, can you tell her that? Everyone's worried sick about the little girl, that's all."

Holly Young went pale. "God, you don't think she'd hurt Flossy do you?"

"Do you?"

"No. Course not," Holly said, looking away from Kinnear.

"You don't sound too convinced, Holly. Sam's dad was adamant that she couldn't possibly harm Florence. Do you know different?"

"I dunno," Holly said. "She's my mate and everything but... well, sometimes she had a temper on her. In school, she decked a lad for just tapping her chair with his feet. In the middle of class it was too."

"We all lose our temper when we're teenagers," Kinnear said.

"Yeah but before she went into that clinic, she wasn't in a good place mentally..." Holly paused and stubbed her cigarette out on the doorstep, carefully picking up the stub.

"Go on, Holly."

"She said she thought she'd hurt the poor kid. Don't say I said or nothing, will you?"

"What did she say exactly?"

"I dunno. Something about being a danger to her. She said that she had dark thoughts about Flossy. Like angry thoughts. She said she had horrible dreams about drowning her. But I don't think she'd ever do nothing like that. Honest."

"Well if she gets in touch, let us know. Persuade her to contact us," Kinnear said, handing Holly a card. "Thank you, Holly. You've been really helpful."

Holly smiled. "That's okay. Sorry I was a cow before…"

*****

It was gone two in the morning by the time Blake pulled up to his house in Rock Park. A cold wind blew off the River Mersey and pushed icy drizzle down the back of his neck as he climbed out of the car. The house was a black silhouette and Blake wondered if Laura had stayed or gone back to her own flat. Things were difficult recently since his colleague DCI Matty Cavanagh had revealed that she had been married to a small-time criminal called Kyle Quinlan. It had troubled Blake that Laura hadn't trusted him enough to tell him herself. But that hadn't been all; Cavanagh was investigating Quinlan's disappearance several years ago. Laura was the last person to have seen him.

From Laura's account, Quinlan had mistreated and abused her which explained why she could appear insecure sometimes. Cavanagh didn't have any concrete evidence that Laura had done anything illegal but his investigation had dredged up horrible memories and she'd distanced herself from Blake for a while. Things were settling down again, though. Or they were until she brought Charlie the Jack Russell into the equation.

Fumbling with the keys in the dark, Blake let himself in. A growl from the shadows warned him that all was not well, and he froze. He reached for the light just in time to see a smoky shadow hurtling straight at him. Serafina landed heavily on his shoulders, knocking him back against the door and clawing at his head, then she sprang away with a furious meow landing with a thump on the stairs. An excited yapping erupted from the kitchen as Blake picked himself up.

"Jeez! It's not my fault," he said to Serafina who just growled and turned tail on him, running into the living room to find somewhere high to hide. "Anyway. I thought you'd have shown him who's boss by now."

A light from the kitchen filled the hall and Laura emerged holding Charlie who wriggled and panted to get at Blake.

"You're late," she said, rubbing her bleary eyes. She gave him a hug and Charlie took the chance to lick Blake's cheek and ear.

Blake grinned in spite of himself. "What're you doing?"

"Charlie's only little. I thought I'd stay in the kitchen with him until he's used to the place. I set up a little bed next to his."

Blake looked startled. "Gets used to the place? He's only here a week."

"Yeah," Laura said. "I just meant, you know, it's strange to him."

"He looks happy enough to me."

"I saw you on telly. Bad day?"

Blake nodded. It was only exhaustion and a promise from his team that they'd keep looking that had sent him packing. "Bloody frustrating. Anyway, I'm off to bed; early start in the morning. Watch out for that cat. She's seriously pissed off."

"She's been fine with me," Laura said, raising her eyebrows.

"Yeah well, she just gave me her verdict on our new houseguest, and I don't want that reception every time I come home!"

"Will…" Laura said, a shadow crossing her face.

"I'm sorry. It's just this case. I hate it when little kids go missing. The idea of losing a child like that. It's bad enough when it's illness or an act of God but the idea of her being snatched by someone so depraved and evil..." Blake looked up. "What is it?"

"Nothing," Laura said, giving a tight smile. "You go and get some rest."

CHAPTER 13

Leonard Hill peered through the blinds at the road outside. Something had hit the window, smearing the glass. He suspected it might be an egg. Some of the kids seemed to think it was funny to go pelting people's houses with eggs around Hallowe'en and often, the tradition extended beyond the end of October. But it wasn't kids this time. Silhouetted by the yellow streetlights, a dark figure stood across the road from the house, hands in his jacket pockets, legs wide in a defiant posture.

"We know what you did, you little nonce," the figure shouted. "We saw it on the telly. We don't want your sort round here." He took something from his pocket and threw it. Leonard flinched away from the glass as another egg splattered close to his face.

The letterbox clanked and a sudden movement in his front garden to his right caught his eye. Someone else was scurrying away from his front door. They'd thrown something through.

A deafening bang made Leonard shriek with terror as the room erupted into a howling storm of sparks and smoke. His smoke alarm screamed, adding to his panic. He sprinted into the kit-chen, dodging past the spitting, multicoloured fire that grew on his doormat. Grabbing a jug of water, he ran back into the hall and doused the flames, spluttering and coughing in the acrid fumes that filled the room. The flames died with a hiss and Leonard doubled up, panting and spluttering as he stared at the blackened fire-works melted into his doormat.

How did they know? "It must have been that policewoman," Leonard hissed, wiping his eyes. He'd been through this before, though. He'd weather the storm and once everything calmed down, they'd go and pick on someone else. He just had to be careful for a while, that's all.

Leonard opened his back-room windows and the kitchen window. He didn't dare open the front in case more fireworks were thrown into his house. He pulled on a pair of gardening gloves, scooped up the stinking, charred re-mains of the doormat and threw it in the wheely bin. Opening a can of lager, he slumped down in his armchair and, trying to ignore the haze in the room, put the TV on.

The local news showed a picture of a miss-ing little girl and her parents. Leonard held his breath and bit his tongue. It was bound to happen. He forgot how quickly news like this spread. Lying low wasn't an option.

"Laura Vexley was never an innocent party in their relationship. When I knew her she was hard as nails. She had a mouth on her and wasn't afraid to use her fists. I was afraid of her," Leslee Quinlan said, cradling her teacup in her hands.

Jeff Blake blinked. "People can change, I suppose…"

"Just before my brother, Kyle, disappeared, he told me that he was closing a 'big deal.' I never knew what it was but it clearly involved a lot of money…"

"Maybe his ship came in and he scooted off with the money, then."

"I thought that, too but he was worried about Laura. Saying that she mustn't find out. He was genuinely scared of her."

"Why would he be scared of her?"

"I've told you, she's not the sweet and innocent that you think she is. And she's handy with her fists, too."

"I've seen that," Jeff said, remembering when Laura stopped Blake from fighting with Jeff by knocking him down.

"I don't know why but Kyle wanted to keep this deal, whatever it was, a secret from Laura. He told me that she mustn't find out. I got the impression he was going to hide the money from her. She was using a lot of substances at the time and I think he worried that she would blow it all."

Jeff sat down, running his fingers through his hair. "I'm finding this hard to process, to be honest. But in another way, it would make sense if she did have that money; Laura has a part time job but never seems short of cash. In fact, I suspect she volunteers more than she gets paid. If she had got hold of that cash somehow."

"The only way she would have done that was over Kyle's dead body."

"Who might know what happened to him? Who else could I talk to?"

Leslee sipped her tea. "There's one place. The Seraph. A pub down in the North End of Birkenhead. It's a dodgy place but Kyle was welcome there. I wouldn't dare go there myself. The landlord knew my brother well. If it's the same person, he might have some knowledge…"

Jeff took a breath. "Then I'll pop down there and pay them a visit, shall I?"

CHAPTER 14

It was still dark outside as Blake stood before the team in the Major Incident Room again. The smell of coffee mingled with bacon butties and deodorant, a testament to those who'd woken hastily from scant sleep or those who had pulled a caffeine-fuelled all-nighter.

"Okay, people what have we got?"

"Sam Percival is on the Wirral for sure. I spotted her at her parents' house in Leasowe but she got away from me," Kinnear said. "She also visited a friend, Holly Young, who said she had asked about staying with her. Her friend got the impression that Sam was planning to take Florence, but she was looking for somewhere to stay."

"Which suggests that she hasn't got Florence. There's no CCTV of Florence with her mother," Blake said. "At least not on Ashville Road."

"Holly Young also said that Sam had quite a temper. Sam told Holly that she worried about hurting Florence before she went into the clinic. She could have the child somewhere but was concealing that from her friend. I do think we need to treat her as a threat."

"What else?"

"The two boys gave us a description of a man who hanging around the playground at that time. It sounds worth pursuing," Manikas said.

"Not the only thing you thought was worth pursuing," Vikki Chinn said, smirking. "What about that teacher, Miss Zander, wasn't it? Did you get her number?"

"I couldn't possibly comment," Manikas said, wiggling his eyebrows.

"Well, try and keep your mind on the matter in hand," Blake muttered. "I'll be glad of anything that leads us to Florence Percival."

"We've got a preliminary image of the man the boys saw, based on their description," Manikas said, passing around some copies of the picture.

"Oh my God. It's him," Kath said.

"It's who, Kath?" Blake said, feeling nettled. Kath Cryer was a good detective, but she was partial to a touch of melodrama.

"Leonard Hill. In and out of prison for grooming minors and possessing indecent images of children. I visited him yesterday," Kath said. "He was lying about something. I was going to run an ANPR check for the Birkenhead Park area to see if his car was around there at the time of the disappearance."

"Make that ANPR check a priority, Kath. I don't

want to drag anyone in unnecessarily but if there's even a faint chance Hill was in the area, we'll be all over him like a rash."

"Will do," Kath said.

"And get more background on Hill. See what kind of threat he poses," Blake added. "I don't know if this child's been snatched by her mother or by a paedophile or if she's just wandered across the park into the lake. We need to organise divers for today."

A phone rang on a desk next to Blake and an officer answered. "Sir," he said, putting the receiver down. "Paul Percival is downstairs. He wants to talk to you urgently."

*****

If Paul Percival was worried sick about his daughter, it wasn't immediately apparent. He looked immaculately groomed, not a hair out of place, and clean shaven. He wore a brown suit with sharp creases and a pale pink shirt. An overcoat hung on the crook of his elbow and he leaned on the enquiries counter chatting casually to Marge the receptionist. He straightened up as Blake approached and extended a hand.

"DCI Blake, it's a pleasure to meet you. I remember you on that television programme," he said. "Searchlight, wasn't it?"

Blake couldn't help frowning. "Yes, Mr Percival..."

"Call me Paul," he said. His brow creased slightly as though he was trying to solve a crossword puzzle. "Brendan called me and said that Flossy has gone missing..."

Blake looked around, the reception area at Police HQ was busy with all kinds of people, including a few journalists eager for a scoop. He could see their ears pricking up. Obviously they hadn't recognised the relaxed, suave character strolling into the building as though he was on a sight-seeing holiday as a worried and anxious father. "Shall we take this inside, Paul?" Blake said. "I'll see if a meeting room is available and then we can bring you up to date."

After a little searching and with a little help from Marge, Blake and Paul Percival located and settled in a meeting room. Blake explained everything they had done and the lines of enquiry they were following. Throughout it all, Paul Percival looked calm and the gentle smile never left his face. Blake could see a vein pulsing in his forehead, though and the man's jaw muscles clenched and relaxed far too often.

"So," Percival said at last. "You think Sam may have her. I really hope that isn't so, detective. Sam is very unstable..."

"Can I ask where you've been, Paul? We've been trying to contact you and I know your father has, too. We checked the hotel you told Brendan you were staying at and they hadn't heard of you at all. Nor was there a conference happening there."

Percival gave an embarrassed smile. "Ah, that is something of a delicate matter, detective. Suffice to say, it concerns the honour of a lady and so I'm not at liberty to say."

"If I may say so, Paul," Blake said through gritted teeth, "you don't seem particularly alarmed at the absence of your child."

This time, Percival went pale. "I have a saying, 'never lose your shit in public.' It's stood me in good stead in the past and I'm sure it will help me through this. Now in all likelihood, Flossy is with Sam and, whilst that is alarming, me going off the rails about it isn't going to help."

"I can see the wisdom in that, but I have to insist. You see, in many of these cases, parents or close relatives are involved and I really need to know where you've been and who with in order to rule you out of the list of suspects."

Percival blinked, clearly close to 'losing his shit' with Blake. "But I'm her father..."

"Nevertheless."

"Very well. I was in the Lake District. The Lodore Falls Hotel..."

"With?"

"You have to promise me that you'll be discreet, Blake," Percival said. "The lady is happily married and wants to remain so."

Blake allowed himself a look of confusion at the idea of a happily married woman sneaking off to a hotel with Paul Percival, but kept any comment to himself. "I'll be as discreet as possible."

"Mrs Davina Allisen. She's the wife of a client of mine. I work in investments; stocks and shares and such."

"And you have contact details for this Mrs Allisen?"

"Yes but... why do I feel like I'm under suspicion here?"

"Because I have a suspicious mind, Paul and I like to be thorough. I just want to get your daughter back, believe me. If I can do that without upsetting your private arrangements, then that's fine but this is a police investigation, and nothing will get in its way."

Paul Percival seemed to shrink in his seat. "I understand."

"Good. Now, Brendan Dockley. How well do you know him?"

Percival shrugged. "Fairly well. He lives in my house. Mum and Dad chose him to calm Sam's nerves. Sam was convinced that I was having it away with the previous nanny and the one be-fore that."

When actually, you were having it away with Mrs Allisen, Blake thought. "But you find him dili-gent? Trustworthy?"

"Yeah. Flossy seems to like him. He kept her busy and out of my hair. Makes me seem very 'equal opps' to clients, having a male nanny, too." Percival's face twisted and Blake thought he saw the mask slip a little. "But he's cocked up bigtime here, hasn't he? I mean he had one job yesterday. One job."

"Yes," Blake agreed. "He did. He hasn't actually met your wife, has he?"

"No but Mum and Dad wanted him in place so Sam could go to the clinic without worrying about my fidelity."

"So your mother and father hired him. Not you," Blake said, trying not to get distracted by Percival's seeming lack of concern about his ac-tual and obvious infidelity.

"Yes, I was mad busy and left it to them. Look, why are you asking questions about Brendan, now?"

"As I say, I have to eliminate everyone from our enquiries. Right now, we're combing the area for your daughter and the person who last saw her is Brendan Dockley."

"D'you think he might be responsible for her disappearance?"

"I'm just finding out the truth about what happened, Paul. I'm not here to apportion blame. Brendan's concentration lapsed, and maybe someone took advantage of it. I just want to find Florence and bring her home safe and sound."

"Yes. I can see that. It would be interesting to find out who took her in the first place as well, don't you think?"

Blake ignored the jibe and the indignation that was growing in Paul Percival's voice. "Your father said that he saw bruises on Florence. Where did they come from?"

"Her mother, most likely. I told you, she's unstable."

"That must have put you in a worrying situation..."

"I love the woman, Blake. I did everything I could. Gave her all the support possible but it wasn't enough. In the end the clinic seemed like the best option."

Before Blake could answer, there was a knock and Kath Cryer put her head round the door. "Sorry to interrupt but could I have a quick word. It's important."

Outside, Blake shut the door behind him. "Leonard Hill," Kath said in a low voice. "His car was in the Birkenhead park area yesterday. Andrew's rechecking the CCTV of Ashville Road to see if we can see his car there but it's him. I'm certain!"

"Okay," Blake said. "Good work, Kath. I'll finish up here and then we'll get a warrant for Hill's house. We can bring him in too. He's got a bit of explaining to do."

CHAPTER 15

Leonard Hill looked as though he expected to see Blake flanked by Cryer and Chinn. His shoulders sagged in weary acceptance, and he pulled his front door wide.

"Morning Leonard, I'm DCI Blake, this is DS Chinn and DI Cryer who I think you've already met. We have a warrant to search these premises for Florence Percival who is currently missing. We're also looking for any evidence that she has been here."

Hill stepped back and let them in. Kath gave him a tart smile as she brushed past him. "You won't find anything," Leonard said.

Blake paused. "Can you wait in the living room with DS Chinn, please, Mr Hill, whilst our officers conduct a thorough search?"

Hill shuffled into the living room and sat on the edge of his armchair, watching the officers come in. Blake glanced down at the floor and sniffed. "You had a fire?"

"That was my lovely neighbours after your Detective Inspector's visit. Put a few fireworks through my front door just to cheer me up."

"If you want to make a complaint…"

Hill held up his hands and closed his eyes. "Just do your searching and then go. Complaining about things only makes it worse."

Blake was puzzled. For someone who was on the verge of being arrested for abducting a child, Hill seemed more fed up than anxious. As though he was resigned to his fate. He also seemed sure they would leave empty handed. "Do you want to have a chat with him, Vikki?"

Blake made his way upstairs. As Kath had told him, the house was a blank canvas. Anyone could have lived there. That was one of the downsides of living in rented accommodation, especially fully furnished. It was fitted out to suit everyone and no one. Every room had the same shade of oatmeal on the walls. He thought of his own décor at home or rather the flowery wallpaper that his parents had put up, given that he'd never done any decorating in the place since his father died.

Drawers were emptied, cupboards were opened, tables turned over but nothing suspicious was found. They even checked the roof space and found it empty apart from some packing cases that Leonard Hill said he'd used to bring his belongings to the house.

"He still hasn't explained what he was doing around Birkenhead Park yesterday, sir," Kath said. "Let me have a crack at him."

"Vikki's talking to him now, Kath. Why are you so sure he's taken Florence?"

"It's just a feeling, sir. A hunch. You know?"

"Yeah, I know what you mean Kath, but we can't just arrest him on a hunch. We need hard evidence. He could have been driving past the park for a whole host of reasons that he didn't want to share with us. It doesn't mean he abducted the girl does it?"

"Sir!" One of the uniformed officers called from the spare bedroom. Blake and Cryer hurried across the landing. Under the mattress on the bed was a jiffy bag. The officer held it between his gloved finger and thumb.

"Put it on the bed, let's see what it is," Blake said.

Carefully, they teased open the bag and slid the contents out. Blake held his breath. A small pair of girl's briefs tumbled out followed by two bloody tissues and a lock of dark hair in a bobble. "Okay," Blake sighed. "Let's get CSI in and take Hill into custody."

Outside, Blake watched as Kath Cryer and Vikki Chinn ushered Leonard Hill into the back of a car. Why would someone keep those items, so personal and intimate? Even after all his years in the force, he couldn't understand why anyone would do that. He'd heard all the explanations, reliving the moment through trophies, keeping the victim close in some way but it just didn't make sense to him. Also the stupidity of where criminals hid their mementos never ceased to amaze him. Hill obviously hadn't thought long or hard about where he was going to conceal the jiffy bag. Or maybe they'd caught him out before he could shift them. Maybe that was what Hill's look of weary acceptance was all about when he'd first let them in. He knew he hadn't moved the package in time and that they'd find it.

A movement across the road dragged him from his thoughts and he realised someone was filming Leonard getting into the car. He was a tall but thin character, bony and unshaved, dressed in sweatpants and hoodie. His attention was focused on Hill clambering into the car so he didn't notice Blake cross the road.

"Can I help you, sir?" Blake said, making the man jump and lower the phone.

"No. I've got all I want, thanks," the man said, staring evenly at Blake with large, poppy eyes. "Have you nailed the dirty bugger, then?"

"I'm afraid, I can't discuss that. What's your name, sir?"

The young man's toothy grin faded, and Blake watched the internal struggle written on his face. Clearly, this man had been in trouble with the police before and knew the perils of not supplying a name.

"Ian Vale," the man said at last.

"Thank you. And why were you filming the police car?"

The grin returned. "I'm an enthusiast, aren't I? I love police cars, I do."

Blake narrowed his eyes. "Right. You seemed more interested in the occupants, Mr Vale. Do you know any of them?"

"Nah," Vale said, with a shrug. "I know the fella in the back is a nonce, though. A bloody kiddy-fiddler and he's getting what's due to him."

"And how do you know that?"

"Everyone round here knows," Vale said. "And if they didn't they soon will, once word gets around. Social media's a wonder, isn't it?"

"I'd be careful what you post, Mr Vale. Nobody has been charged with anything. I'd hate for you to get into trouble for libelling anyone. I suggest you move on and try not to cause any trouble…"

"Okeydoke," Ian Vale said, stuffing his hands in his pockets and sauntering away from Blake. "He better have the book thrown at him, though," Vale said loudly, without looking back. "What he's done isn't right. Needs more than a slap on the wrist."

"I agree," Blake muttered quietly to himself. "If he's guilty."

*****

Blake was beginning to think that bringing Kath Cryer into the interview room with Leonard Hill was a bad idea. She seemed edgy and snappy. Hill leaned forward and looked into his paper cup of coffee. Leonard Hill's brief sat next to him

"So where is she, Leonard?" Kath said before Blake could even open his mouth.

"Where's who?"

"You know very well who. Florence Percival. The little girl you abducted yesterday morning from Birkenhead Park," Kath said. Blake gave her a sidelong glance but she didn't seem to notice.

"I don't know what you're talking about."

"Really? When I spoke to you yesterday, you told me you'd not left the house except to walk the dog first thing."

"That's the truth," Leonard said, licking his lips. Blake had to admit, he suddenly looked very shifty.

"Is it? Then how come our ANPR cameras picked up a car with your registration number driving down Park Road North at 8:20 yesterday morning?"

Hill looked startled. "They did?"

"Yeah, Leonard, they did. And we have CCTV footage of you driving down Ashville Road where the little girl disappeared not long after."

He glanced at his brief. "No comment."

"How come two schoolboys saw you hanging around the children's play area around 9?"

"No comment."

"And what about the little girl's knickers? How did they end up in your house, Leonard?" Kath snapped.

"No comment."

"It's not looking good, Leonard, just tell us and be done with it."

"Kath..." Blake muttered.

"Come on, Lenny, you know you want to. Get it off your chest..."

"I don't know. You must have planted them there..."

"Ha!"

Blake raised his voice. "DI Cryer, can I have a word outside?"

They rose and stepped into the corridor, Blake closing the door behind him. "What is your problem, Kath?"

She folded her arms and looked at the floor. "I dunno what you mean."

"Yes you do, all that ranting at him. What are you trying to do, get any chance of a case thrown out?"

"It just boils my piss when men like him think they can get away with…"

"With what? We don't know what he has or hasn't done yet. He may have abducted Florence he may not. But if he has and she's still alive, then browbeating him like that isn't going to help and it'll just get us in trouble."

"Sorry," she said. "But he's lying sir and you know as well as I do that time's running out for that little girl, if it hasn't already."

"I know but just cool it. Keep schtum and let me do the talking, okay? Otherwise I'll get Kinnear instead."

Back in the room, Blake sat back in his seat. "I think you're frightened of something, Leonard. Can you tell me what that is?"

Leonard pursed his lips. "No comment."

"You see, there is a little girl missing, isn't there and you'd want to do all you could to help her wouldn't you?"

Hill winced and glanced at his brief. "Yes, of course," he said at last.

"So, we know you were in the Birkenhead Park area yesterday. If you weren't there to abduct a child, why were you there? Once we know that, we can unravel what on earth is going on here." Blake gave a theatrical sigh and ran his finger through his hair. "I don't know about you, but I'm bone weary and worried about Florence Percival."

"I was meeting someone. A woman."

"Okay. And who was this woman?"

"She's called Geri Sharpe. I met her online. We spoke for a bit," Hill looked away and reddened. "Exchanged a few pictures. We've hooked up a couple of times before. We always meet at the playground in Birkenhead Park at 9 am."

Cryer opened her mouth, but Blake gave her a look and she sealed her lips, glaring at Hill like she wanted to strangle him.

"So, if we contact this Geri Sharpe, she can vouch for you and verify your story, can't she?" Blake said.

"That's the trouble," Hill said. "I stood there for ages in the drizzle, waiting for her but she didn't turn up."

"That's unfortunate," Cryer muttered.

"What were you going to meet up for?" Blake said, ignoring Cryer.

Hill glared at Blake. "What d'you think? Sex of course. I texted her and she said she'd been delayed. We met up at my house, later."

"So to get this straight, You hung around Birkenhead Park until what time?"

"About 9:30. Then I went home and met Geri."

"And what time did you get back home?"

"About 9:50 something like that? If I'd snatched that kid, how could I have got back so quickly?"

"That doesn't explain the underwear, the tissues and the lock of hair in the jiffy bag under your mattress, Leonard," Blake said. "Where did they come from?"

"You tell me."

"Why are you being so reticent about them, Leonard? You know that we'll be running a forensic examination on them. Any DNA will tell us who they belong to."

"No comment."

"Do they belong to Florence Percival?"

"I wouldn't know."

"Have you harmed her, Leonard?"

"No… no I haven't I haven't seen her or those knickers before. Someone planted them there. I'm not going to say any more. If you want some answers, go to the Percivals."

"What do you mean by that?"

"No comment."

CHAPTER 16

Brendan Dockley carried the heavy bags of shopping up the step to the front door. It was all he could think to do to take his mind off the waiting. Maybe, too, if he presented Paul Percival with a well-stocked fridge, it might soften the man's judgement of him. Brendan doubted this, though. Paul Percival was anything but forgiving.

Rattling the keys against the door, he struggled into the hall and dumped the bags on the floor. He stopped and stared into the living room. Shards of glass sparkled on the floor in the otherwise grey twilight of the November day. The tubular steel frame of the coffee table lay on its side. A chunk of shattered vase lay there too. The TV lay facedown in the debris and furniture was upended. It looked like a hurricane had struck the room. Cushions had been emptied of their stuffing, torn books slumped on the shelves that still remained horizontal. The light, minus bulb and shade, swung gently above the carnage.

In the midst of all this, Paul Percival perched on the upturned sofa, staring at the floor. His face was pale and a single coil of hair had slipped out of place across his botoxed forehead. He sat so still, he looked like a wax work. Brendan swallowed and raised a hand.

"Hi Paul," he said. "Erm...Are you okay? Can I make you a coffee or something?"

"Yes. A coffee would be fine. Thank you," Paul said, his voice distant and haunted.

Brendan picked up the shopping and wandered into the kitchen, trying to process the destruction in the other room. Paul was usually such a calm and collected person. Cold almost, unless he was talking to someone in authority or someone useful to him, then he became animated and alive. With Brendan, he was always polite, but the hierarchy had been made abundantly clear from the outset.

He filled the kettle and switched it on. He twisted the lid of the coffee jar, turned and had to stifle a scream. Paul stood directly behind him. He hadn't heard him come out of the living room.

"You gave me a shock," Brendan said, with a nervous giggle.

"So, what did you tell them?" Paul said, not taking his eyes off Brendan. The kettle rumbled behind him.

"I- I told them what happened... that she just vanished... that I didn't know where she went..."

"Only, the way the police have been talking to me, I'd say they even suspected me!"

The water started to bubble and wisps of steam escaped from the spout of the kettle.

"That's ridiculous, Paul. Why would they?"

"Yes. Why?" Paul said, frowning a little. He gripped Brendan's wrist and pressed it against the boiling kettle. Brendan gave a strangled cry. "I'll ask you again. What did you tell them?"

"Get off me!" Brendan yelled, trying to drag the back of his hand away from the heat. The pain seared into his skin and up his arm as the kettle hissed and steam billowed from its top. Paul's hold was strong and in desperation, Brendan swung his lose hand up, punching Paul in the side of his head. Paul's grip slackened, giving Brendan a chance to snatch his burning hand away and stagger back across the kitchen.

It all happened so quickly. Brendan's leg became entangled in the shopping bag and he fell backwards cracking his head on the hard tile floor. Paul leapt on him, grabbing him by his jacket. "Tell me!" Brendan lay staring at Paul with glassy eyes. Paul shook him. "Brendan?" He pulled him to a sitting position but his head lolled to one side. "Come on, what are you messing around for? Are you okay?" A small line of blood trickled from Brendan's ear. Paul checked the pulse in the man's neck and found nothing.

"Oh, shit."

He pulled a tissue from the kitchen work surface, ripped it in half and poked the two pieces into Brendan's ears before the blood could get on the floor. Already his mind was working overtime. The young man was dead, his body cooling already. Like every other time he'd felt a surge of panic, or guilt or sadness, he squashed it down so he could remain effective and efficient. He'd been doing this since he was a boy. Battening down the emotion, figuring out the best course of action. The best way of getting out of trouble.

His first thought was that he mustn't be caught. He hadn't meant to kill Brendan, but he had and there it was. So he wouldn't be done for murder; it would be manslaughter. Paul didn't know what the sentence for manslaughter was but he mustn't go to prison. He was sure it wasn't his fault. If anyone was to blame it was Brendan. Yes, the lad had brought this on himself.

But if Paul just dumped the body somewhere, he'd be a prime suspect if it was found. And how feasible would that be right now, anyway? The press were still lurking around, the media filming the policemen and the divers who were searching through the park's two lakes. He wouldn't be surprised if there was a camera trained on the house either at the back or front.

He scurried over to the back of the house and

the conservatory, peering out beyond the garden but the wall obscured any view from the park. A sudden spark of panic flared in his chest and he ran to the front. What if a hovering journalist had seen Brendan come into the house? The less that was known about his movements, the better. Paul peered cautiously out of the front window but couldn't see anyone.

What if he faked Brendan's suicide? Or made his death look like an accident? Like he'd just come in and found Brendan like that? Paul pulled at his bottom lip as he stared at the back of Brendan's hand. It was scorched red. Paul was no detective but even he'd guess that it would take quite prolonged contact with a hot surface to burn that much. Any thought that Brendan burnt his hand, staggered backwards in shock and tripped would be undermined by just how serious that burn was.

He'd just have to hide the body and then dispose of it somewhere far away when all this was over. Then people would just think Brendan had run away, unable to bear the shame of losing Flossy. For a few seconds, Paul stared at the body smiling faintly and marvelling at how clever he'd been to work all that out under pressure. He shouldn't be, though; he'd wriggled free of fixes like this before and come out smelling of roses.

Then he snapped out of it. Time was of the essence. There were things he needed to do. He took out his phone and called his father.

"Paul? Where the hell have you been? We've been worried sick. Have there been any developments about Flossy?"

"No," Paul said. "I saw that Blake character before. Looks more like a gardener than a policeman if you ask me. They hadn't got any further. Listen, have you seen Brendan? I expected him to be at the house when I got in from the station but he wasn't here. He's left some shopping but then I don't know where he is. Any idea where he's gone?"

"I haven't," Roland said. "Don't worry, Paul. I'm sure everything will work out for the best…"

"Yes," Paul muttered, looking down at Brendan's body. "I think it will in the end."

*****

Blake was pretty sure he could do without Kath Cryer's 'I-told-you-so' face. His softly-softly approach hadn't proved as fruitful as he had hoped. All the same, Kath had risked being downright aggressive. Leonard Hill could have put a complaint in. But there was still something nagging Blake about Hill.

"We need to talk to this Geri Sharpe. The woman Hill claimed he was meeting."

"If she exists at all," Kath Cryer muttered. "He's probably sending us on a wild goose chase just to buy himself time. I'm telling you, sir, these people know the ropes. They're clever and manipulative."

"Then why did he give us full access to his mobile phone?"

"Leonard Hill is a computer nerd. He keeps all his filth on a PC, I bet you."

"Is there something I'm missing, here, Kath? I mean, I'm no fan of paedophiles but you seem to have it in for Leonard Hill."

"Just don't like 'em, sir. Like I say, they're sneaky and manipulative. I'd lock 'em up and throw away the key."

"But if Leonard Hill didn't abduct Florence, then he's an innocent man…"

"Is he? Innocent of everything? I bet you he's up to all kinds of evil. People like him are never satisfied."

"But we aren't judge and jury, Kath," Blake said. "We just establish the truth. The law will take care of the rest."

"If the law took care of people like Hill properly, then he wouldn't be out on the streets harming little girls," Kath said, folding her arms.

"Looks like you've solved this case then, Kath. It must be Leonard Hill because you said so. Just humour me, okay? Pretend he is innocent. What do you think he meant by saying that we should ask the Percivals."

Kath pursed her lips. "Well, you know what I think. He's being manipulative. He's throwing the shadow of suspicion back on the family. Only a real sicko could do that and he's a real sicko."

"But didn't you think the way he said it was odd? He sounded like he was familiar with them."

Kath gave a non-committal shrug, spun round in her chair and typed into the computer. "Oh my," she whispered and turned the screen to face Blake. "Hill has a string of offences connected with inappropriate images, but I didn't go that far back in his record. Look at the first offence."

Blake's mouth hung open. "Hill was right. We do need to go and talk to the Percivals again."

CHAPTER 17

Blake had been to Caldy several times in a work capacity, whether to question witnesses or, on one occasion, to investigate a grisly murder. "It's well-posh round here, sir," Kath Cryer said, looking around at the extended and almost fortified houses along the road.

"Bit of a contrast to the rows of terraces around Birkenhead Park, eh? I wouldn't live up here for a big clock, though."

Kath pulled a face. "Why not?"

"No shops to walk to."

"Where's the nearest shop to your house?"

"Hmmm. Good point," Blake said, smiling. "And I can't think of the last time I walked to the shops anyway. Maybe I will buy a place here when I win the lottery."

"You have to do the lottery first, sir."

Roland Percival's house wasn't as big as Blake had expected. Nor was it as old. It was a bungalow probably built in the 1960s set in extensive, well-maintained grounds.

Roland Percival was waiting for them at the front of the house and ushered them in through the side gate into the back of the house. Blake found himself in a large kitchen-cum-dining area. It was all stripped pine and Welsh dressers covered in plates. It reminded him of his mother's house. Roland offered them a seat at the kitchen table. He seemed jittery and on edge, smoothing the gingham tablecloth down and almost dancing from toe to toe.

"I'll just tell my wife, Xanthe, you're here," he said.

"It's all right, Roland, I heard them come in," a voice said from the door. Xanthe Percival was a tall, elegant woman with pure white hair tied up in a bun. Her high cheek bones and long neck gave her an exotic beauty that made Blake think of a fairy queen he'd once seen pictured in a children's book. She wore a long dress and Victorian boots. Her heavy eyelids made her look as though she was bored with Blake already.

Blake stood up without thinking. "Hello, Mrs Percival, I'm DCI Will Blake, this is my colleague, DI Kath Cryer."

Xanthe Percival nodded and sat down at the table. "Very pleased to meet you Mr Blake. Tell me, were you named after the famous poet?"

"Not especially, Mrs Percival but it has been mentioned before."

"I was an English lecturer at Liverpool University many years ago. I used to love teaching

Blake but not the obvious ones, The Tyger and Jerusalem..."

"I'm not really that familiar..." Blake began. Which wasn't entirely true. He'd learnt The Tyger off by heart basically so he could make people squirm when they began reciting it to him but then realised they couldn't continue.

"A Divine Image is a favourite of mine, Mr Blake," she said. "Cruelty has a human heart, And Jealousy a Human Face, Terror, the Human Form Divine, And Secrecy, the Human Dress..."

"I see," Blake said, not seeing at all. "If I may..."

"It's about human nature, Blake. You should know all about that in your line of work. Humans are beasts, capable of the harshest cruelty and the tenderest love."

"A fearful symmetry," Blake said.

Xanthe Percival smiled and Blake couldn't help thinking of the Tyger in the poet's illustration. "I thought you weren't familiar, Mr Blake."

Blake shrugged. "I suppose sharing the poet's name made me curious to find out a bit more, at one point," he said. "It's not something I've pursued for a long time."

"You said on the phone that there was something you wanted to discuss," Xanthe Percival said. "It must be important. Have you found Florence?"

Blake shook his head. "I'm afraid we're still searching. Can I ask you, does the name Leonard Hill mean anything to you?"

Xanthe Percival looked as though Blake had slapped her. She glared at him. "I'm guessing that you know it does mean something, Mr Blake otherwise you wouldn't be asking."

"I know it may be painful but if you could explain your family's connection to him, it would be very helpful."

"Why are you asking us to drag up the past like this, Blake?" Roland Percival said. "It's not on, you know."

"It's all right, Roland," Xanthe said, holding her hand up. "Is there a reason, Mr Blake?"

"We have Hill in custody under suspicion of abducting Florence but we can't be sure as he is reticent about explaining himself."

The old woman straightened up in her chair. "Leonard Hill murdered our daughter, Undine, twenty years ago..."

"I wasn't aware that he'd been convicted of murder," Blake began.

"We know he did it," Xanthe Percival spat. "He was a friend of Paul's. A loner, more interested in computers than people. I don't know what Paul saw in him, but he let Leonard tag along with him."

"What we didn't know then was that Hill was a deviant…"

"The boy was a monster, Roland. Undine was only a toddler, nearly three. She had Down's Syndrome, but Hill would seek her out whenever he visited and make such a fuss of her."

"It wasn't right," Roland muttered, shaking his head. "At the time we just thought he was being nice but with hindsight, we know that Hill was a paedophile."

"We lived in Birkenhead then, on the park just as Paul does now. I never understood why he chose a house there. We had gone shopping and told Paul to look after Undine. Paul was distracted and went off to see a girlfriend, leaving Leonard Hill to look after her. A few hours later, they found her body in the lake."

"Paul must have felt terrible about that," Blake said.

"Hill tried to blame Paul," Roland Percival said. "He tried to claim that Paul had pushed Undine in and let her drown. Luckily Paul had this girl who was able to swear that he was with her all the time. But in the end, the jury found Leonard guilty of manslaughter. They said he hadn't meant to kill her but his carelessness had led to her death. We know better though."

"Leonard Hill tried to destroy our family. He tried to drag Paul into the mire. When they searched Hill's room at his parents' house, they found all manner of unsavoury pornographic material. Hill turned out to be in a number of chatrooms associated with child porn. He'd even taken photographs of Undine and stuck her head onto pornographic pictures. It was absolutely horrible, Mr Blake."

"I'm sorry…"

"To rub salt in the wound, Hill tried to imply that Paul hated Undine. That he had said that killing her would be a kindness," Roland added. "It was a terrible time and we've never recovered."

"Can you think of any reason why Leonard Hill would target your granddaughter?" Blake said.

"Revenge," Xanthe Percival declared, slapping her palm on the table. "Plain and simple. In his warped mind, he blames Paul for his incarceration. At the trial, he called us monsters and said we had stolen his life from him. But it's he who stole Undine away from us and left us in limbo and now it seems he's robbed us of Flossie too."

"I see," Blake said. "I'm aware that you requested to be notified of his whereabouts."

Xanthe Percival's eyes hardened. "I want to keep as close an eye on that creature as possible. We know that he has been in and out of prison for various hideous offences and he was caught attempting to take a child from a playground recently. Prison doesn't seem to discourage him, though."

Outside, Blake sat in the car, digesting every-thing that had been said. Kath Cryer sat next to him in silence. Finally, she said, "So, you see. The bastard's taken that poor girl. Probably killed her just to get back at her father. And to satisfy his own sick desires. It's plain as the nose on your face, sir."

"It is, Kath," Blake said, staring off into space. "It is, isn't it? But what would he get from that? I mean, he would know that we'd catch up with him eventually. He'll be banged up for good this time. And why keep the knickers or the hair in such an obvious place?"

Kath shrugged. "You could ask why do any of it. I mean, he's not right in the head is he, to do what he does to kids..."

"I don't know," Blake said, starting the car. "It still seems odd to me. Let's go and talk to Paul Percival about the incident. He struck me as unusually composed given that his daughter is missing and might be dead."

"But you can't think that Florence's father took her when the weight of evidence is against Hill, surely?"

"I'm trying not to think anything, and neither should you, Kath. Not until we've nailed this down completely."

"We have, Will. All we have to do is wait for the DNA."

There's more to this than meets the eye, trust me."

They drove in silence for a while. Kath staring out of the window at the passing hedgerows. Pretty soon, they were driving through suburban estates and then the urban sprawl of Birkenhead. "It's funny to think that this used to be such a trend-setting town," Blake said. "You know, first public park in the world, one of the first out of town cemeteries. It had the tallest iron tower, once too, bigger than Blackpool."

Kath just grunted, not in the mood to change the subject to something less contentious. Blake was teased and even mocked by some for his 'mini lectures' on Wirral history but Kath normally enjoyed them. Right now, she wasn't in the mood.

Blake turned the car into Park Road and immediately slammed on the brakes. Two people wrestled with each other in the middle of the road. One was Paul Percival, the other a woman who Blake recognised as Percival's wife, Samantha.

CHAPTER 18

The Seraph was an old street corner pub in the part of Birkenhead trapped between the park and the docks. The area was a strange mixture of sixties infill building and old Edwardian terraces. These were the houses of dock workers and the shipbuilders, ravaged in the Blitz and rebuilt. Many of the corner pubs had gone to the wall in recent years as people took to drinking at home or preloading before going over to Liverpool on a night out. Propped up by local drinkers and a few shady types who needed a place to meet, The Seraph kept going. Reviews for it online made it clear it was a local pub for local people and outsiders weren't to expect a warm welcome.

Jeff felt out of place the second he stepped out of the taxi. A few kids kicking a football in a side road stopped to eyeball him in his tweeds and cord trousers. Then they carried on bouncing the football against the pub wall. Back at Leslee Quinlan's house, supping tea yesterday, it had seemed like a simple task to pop to a pub and talk to the landlord. Now the pub squatted in front of him, its door like an open mouth waiting to swallow him up. Above the door a faded notice announced that Dougal and Ailsa McClague were licensed to sell intoxicating liquor for consumption on the premises.

"Come on, Jeffrey," he muttered to himself. "Think of the royalties." He stepped inside.

It was a murky twilight outside and it didn't get any brighter inside the pub. As Jeff's eyes became used to it, he could see just how tiny the place was. A small bar squashed itself against one wall and little round tables, barely bigger than the stools that surrounded them, dotted the floorspace. Men crammed in at the bar and hunched over the tables. The place didn't look like it had been decorated for a hundred years. The other thing that struck Jeff was the silence that had fallen.

"Oh come on," he muttered to himself. He felt like he was in American Werewolf and had just enquired about the pentagram on the wall. He squeezed past the bodies to get to the bar to see a young girl with a black dress and an enormous cleavage polishing a glass. "Yeah?" she said, not looking up.

"I'm looking for Mr McClague..."

The girl turned her back on Jeff and yelled, 'Boredom!" at the floor. Jeff blinked, wondering what was happening. "Boredom!"

"What?" a voice drifted up from below.

"Some bloke here wants a word."

"Who is it?"

"Dunno, never seen him before. He looks like a bit of a tosser, should we chuck him out?"

Jeff stiffened as a few curious faces looked up.

"Don't be daft, girl, I'm coming up," the voice said. Slowly, the man's face appeared from below the bar where Jeff assumed he'd been working in a cellar. As soon as he saw the man, he realised that Boredom was the man's nickname and he also realised how he'd acquired it. Boredom McClague had a long face, made even longer by his grey beard. His eyes drooped and his down-turned mouth gave him a look of perpetual weariness.

"Can I help you?" he said, his voice a gentle Scottish lisp.

"I wondered if I could have a quick word," Jeff said, looking over his shoulder. "In private."

"I can't leave the bar," Boredom said. "What is it you want?"

Jeff lowered his voice. "I'm looking for Kyle Quinlan..."

"Really?" Boredom said, pulling a pained face. "Why would you be doing that?"

"He vanished about six years ago and I'm trying to find out what happened to him..."

Someone placed a glass down on the table noisily and got up. Jeff looked round in time to see the door swing shut.

"Sounds like you know as much as I do, young man. Sorry, I didn't catch your name, Mr...?"

"Blake, Jeff Blake..."

More glasses hit the table and more men got up to leave. Boredom licked his lips, his eyes suddenly awake. "Would you be any relation to Will Blake? You have a look about you."

"He's my brother but..."

There was a scraping of chairs and a general exodus from the pub. Jeff looked at the empty room in confusion.

"Listen, Jeff Blake. Kyle Quinlan is gone and I don't know what happened to him. Maybe you should have a chat with his sister..."

"She said to talk to you..."

"She would. Look, you may have a tough guy detective for a brother, but I can't guarantee that will protect you round here. If you want to know more about Kyle Quinlan, you have to ask Harry Thorpe. Your brother will know how to find him. Mind you, talking to Thorpe might be a shortcut to a one-way trip out into the estuary. But that's your lookout. Now, out of respect for your brother, I'll phone you a taxi and then you get out of here sharpish. To put it mildly, Mr

Blake, you aren't safe. "

CHAPTER 19

Pulling the car into the kerb, Blake launched himself out and sprinted towards the grappling couple. Kath was close behind him. Paul Percival seemed to be getting the worst of the attack, lying on his back and fending off the blows as Samantha straddled his waist. "Where is she you bastard? What have you done with her?" she screamed. Blake grabbed Samantha and pulled her away but Sam tried to lunge forward sending them both sprawling onto the floor. Kath caught up and put herself between Sam and Paul.

"Okay," Blake said, clambering to his feet. "We need to stop this now and calm down."

Sam stood up too, panting for breath and glowering at Paul through her dishevelled hair. "He needs to tell me what happened to Florence."

"I wish I knew," Paul said, dabbing the corner of his bleeding mouth with the back of his hand. "I thought you'd snatched her."

"You..." Sam hissed and lunged at him but Blake grabbed her and Kath shielded Paul.

"Stop!" Blake snapped. "We all want to find Florence, Mrs Percival, and you need to explain what happened at the clinic."

The mention of the clinic took the fire out of Sam and her shoulders slumped. "I'm just worried about my daughter, that's all." Her body shook and her face crumpled into tears. Kath put an arm round her. Blake breathed a sigh of relief at the sight of some genuine emotion. "Sam, we'd like you to come back to the station with us…"

Sam Percival stiffened. "You're not going to lock me up… I need to find Flossy…"

"We're all looking for Flossy, Sam," Kath said. "We need to talk to you about what's happened. Okay?"

Sam looked up at Kath and nodded. Paul Percival had limped over to his front door. Blake followed him. "What happened, Paul?"

"She just turned up at my door, shouting all kinds of nonsense about Flossy. I tried to get her to come inside but she attacked me. She's unstable, Mr Blake. I just hope she hasn't got Flossy somewhere…"

"It doesn't seem like she has if she's accusing you of somehow being responsible for her disappearance. Why would she do that, do you think?"

"She's crazy, Mr Blake. Honestly, if you'd seen her a couple of months ago, you wouldn't ask that question. She's capable of believing those two contradictory ideas at once."

"I see. I need to speak with you again, at some point," Blake said. "Now probably isn't a good time. I may pop back later, if that's okay…"

"Or I could come over to you," Paul said, suddenly. "It'd be no problem."

"Okay," he said, surprised. "How about we compromise, and I'll meet you at Birkenhead Station this evening. Eight thirty?"

"Great," Paul said, shivering and nodding at Sam who was climbing into the back of the car. "Watch that one. She's a danger to herself and others."

Driving off, Blake could see Paul Percival watching them from his doorstep, waiting for them to leave.

*****

He must have stood watching the street for a full five minutes after the police car had vanished round the corner before he slipped back into his house. Paul Percival closed the front door behind him and blew out a long breath. That had been close. Too close. Looking down the hall into the kitchen, he could see Brendan's feet still sticking out of the cellar door where he'd dropped the body.

He had just been moving Brendan downstairs

when Sam had arrived, hammering on the door. Demanding to come in, Sam had lunged at him and the only thing Paul could think of was to turn it into a fight. When Blake arrived, that saved his bacon, and Paul was relieved that Blake didn't want to come in. He looked at the stiffening body. He needed to get it bound and bagged up before it started to smell. There was an old chest freezer down in the cellar and it wasn't very full. He could keep the body in there.

Steadying his nerves, Paul clambered over the body and dragged it down the cellar steps, wincing every time the head bumped on the step. It amazed him just how heavy the body was. He could see where the term, 'dead weight' came from. He paused, exhausted from the fight with Sam and the stress of dealing with Blake. He mustn't forget to go to the station this evening. Brendan's eyes stared up at the ceiling, blank and empty. It wasn't the fact that Brendan had gone and got himself killed that bothered Paul. It was the inconvenience it caused, in the middle of everything else. Blake seemed to eye Paul with suspicion and Paul realised that he had to keep calm and cool when he went to the station later. He smiled. That was easy. At least there were no witnesses and Dockley wasn't going to say anything, was he?

"How did the old saying go?" he said, looking down at the corpse. "Dead men tell no tales, that's it."

*****

Interviewing Samantha Percival was going to be tricky, Blake knew that. On the one hand, she could be a worried parent frantic about the whereabouts of her daughter. On the other she may be the one who was holding Florence somewhere.

"To be honest, Kath," Blake said, before they went into the interview room, "she's the only member of the family who seems actually upset that Florence has gone missing. Everyone else just seems angry but trying to keep things together. As though remaining calm was the imperative. If it was my daughter, I'd be in bits."

Sam Percival sat in the interview room, dabbing her eyes with a tissue. She had been offered a brief but had declined. "I'll tell you exactly what happened at that fucking clinic and at home with Paul," she said. "I don't have anything to hide."

"So you admit assaulting Dr Gillespie?" Blake had said. "And stealing his car."

"I had no choice. I had to escape."

"You weren't being held there against your will," Blake said. "Surely you could have left at any moment. That was our understanding."

Sam Percival gave a cynical smile. "Yes, you'd

144

think so, wouldn't you? I'm not paranoid, Mr Blake. The clinic is in the middle of nowhere. You can't just walk away from it. I did try to leave on several occasions; the taxi I booked never turned up and shortly after, Paul would call me out of the blue and talk me out of leaving. If I was adamant about leaving, he would come up and we would have a 'meeting' about the wisdom of my choice to discharge myself. I was bullied into staying."

"Why didn't you ring your father? Surely he would have come for you," Kath said.

"There's a no mobile phones rule up there," she said. "It's meant to be a retreat. The signal was poor at the best of times, anyway. Besides, my dad is full of good intentions but when it comes down to it, he goes AWOL. No, believe me, the only way I was getting out of there was to steal that car."

"We'll have to charge you with those offences, Sam. Assault is a serious business," Blake said. "You traumatised that man, not to mention the physical injury."

"He deserved it," she said, darkly. "That man held me against my will at the behest of Paul Percival."

"Can you explain why your husband would do that?" Blake said.

"He's a narcissist," Sam said. "Totally self-obsessed. He was jealous of the love Florence and I shared. He wasn't happy about my 'weakness' as he called it, either."

"What did he mean by that?"

"He meant my epilepsy. He saw it as a flaw; something to be embarrassed about. His mother and father weren't much better, to be honest. I had it under control but, of course, during pregnancy, I had to come off my medication. He treated me as if I had cheated him in some way. I was no longer his 'trophy wife.' That was when the gaslighting started."

"Gaslighting?"

"You know, telling me I'd hurt Florence during my absences. Moving things so I couldn't find them. Telling me things that just weren't true. He even slipped me tranquilisers in my drinks. I didn't know what day it was sometimes. It was only when I got my medication sorted at the clinic and got my head straight, that I realised what had been going on. I suppose I should be grateful to them for that."

Kath looked unconvinced. "But you told your friend Holly Young that you were afraid of harming Florence."

"I did but that was when Paul was messing with my mind. I believed those things he told me."

"Roland Percival said that Florence had unexplained bruises on her..."

"That wasn't me. I'd never hurt Flossy. Ever. I realise that now. It's possible that I'd have short absences when I was looking after her but I can feel them coming on and I'd make sure she was safe. I'm telling you, Paul did a proper number on me. I even began to believe that I'd hurt Flossy; that I'd caused those bruises."

"Then where did they come from?"

Sam shrugged. "Paul. He's heavy-handed. A control freak. We'd had arguments about him laying hands on Flossy because of some little thing she'd done wrong. He never did it in front of anyone else, though. He blamed the bruises on me because he wanted rid of me."

"Why not just divorce you, then?"

"Have you spent any time with my husband, Mr Blake?"

"I have."

"Then you'll know that my assessment of him as a narcissist isn't far off the mark. He doesn't want me anymore and yet he's jealous and possessive of me. But he doesn't want anyone else to take me away from him. He's the original dog in a manger."

A moment of silence fell over the interview room as Blake digested this information. It rang true to him. Paul Percival was a curious character, there was no doubt.

"We have to ask you this, Sam, are you holding Florence somewhere?"

Sam glared at Blake. "No. God, if I had Florence with me already, I'd be on the other side of the country by now. I swear. The further away from the Percivals we both are, the better."

Blake frowned. "Why do you say that?"

"It's so toxic. Xanthe rules the roost but Paul's need to control is so strong and yet, he has no real interest in Florence. He ignores her most of the time. He was more interested in flirting with her nannies, who *he* insisted on hiring. No, I'm telling you, if Florence was with me now, I wouldn't be here. Oh God..." she dissolved into tears at the reminder of Florence's absence. "Where is she? Have you any idea?"

"We're still searching, Sam. We won't give up until we've found her," Kath said.

"Does the name Leonard Hill mean anything to you?" Blake said.

Sam shook her head.

"Did Paul ever mention his sister?" Kath added. Blake winced, hoping that Sam wasn't astute enough to make a link between the two fragments of information.

"Yes. A terrible accident..."

"Accident?" Blake said, glancing at Kath.

"Yeah, Undine drowned in the lake when he was a kid," she said. "Paul didn't talk about her much. I think he just didn't want to go there. Xanthe mentioned her more... why?"

"Family history often helps us work out the dynamics," Blake said vaguely. "So can you give us an idea of your movements in the last couple of days?"

Sam shrugged. "Once I'd escaped from the clinic, I drove down here. I slept in the car and then booked into a B&B. I watched Paul's house for a while, hoping to see Florence. I fully intended to take her away. There's nothing to stop me doing that. I'm her mother. Then I heard the news..."

"Why didn't you come to us when you heard?"

"I knew Paul would have done a good job in making me sound like a total psycho. And I wanted to find Florence myself..."

"When you were fighting with Paul, you seemed to be implying that he knew where Florence is. Can you explain that?"

Sam shook her head wearily. "I don't know. I suppose I was blaming him for her disappearance. The way he could just shrug off his responsibility for her to that careless idiot of a lad. But, to Paul, Flossy's just a pawn in a power game with his parents. He virtually charges them to see her. If they upset him, he stops them seeing her. If someone told me this was all an elaborate game to punish Xanthe and Roland, I'd believe it. With Paul, nothing would surprise me."

CHAPTER 20

The interview room at Birkenhead station was sweltering. Blake assumed that there must be something wrong with the heating and made a mental note to report it on his way out. Paul Percival didn't look quite as well-turned out as he had that morning. A shadow of stubble covered his chin now and his clothes looked crumpled. Paul's aftershave struggled to cover the body odour. The heat in the room wasn't helping either.

"Thanks for agreeing to meet me, Paul," Blake said. "I just wanted to get a bit of background. I don't like bringing this up but I think it's important that you know, we've arrested Leonard Hill on suspicion of abducting Florence."

Paul went pale. His reserve left him, and his face twisted. Blake saw the man for a second. "That… that…"

"As I understand it, Hill was accused of murdering your sister twenty years ago but wasn't convicted."

"He's a paedophile, Mr Blake. If I'd known I would never have left him alone with my sister. He tried to twist things and make it sound like I was the one who pushed Undine into the lake."

"So what were your movements on that day?"

"Is this entirely relevant?" Percival said, wiping his brow. "That was a painful time for me. I'd rather not dredge up the past."

"Unfortunately, it seems that Mr Hill has dredged it up for us. So, if you could humour me, Paul, I'd be very grateful."

Percival's shoulders sagged. "If you insist. It was this time of year. Mum and dad had gone Christmas shopping. I was left looking after Undine," he said. "I was only 16, Mr Blake, just a kid. You probably know, but my sister had Down's Syndrome. She was a handful. I suppose I resented her for cramping my style. If I could turn back time and change things I would. But I was desperate to see Tanya, my girlfriend at the time. It was around six o'clock and my parents were still out. I made a mistake and left Undine with Leonard. I spent the evening with Tanya and the next thing I knew, Undine was missing. They found her floating face down in the lake."

"I'm sorry to rake it all up again," Blake said. "And Leonard Hill, what was his version of events?"

Paul Percival snorted. "He tried to say that I got him blind drunk on my parents' vodka and then took Undine across the park and threw her in the lake. I mean, why would I do that to my own sister? Hill said that when he came round, he was by the lake and my sister was floating in the water. He has a sick imagination, that's all I can say."

"So what do you think happened? You must have considered what the truth was."

Percival was quiet for a moment as though gathering his thoughts. "This is difficult for me to remember, Mr Blake and painful on top of everything else that has happened to me in the past couple of days..."

"I understand, Paul," Blake said. He was beginning to see the man through Sam's eyes. Never once during the interview had Paul uttered Florence's name or asked if they'd found her. And he'd referenced his own suffering twice. "If you could indulge me..."

"Leonard had always had a 'thing' about Undine. She was just a toddler but Leonard always sought her out when he came to ours, always said hello and chatted to her..."

"Is there anything wrong with that?"

"I just thought he was being friendly. Leonard was always befriending the younger kids in school, you know, the waifs and strays who got bullied. He started a computer club. Again, looking back, alarm bells should have been ringing then but we didn't know that Leonard was a paedophile then, did we?"

"So Leonard had an unhealthy interest in Undine?"

"I would say so. Undine was loud and demanding. Mum and Dad spoilt her rotten. I know it was her condition and it's an awful thing to say, but she was a pain. Maybe he felt superior to her. Leonard was at the bottom of the food chain at school, that's for sure. Maybe Undine made him feel better about himself. I don't know."

"Right," Blake said, keeping as quiet as possible and letting Paul fill in the gaps.

Percival shrugged. "I don't know what happened that night. Maybe he got drunk and carried away with himself. Maybe he drank the vodka after he'd killed her. She wouldn't have known what was going on. It would have been pitch black in the park. He could have done what he wanted to her, she wouldn't have been able to tell anyone. Perhaps he felt guilty or revolted at himself and what he'd done. Perhaps that's why he pushed her in the lake."

Blake nodded. "Undine wouldn't be able to swim."

"No. And she hated swimming pools or large expanses of water. Quite ironic considering her name meant some kind of water nymph or something."

"Why do you think Leonard Hill said you were involved too?"

Paul shrugged. "I don't know. I was always kind to him. I don't know why he would turn on me like that. Maybe he wanted to spread the blame and confuse the jury. It was a terrible time, though. For a moment, I thought they would actually arrest me."

"Must have been difficult."

"So can I ask," Percival said. "Why have you arrested Hill now? Is there evidence?"

"We've only arrested him on suspicion. Our investigations are ongoing so I can't give you any more detail, I'm afraid."

"God, if he had Flossy, then she could be dead."

"We don't know that, Paul," Blake said, unconvinced by Percival's dramatic outburst. "My team are questioning him as we speak. If he does know anything about her whereabouts, then we'll find out. Can I ask you about Samantha?"

"What about her? Deceptive and manipulative. That's all you need to know. She got me to marry her and never told me about her illness. You'd think someone would warn a potential partner about that, wouldn't you?"

"It's not really an illness, is it? But, yes, I think it would be preferable to make you aware of a condition like that. Why did you send her to the clinic in Scotland?"

"I didn't send her, Mr Blake. She booked herself in."

"Sam tells a very different story. She believes that she was bullied into going."

"That's Sam for you. As I said, manipulative. She was falling apart. Paranoia for a start. She accused me of having affairs…"

"To be fair, Paul, that isn't unreasonable, given the reason for your recent absence when Florence went missing."

Percival's cheeks coloured. "Fair enough," he said. "But you have to understand, Sam had trouble with her memory, with these absences while she was handling Florence. She wasn't safe."

"Was Sam able to leave The Pines whenever she wanted?"

"Absolutely. She could have phoned me, and I would have picked her up. It was totally up to her."

"She told us that you persuaded her to stay whenever she rang you up or you came to see her."

"Well, of course I did. She isn't well. It might sound cruel, Mr Blake but it was in her best interests."

"What was the fight about earlier?"

Paul shook his head. "She came to the door saying I knew where Flossy was and wanting me to give her back. It was madness. Literally. I told you she was paranoid. She wanted to search the house…"

"Wouldn't it have been easier to let her have a look around? It's her home too, and it would have proved to her that Florence wasn't there."

"No," Paul said, licking his lips. "She would have caused all kinds of trouble if she'd got into the house…"

"What like?"

"Throwing things for a start," Paul said. "At least outside, she wouldn't have ornaments and cutlery to throw at me. It's happened before, Mr Blake, believe me. You've met her once. I've lived with her and it's no picnic."

"But it seems clear that she doesn't have Florence," Blake said. "Otherwise, why turn up at your door?"

Paul Percival shook his head. "I still wouldn't be sure, Mr Blake. I don't know what goes on in her head. I wouldn't put it past her. Put it this way, unless you've got concrete evidence that Leonard Hill has my daughter, I still wouldn't rule out her mother."

CHAPTER 21

It was late but Blake wanted everyone allocated to tasks the following morning. He felt bone weary and his stomach growled. He was no nearer finding Florence.

"Okay, people," Blake said. "We have the forensic report back on the knickers, hair and tissues found in Hill's house. DNA on them belongs to Florence Percival. There's also semen on them belonging to Leonard Hill."

Kath Cryer sat back in her chair and folded her arms as if to say, 'case closed.' She raised her hand. "He's kept it up with the, 'no comment' routine since you left. No wonder."

"Anything else at the house?"

"Clean as a whistle. He even let us look at his phone. Nothing mucky on there. Apart from some dick pics sent to this Geri Sharpe." A groan of disgust rippled through the group at the thought.

"She's the woman he said he was meeting at the Park, right?" Blake said.

Kath nodded. "Yeah but she never showed up. She met up with him at his house. The texts match his account of things except a couple of texts sent from her asking where he was."

Vikki Chinn straightened up in her chair. "We've got more on Geri Sharpe. She has convictions for prostitution and possession. Want us to bring her in and have a chat?"

Blake nodded. "We need to establish a timeline and figure out what happened between Hill taking Florence and him arriving at his home to meet Geri. If she was wondering where he was, that suggests he was late. So he must have hidden or... dumped... Florence somewhere between the park and his house. Alex and Andrew, can you have a look at possible routes he could have taken and any possible locations where Florence might be?"

Kinnear and Manikas nodded.

"What about the divers. Have they found anything?"

"A whole pile of rubbish, but no sign of Florence," DS Vikki Chinn said. "They've covered the lake in the lower park but not the one in the upper park. I can't imagine Hill disposing of her in the lake in broad daylight. Surely there'd be too many people around and how would he have the time?"

"I don't know, Vikki. It's troubling me, too. I'll go through things with Hill again tomorrow, see if I can get something out of him."

*****

The lights were all on when Blake got home. For a moment, he felt the old gut twist of anxiety that he used to experience when his mother was still alive. Some nights every single light would be glaring at him through the darkness and he'd find her in the garden in her nightie calling for Jeff or his father. But his mother had gone, so it puzzled Blake that so many lights were on.

Inside, Laura was frantically searching under the front room sofa. "Charlie? Come on, boy. Where are you?"

"Problem?" Blake said, making Laura yelp.

"Jeez, Will. You frightened me. I can't find Charlie anywhere."

"Really? He can't be far. You've kept all the outside doors closed, right?"

"Of course I have. I just went to the loo and when I came back, he was gone. Serafina was sat in his place, purring."

Blake raised his eyebrows. "His place? He hasn't got 'a place' in this house. Perhaps she ate him."

"Don't," Laura said, smacking him playfully on the arm. "He'll be around somewhere. Help me find him."

Blake rolled his eyes. "It's gone midnight, Laura. It's been another stinker of a day. Still can't find Florence Percival. I think we might be too late."

"Will, that's awful," Laura said, wrapping him in her arms. "You can't blame yourself. You did all you could."

"I know, I know. It doesn't make it any better, though. How can someone do that to a child? Steal them away like that?"

"I don't know... wait... listen..."

Blake strained his ears and heard a faint whimpering coming from the hall. "Sounds like your puppy," Blake said. They went out into the hall.

"It's coming from the cellar," Laura said, frowning.

Blake pulled open the cellar door and Charlie bounded out, wagging his tail and leaping up at Laura. "How did he get in there?" Blake said, frowning.

"I blame the cat. Charlie must have nosed his way in there and she pushed it shut on him," Laura said.

"Sounds a bit far-fetched to me," Blake said, glancing over at Serafina who lay curled in her armchair asleep.

"Believe you me, Will, jealousy is a deep animal emotion. It's tied up with survival and ranking within the pack. I'd never underestimate it as a motive for skulduggery."

Blake paused, letting what she had said sink in. "Good point. But shutting the cellar door would require opposable thumbs, I'd have thought…"

"A good shove with a big enough body and that cellar door would click shut on its own," Laura said.

"So you left all the lights on when you were searching for Charlie?"

Laura blushed. "Well, no. It's this house, Will. It gives me the creeps sometimes…"

"Fair enough. But, you don't have to stay here, you know. I've offered to come to your…"

"It just feels like a mausoleum, sometimes. You need to sort it out, one way or the other, Will. Redecorate or sell. Maybe both. It would sell better if you redecorated it."

Blake looked into Laura's eyes. "There's something else, isn't there? What's up, Laura?"

Laura hugged Charlie to her, turning her head away as he frantically licked her chin. "There was a car the other day. It slowed down and the driver stared at me while I was in the front garden. It just gave me the creeps, that's all. I thought I saw the same car again tonight. I dunno. I suppose I put all the lights on to make out there was a party or a gathering or something. The house felt less empty."

"What kind of car was it? Did you get any details? What did the driver look like?"

"No. I'm not a detective! It was a black car with tinted windows. I'm pretty sure it was a man driving it. It just freaked me out, that's all."

Blake put his arm around her. "That's okay. Completely understandable given what happened." Josh Gambles had taken Laura hostage in this house and Blake himself had nearly been killed not far from here. "Nothing wrong with feeling anxious. You never know who is lurking about. I believe Gambles has his own twisted fan club these days. It could have been a sightseer, some kind of ghoulish tourist."

"Wow, thanks. I feel much better about it now," Laura said, smiling and scratching Charlie's chin. "God, I'm so tired. I'd better get this one back in his basket."

Blake paused and then looked at the dog. "Bring his basket up to our room," he said at last. "You need some rest, too."

"Really?" Laura's face lit up. Over her shoulder, he saw Serafina blink at him and lick her lips. He wouldn't have been surprised if she'd shaken her head in disappointment at him.

"Come on," Blake said, glancing out of the windows into the darkness. "Let's put this day to bed." But something had slotted into place. Maybe he was getting somewhere. He'd see to-morrow.

Jeff Blake saw the private hire car pull up outside the Seraph and breathed a sigh of relief. Boredom McClague nodded towards the door. "Off you go, now," he said. "Get straight into the taxi and don't talk to anyone. You've got about four feet of pavement but I think you'll make it."

What worried Jeff the most was that McClague wasn't joking as far as he could tell. "Thanks," Jeff said and hurried outside. The cold air hit him and he was conscious of a few dark figures lurking in the shadows on the other side of the road. He ignored them and climbed into the back of the car. The door lock clicked and Jeff instantly realised his mistake. The seat next to him was occupied by a burly, bearded man in a black leather jacket. In panic, Jeff scrabbled at the handle but it didn't open the door for him. Instead a hessian sack went over his head, scratching his face and plunging him into darkness. "Keep still," the man said and Jeff felt the sharp point of a needle in his neck. He thought to himself that this would make one hell of a chapter or the book would never get written. Then darkness consumed him.

CHAPTER 22

Leonard Hill looked weary. His brief looked similarly wrung out. It was clear she didn't relish representing a potential child-killer and was doing mental gymnastics trying to justify her role. But Blake believed that everyone deserved a fair hearing.

"My brief says that unless you're going to formally charge me, you can't keep me here much longer," Hill said, picking at his thumbnail.

"I don't think you'll be going anywhere, Leonard," Blake said, sharing a look with Vikki Chinn who sat next to him. "We've had the forensic results back and the underwear has Florence's DNA all over it. And traces of your semen. Care to explain that?"

Hill went pale and swallowed hard. "That's impossible."

"Not from where I'm sitting, Leonard. It looks like you took the girl from Birkenhead Park and sexually assaulted her. Where did you dump her, Leonard? Where's Florence's body? Did you drop her in the lake like you did Undine Percival?"

"No comment."

"What is it about the Percivals that brings out the worst in you, Leonard?" Blake said, leaning forward on the table. "Did it give you more of a rush, thinking of how devastated that family would be, again?"

"Devastated?" Hill sneered. "Ha! You have met them, haven't you? The Percivals don't do 'devastated.'"

"Then why did you take Florence? Or was it just a massive coincidence?"

"No…" Hill began to say and then his shoulders slumped. "No, it wasn't because I didn't take her. I never even saw her. I waited for Geri and then, when she didn't turn up, I went home to meet her. You've seen my texts on the mobile phone."

Blake produced the phone. "Yes, including two texts from Geri asking where you were. Obviously you were late back from the park. Something very important must have detained you. What was it Leonard?"

Hill blinked at Blake as if he hadn't understood. "What do you mean? What texts?" Blake scrolled through and turned the screen to face Hill.

"You see my problem, Leonard. You lied to us about being at the park at first. Then you told us you waited there maybe half an hour until 9:30, arriving home at 9:50. But Geri texts you twice asking where you are, the last one at 10:30. So you can't have been at home before then, can you?"

"I-I was… I've never seen those texts before…"

"Look now. They're there, large as life. Maybe you were too preoccupied with something else to notice them. Do you want to tell me about that?"

"I can't."

"Can't or won't?"

"I can't because I arrived at my house about 9:50."

"Tell me about your friendship with Paul Percival," Blake said, hoping a change of tack would wrong foot Hill.

Hill shrugged. "We hung around together in school. After he killed Undine, I had nothing to do with him. He's a psychopath."

"You say, Paul Percival was responsible for his sister's death but you were arrested for that, were you not?"

"I was framed…"

"Bit of a pattern forming here, don't you think?"

Leonard Hill pushed his glasses back up his sweaty nose. "I don't care what you think. I didn't kill Undine or Florence Percival."

"So take me through your version of what happened to Undine."

"It was horrible," Leonard said and Blake was struck by the sorrow in the man's voice. "Paul hated her. He was so jealous of her. Mr and Mrs Percival were totally focused on her, you see. That wasn't on. Paul constantly moaned about how she got special treatment from their parents. Paul is a very selfish person, you see, Mr Blake. I remember him grumbling about how he could have gone to a 'decent' private school instead of the Birkenhead School we went to. He wanted to go to a 'proper boarding school,' but his parents said that they had to save for Undine's future. He resented that. Never shut up about it."

"Why did you hang around with him then?"

Hill reddened. "Because I had nobody else and... I was lonely. The Percivals were rich. Everyone at that school was rich except me and a couple of other scholarship kids. He got all the latest computer and video game stuff. I helped him set it up and he pretended he'd done it."

"Right," Blake said, unimpressed. "And Undine was there, too. Helpless and, maybe one day, she'd be at your mercy..."

"No," Hill said, squeezing his eyes shut and shaking his head. "She was cute and innocent. I was just nice to her. You couldn't help it, Blake. She brought out the best in most people. Not

Paul, though. Then one night, we were asked to babysit her. Paul was disgusted but agreed. When his parents had gone, he suggested a drinking contest with some of his mother's vodka. Paul was always doing stuff like that, little dares, or downright dangerous stuff just for a laugh. I thought we were both drinking the vodka, but I reckon now that Paul had filled his bottle with water."

"So he got you drunk…"

"Very drunk. I wasn't used to alcohol. I can't remember much of that night. But I do remember waking up by the lakeside and Paul pointing at Undine's body floating in the water. I'll never forget him shaking his head and saying, 'what have you done?' like I was a naughty kid who'd broken a window rather than doing anything to try save his sister. He ran off then, leaving me to thrash around in the lake, and pull Undine out. She was dead, though."

"The jury found you not guilty of murder."

"Manslaughter. That was the best I could hope for according to my brief. Everything was stacked against me. Dysfunctional family background, a loner, my unhealthy obsessions. D'you know, Blake. I truly believe that, if Paul hadn't murdered Undine, I would have come to my senses. I was young. Maybe I could have got help or even grown out of it. Instead, I was branded a pervert and dumped in a secure unit with a load of other perverts. It did me no good and set me on the path I'm on now."

"So, imagine for a moment I believe your version of events, that could easily explain why you took Florence. Revenge is the oldest motive in the book."

"Except I didn't," Hill's eyes were glittering with tears of frustration. "All I can say is this is exactly like the first time. Somebody has set me up and I don't know how or why."

*****

A loud cough brought Jeff Blake to his senses and he instantly wished he was still unconscious. The bag over his head rendered him sightless but he didn't need his eyes to know that he was tied to a chair. His head throbbed and his mouth felt like it was full of cotton wool. One gangster torture film scene after another played over in his head and he suddenly felt the need to urinate. Any minute now, the bag would be torn from his head and a gorilla holding a pair of bolt cutters would be leering at him. He squeaked and clenched his fists at the thought. Then the bag was ripped from his head.

Jeff winced in the sudden light and groaned. He was in a plush office with a green carpet. A large oak desk sat at one end of the room and a couple of chairs faced it. There were bookshelves filled with files, a drinks cabinet and a TV screen. He could have been in his agents office if it weren't for the three burly men dressed in dark trousers and leather jackets. Jeff scanned their hands and breathed a sigh of relief at the absence of bolt cutters.

A man stood at the other end of the office, wearing loud check trousers, a pale blue Pringle tank top and a pink, open-necked shirt. His silver hair was slicked back over his scalp and made his tan look deeper than it probably was. He held a golf club and was concentrating intensely on putting a ball into a paper cup.

"Ah, you're awake, Jeffrey," the man said, popping the ball neatly into the cup. "Yuss!" He punched the air, even though there was no way he could miss. He held up the club. "Gotta keep up to scratch. Little and often that's my motto when it comes to practise. Wouldn't you agree?"

"Yes, I would... little and often..."

"I think someone overdid the dose of that tranquiliser. What did you give him, Bjorn?"

Bjorn shrugged. "Dunno, boss, it was in the back of the fridge. First thing that came to hand."

Harry shook his head. "Blimey, Bjorn, that could've been my Hep B vaccination for my holidays, you pillock." He turned back to Jeff. "You've been out for the count all night. Did you know that? You hungry?"

"N-not really," Jeff said. "But th-thank you..."

"Manners," the man said, shaking his golf club at the big men. "I like that. You can tell you're a man of culture, Jeffrey." He squatted down in front of Jeff. "I'm Harry Thorpe."

"Pleased to meet you," Jeff said, hoping he didn't sound sarcastic or too flip. The fact that he was still tied up told him that his fate hung by a thread."

"I'll get to the point. One of my chaps here heard you blabbing in the pub last night. Asking questions about Kyle Quinlan. What I want to know is why are you interested?"

Jeff pursed his lips. If he got out of this in one piece, he'd give Josh Gambles a kick up the arse for getting him into all this trouble. "I'm writing a book. A biography of Josh Gambles. You might have heard of him."

Harry Thorpe pulled a face. "I read about that bloody psycho. What you writing about him for?"

"Crime pays," Jeff said, smiling and trying a little of his old charm usually reserved for female editors and agents.

"That loony gives criminals a bad name. It's worse than the films. I mean, I bet you thought we were going to torture you and cut your fingers off with a bolt cutter or something..."

Harry Thorpe looked round at his men who all laughed.

"No, not at all," Jeff said, his voice hoarse.

"Get the bolt cutter, Bjorn," Thorpe said, his face deadly serious. Jeff felt his stomach lurch and he gasped, only for Thorpe's face to crack into a huge grin. "Ha! See! I told yer. Honestly, what kind of monster do you think I am?"

Bjorn reappeared with a pair of bolt cutters. "Here you go, boss."

Thorpe closed his eyes and shook his head. "It was a joke, Bjorn. I'm not going to cut Jeffrey's fingers off." Bjorn looked slightly puzzled and Jeff wondered if he was confused or just disappointed or both. "So," Harry Thorpe continued, "you're writing a book about this Gambles character. Where does Kyle Quinlan come into it?"

"He's an old friend of Gambles. Apparently, he's gone missing and Gambles wants to know where he is."

Thorpe pulled a face. "So he asked a writer of literary fiction to hunt him down. What a plonker."

"It's a bit complicated. You see, Gambles has a bit of a fixation on my brother..."

Thorpe's eyes narrowed. "Yeah, I heard you were Will Blake's brother. To be honest, that's the only reason you aren't in Arrowe Park breathing through a tube. I don't want plod trampling all over me. So I'm still none the wiser. What does Gambles getting a stiffy over your brother have to do with Quinlan?"

"His ex, Laura Vexley, is my brother's girl-friend..."

Harry Thorpe raised one eyebrow. "Well, well, well," he said, quietly. "Now you're talking. Bjorn, untie the man. What're you thinking of leaving him all trussed up like a Christmas turkey? Cut him free."

Bjorn pulled a knife from his pocket and sawed through the ropes. Jeff shook the blood back into his hands and feet as the bonds fell to the ground. Harry Thorpe brought a decanter of amber spirits down from the cabinet and two heavy tumblers and went and sat at his desk. "Come and tell me all about the lovely Laura Quinlan. I've been dying to catch up with her."

CHAPTER 23

When Vikki Chinn had asked whether or not Blake wanted Leonard Hill's girlfriend bringing in for a chat, Kath had smirked. Geri Sharpe wouldn't be the kind of person you 'brought in.' She did have a record for prostitution, and possession but she'd also knocked out a police officer whilst resisting arrest and Kath noticed a complaint against her from a neighbour for smashing windows. Her name cropped up as a peripheral witness in numerous altercations and cases of public disorder.

Just out of courtesy, Kath tried to phone the number they had for her from Leonard Hill. A continuous tone told Kath that the phone was dead. Maybe ditched once she realised what Leonard was involved with. Kath hoped that Hill's star witness had done a runner, to be honest. As far as she was concerned, they were wasting everyone's time listening to the man's desperate alibis. The last thing Kath wanted was for Leonard to walk out of the custody suite a free man. He didn't deserve that.

*****

Harry Thorpe sipped at his whiskey and Jeff

passed his own glass under his nose. Even though he'd been out for the count, he was pretty sure it was early in the morning. It was a fine whiskey, not cheap but at this time of day Jeff's stomach lurched. He wondered how he was going to drink it without throwing up on Thorpe's carpet. That might just stretch the man's hospitality to the limit.

"God! What am I thinking?" Thorpe said suddenly, making Jeff jump and almost spill his drink. "Lads, get this man a bacon butty. He must be starving. You can't enjoy that on an empty stomach."

Jeff smiled. "Thanks, Mr Thorpe…"

"Harry. Call me Harry," he said. "So where's Laura been hiding since she left Kyle Quinlan?" he said it as though he was concerned for her welfare and Jeff started to worry that Thorpe had other motives for asking.

"I'm not sure," Jeff said, honestly. "I'll be straight with you, Harry, Will and I don't see eye to eye all the time. So I don't see much of him or her. I think she spends a lot of her time at Will's in Rock Park. She has a flat in Wallasey somewhere."

"Interesting," Thorpe said, swirling his whiskey around in the glass. "Hiding in plain sight. Clever."

"Can I ask," Jeff said. "How did you know Kyle

Quinlan and Laura?"

Thorpe weighed Jeff up. "This goes no further, right? I don't want to open the book about Gambles and find my name plastered all over it."

Jeff put the glass down and held up both hands. "I assure you Harry. I am the soul of discretion. I'm not sure it would ever get into the book, anyway. I think Gambles is just trying to stir up trouble for my brother."

"Oh," Thorpe said, looking slightly crestfallen. "I mean, you COULD write about it. Just don't go naming names and all that."

Jeff nodded and wondered if he was looking at another potential customer. 'Jeff Blake, Biographer to the Underworld,' had a certain ring to it. "I wouldn't dare," he said, winking.

"Quinlan used to work for me. A bit like these chaps," Thorpe said, pointing to the gorillas surrounding them. "He leaned on people when required, kept me safe, that sort of thing. But he had brains." Thorpe looked up at the men again. "No offence lads. You know I love and respect you, but you all have Velcro fasteners on your shoes."

The men frowned and looked at their feet in unison.

"So Kyle Quinlan was one of your security guards?"

"Yeah, that's it. Call him a security guard. I like that. He wanted a bit more, though. I never thought he'd actually steal from me but one day we were moving some cash. All very hush hush and behind the tax man's back. Well, Kyle comes back all bruised and bleeding. Claiming he'd been jumped. The money was gone." Thorpe paused, lost in the memory, his face had darkened.

Jeff kept his voice low, as though he was talking to a bereaved relative. "Can I ask how much money went missing?"

"Seven hundred and fifty fucking grand," Thorpe said through gritted teeth, the mask slipping for a second. "Three quarters of a mill."

"A lot of money," Jeff said, faintly.

"We asked around, did some digging, but nobody knew anything about it. Normally, rumours would circulate if someone had nicked that much dosh. Somebody wouldn't be able to contain their excitement and would blab or buy a flash car or something. But there was nothing. It occurred to me that the reason nobody knew anything was because it had never happened. Quinlan had staged the whole thing and kept the cash for himself."

Jeff glanced around the room, wondering whether he should ask the next question. "So, what did you do?"

"Nothing. Quinlan and the lovely Laura had done a flit, hadn't they? I don't blame them. It would have been game over if I'd caught up with them." He paused. "It's odd her returning to the Wirral, though. She must know I'm not a forgiving soul…"

"Maybe she thought you'd stopped looking for her after six years. Are you certain she was involved in the robbery, too?"

Thorpe shrugged. "They were inseparable. Plus, I know I said Quinlan had brains but she's clever in other ways. She could twist Quinlan, and most men, round her little finger. I bet she hasn't told half of this to Blakey. He'll get a shock if he found out." Thorpe's shoulders shook with mirthless humour. "I think your friend Mr Gambles has just opened a very nasty can of worms. Ah! Here's our bacon butties."

Jeff smiled and took the package from Bjorn, but he really had no appetite as he watched Harry Thorpe tearing at the sandwich.

"Yeah," Thorpe said with his mouth full, a blob of tomato sauce at the corner of his mouth, "it'll be great to see Laura after all these years. So much to catch up on."

CHAPTER 24

A gentle curtain of drizzle had blown in from the Irish Sea as Kath pulled up outside Geri Sharpe's house in Noctorum. It was a big estate of mixed housing, overlooked by a ridge that was the thin end of a wedge that was Bidston Hill. The houses up on that ridge were big and looked down on the humbler dwellings literally and probably metaphorically. She realised that she wasn't that far from Leonard's house in Woodchurch, but the motorway formed a barrier between the two. She could hear the traffic swishing along the wet tarmac in the distance.

Despite the chaotic background that Geri's Sharpe's record suggested, her house looked surprisingly respectable and innocuous. It was a semi-detached with a small, well-tended front garden. An old Vauxhall Zafira sat in the drive and a child's tricycle stood next to it. Clearly Geri had children, more than one judging by the size of the car; anyone with just themselves to worry about would have a smaller one.

Geri was probably in her late thirties, small, with a flat nose and peroxide blonde hair. Kath thought she looked too skinny to be healthy. It flashed across Kath's mind that the woman could easily pass as a child if not subjected to too close scrutiny. Perfect for Hill. Geri was all smiles when she first answered the door but her face fell when Kath produced her warrant card.

"Is this about Leonard?" Geri said, leaning against the front door.

"It is," Kath said. "Can I come in?"

"You're like vampires you coppers, aren't you?"

"I'm sorry?"

"You can't enter a building unless you're invited, can you?" Geri said, she grinned, relishing Kath's discomfort. The drizzle had developed into a proper shower and the house had no porch. "Okay," she said. "Come in. You'll get soaked!"

Kath pursed her lips and gave Geri Sharpe a hard stare as she stepped into the house. "Thanks," she said, acidly.

They went into a living room dominated by a huge box of Lego. "My Dominic and Bertie," Geri said. "They love making things. You were lucky to catch me. I've only just got back from dropping them off at school."

"Right," Kath said, smiling tightly.

"I've got four of them," Geri said. "You know what they're like, right?"

"No," Kath said. "I don't have any kids. Can I ask you about Leonard Hill?"

"Fire away," Geri said. "Do you want a coffee or something?"

Geri's chatter was beginning to grate on Kath. This might take a while. "No thanks," Kath said. "Need to crack on. So can you tell me what happened the day before yesterday?"

Geri composed herself as if she was trying to remember the details. "Yes. I was meant to meet Leonard Hill at the playground at Birkenhead Park around 9am..."

"That's an unusual place and time. Didn't you have the kids to drop off?"

"No, Sheila the woman across the road said she'd take them. She's good like that if I've got someone to meet..."

"Why the playground and the park?"

Geri shrugged. "Dunno really. I thought he suggested that but maybe I did. I'd taken the kids there a while back, so it was probably just stuck in my mind. Anyway, it was somewhere we both knew. I never give out my address for obvious reasons."

"What was the purpose of your meeting?"

Geri grinned and winked. "You know, good times, a bit of fun..." Her grin faded, quickly. "Except it wasn't that much fun, this time."

"So you were meeting Hill to have sex?"

Geri rolled her eyes. "Yeah, if you want to be so... so what's the word?"

"Factual," Kath said. "What time did you meet him?"

"Well I didn't, did I? Sheila wasn't well. Silly cow had too much Prosecco the night before. Too hung over. I said to her, 'you wanna watch that, boozing on a school night.' I wasn't best pleased. Anyway, she said..."

"So you didn't actually meet Leonard Hill at the park?"

"No. I had to drop my kids off, didn't I? And bloody Sheila's, too. And her little one, Kanye, he's a bloody handful..."

"So what did you do?"

"I told him, didn't I? I said to Kanye, 'don't be undoing your seatbelt when I'm driving along or ...'"

"I mean what did you do about Leonard?" Kath was losing the will to live.

"Oh, yeah. I called him and said I'd meet him at his house. I've been there a couple of times. I went there after I'd dropped the kids off."

"How did you two meet?"

"Oh, you know, one of them apps, swipe right, swipe left," Geri said. "To be honest, he was no looker but I thought, you know, he might have a nice personality. Or a bit of money to spend." She winked.

"Right," Kath said, scribbling a note down. "So you went to his house. Wasn't that a bit risky?"

"That's the chance you take, isn't it? Anyway, like I say, I'd met him a few times, so I was pretty sure I was safe."

Kath paused for a moment. "I don't know, Geri. You go to a stranger's house for a quicky in the morning. I mean aren't there better ways to meet people?"

"Look, I'm not saying it's perfect but it's better than walking the streets..."

"So you were selling sexual services," Kath said.

"I never said that. If a man gives me a few quid as a present, then that's fine by me. I'm not fussy about looks if they're kind and generous."

"So you got to Leonard's house," Kath said. "What then?"

"Well he didn't show up, did he? Not for ages..."

"How long?"

"I dunno. I texted him twice, I think, asking where he was. It was gone half ten by the time he turned up, I remember that because I was hoping to have been on my way home by then."

"Did he give any reason for being late?"

"No. He just looked a bit flustered and muttered something about traffic."

"Did he have anything with him?"

Geri shook her head. "Nope. Oh, wait a minute. Yeah, He was carrying an envelope thing. What d'you call them? The ones that sound like the condoms..."

"What?"

"Or lemons... Jif.. Jiffy, yeah. A Jiffy bag. He had a Jiffy bag in his hand."

Kath scribbled down a note, trying not to think about Geri's thought processes. "Did he say what was in the bag or what it was?"

"Nah. He just left me in the living room and ran upstairs with it," Geri said. "Dunno where he took it."

"So then what did you do?"

Kath expected another saucy wink or a smile from Geri but she looked serious. "We went upstairs, and we undressed. It wasn't very nice, to be honest. He kept saying things... calling me his 'good little girl' and trying to get me to call him 'Uncle Len.' He hasn't done that before. It felt wrong. Anyway, he finished, gave me a few quid and I got out of there as quick as I could."

"And you haven't seen him since?"

"God no. I'd run a flipping mile if he came near me, now. He gave me the creeps. All that talk. He sounded like some kind of paedo. Is that why you're here? Has he been caught with a kiddy?"

"It's just a lead in a serious case. I'm afraid I can't tell you any more than that. Mr Hill may not be involved at all."

"I bet he is, whatever you're investigating," Geri Sharpe said, looking at the Lego on the floor. "God, I'm glad I never let him come here…"

Kath stood up. "Right. Well, thank you for your help, Ms Sharpe, you've been very helpful. I'll get on."

Sitting in her car outside Sharpe's house, Kath flicked through her notes and listened to the rain rattle on the roof of the car. It all fitted together. Leonard Hill had killed the little girl and then gone back to his house and had sex with Geri Sharpe. The poor girl was dead. This man was a monster and needed bringing down.

*****

Alex Manikas and Andrew Kinnear scowled in silence at the map in front of them. Neither of them could figure out how, in the time given, someone could snatch a child, bundle them into a car, take them somewhere secluded and then… what?

"Between the park and Hill's home, there are

more than ten fields, parks or public open spaces that he could have visited. And that's assuming he chose the most direct route home to cut down travel time. But how could he have done it without being spotted?" Kinnear said.

"What about this stretch of woodland alongside the M53. It's not far from his home."

Kinnear shook his head. "But where would he park his car?"

"There, in Manor Drive or Ford Road?"

"And then drag a reluctant child across a busy carriageway and into that scrubland? It's possible, I guess. Maybe worth a search."

"What about Bidston Hill?"

"Being generous and allowing him five minutes to get into his car with the girl, then allowing ten fifteen minutes to get home, assuming the traffic's in his favour. Do you think he'd have time to go up Bidston Hill?"

"It's as possible as anywhere else?" Manikas said with a shrug. "He could have gone the other way, towards the docks. The poor kid could be in the River Mersey..."

Kinnear put his head in his hands. "Or Arrowe Country Park near his house or Prenton Golf Club. We could search for weeks with any number of men and find nothing."

"But he wouldn't have had time to hide her

very well, would he?"

"Unless he prepared earlier."

Manikas grimaced. "Did Hill have any known associates? Someone who lives near the park who he could have dumped the kid with to return to later?"

"The man's a complete loner. He doesn't have a job, he walks his dog and watches TV. Unless there's something dynamite on his computer and we haven't had anything back on that yet. We may as well close our eyes, stab a pin in this map and go and search there for all the good it'll do."

Manikas chewed his thumbnail. "He can't have planned it, though. He wouldn't have known that Florence would run away from Brendan Dockley at that moment. If he did plan it, then either he was going to take Dockley out somehow which seems unlikely..."

"Or Dockley was in on it from the start," Kinnear said, looking up at Manikas. "It's too much of a coincidence that Hill abducts a child from *that* particular family by chance. And he obviously has an axe to grind with the Percivals. What if he somehow concocted some kind of plan with Dockley?"

"It makes as much sense as anything else," Manikas said. "And if that is the case, then Dockley may know where Florence was taken."

"We'll identify some likely areas and then have a word with Mr Dockley. I think there's more to him than meets the eye."

CHAPTER 25

Things had been tense between Will and Jeff Blake for many years but Jeff insisting on being Josh Gambles' biographer really wound Will up. So when his phone rang and he saw it was Jeff, Will almost ignored it. But he'd done that in the past and it had nearly cost him his life. Will answered. "Jeff, this isn't a great time. Is it important?"

"It is Will but I need to talk to you in person about this. Not on the phone."

"Right. How about tonight? I might be a bit late but…"

"Urgently, Will. It's about Laura. I think she might be in danger… I'm in Birkenhead. I could meet you in Liverpool in half an hour…"

Blake looked down at his files. "It better be important Jeff. I really don't have the time. I'll meet you in the foyer…"

"No. Somewhere a bit quieter. I can't be seen to be going to the police station. I've had an… interesting night…"

"There's a coffee shop on the corner of Castle Street. I'll meet you there."

Paul Percival sipped the hot coffee and winced. It tasted bitter and strong, but it kept him alert and awake. He'd need his wits about him today. Last night had been a nightmare but he thought he'd pulled it off.

All he had to do was to sit and wait for the police to come knocking, which they would.

Once they'd found the body.

He'd known that he couldn't keep Dockley in the freezer forever, so he reasoned that dumping his body sooner rather than later was the best thing to do. After all, once it was clear that Dockley was missing, they'd search the house again, wouldn't they? And if Paul could make it look like an accident or maybe a possible suicide, then any suspicion would fall on the young man. True, Brendan had the scald marks on the back of his hand but Paul could just deny any knowledge of where they came from. But if they found the body in the house, in a bloody freezer, then there was no denying that. No, Brendan's body had to go.

It looked like they were going to charge Leonard Hill anyway and Dockley might look like an accomplice then. That would work in Paul's favour, pushing the suspicion away from him.

He'd waited until early in the morning and dragged Dockley's stiff corpse back up into the kitchen. It was awkward and unpleasant. The body was stiff with rigor mortis and had partly frozen. Fortunately, Paul had curled it into a foetal position when he pushed it into the freezer so arms and legs weren't sticking out at awkward angles. But the curled-up position made the body hard to handle. It smelt a bit too and the skin looked a bit grey. After much struggling, Paul had managed to get the body into the barrow.

The riskiest part was pushing the body in a wheelbarrow to the lake in the lower park. It wasn't that far but there could be someone about, even at this time. On the plus side, it was a dark night, and the moon was smothered in a thick layer of cloud. So, keeping to the shadows beneath the trees at the edge of the park, he'd inched his way around. His heart had thumped so hard, he thought someone might hear it. But it was exciting, too. A fox had trotted across his path, pausing to stare at him before scampering away. The park seemed different at this time, twigs cracked and things scuttled in the undergrowth. The occasional bird chirped up in the trees as it roosted for the night.

The edges of the lake were well-worn with children squatting at the banks to poke sticks in the water and feed the ducks. But here and there, the bushes were too thick to allow access and hung over the water. Paul heaved the barrow as close as he could to the bank and then dragged the body into the water, pushing it under cover of the bushes. There would be plenty of dog walkers in the morning but with any luck, it might be a couple of days before it would be discovered. By that time, the water might have done a good job destroying any DNA evidence.

Getting back with the empty barrow had been as fraught as taking the body. The barrow clanged now it was free of any load and the wheel squeaked all of a sudden. Once he got back, he hosed it out and leaned it up in the garden shed, piling a few spades and rakes on top of it to make it look like it hadn't been used for a while. Then he crept back into the house for a shower and to wash the clothes he'd just worn.

Now he sat, waiting for the police to call. He'd practised his concerned look in the mirror. "I wish there was some way I could help you, detective," he said to his reflection and then smiled. But something squirmed in his gut. A worm of anxiety. What if someone had seen him last night? What if there was some tell-tale DNA on the clothes he'd worn? He shook himself. The clothes were clean, there were no tracks, and nobody had seen him last night. He was certain.

*****

Jeff sat at a table in the coffee shop, twirling a mug round and staring into the black liquid, when Will found him. He squashed down a flash of anger at his younger brother. In many ways they were like two sides of the same coin. Will had been athletic at school whilst Jeff had been more artistic. Will was a one-woman man and loyal, but Jeff was a butterfly who flitted from one flower to the next, never really settling. He'd judged Jeff harshly as far as money matters were concerned and overlooked quite how much Jeff had cared for their parents when they needed it, even to the detriment of his own writing career. Meanwhile, Will had been preening himself on television and selling photoshoots of his so-called 'perfect life' to Hello magazine. He'd only really gone back home when all that crumbled to dust and his daughter died. Besides, if Jeff was worried enough to drag Will out of work, then it was probably worth hearing. He pulled a chair up to Jeff's table.

"You look terrible," Will said. "What have you been up to?"

Jeff scrubbed his hands down his stubbly cheeks. "I told you, I had an interesting night. Does the name Kyle Quinlan mean anything to you?"

"This is Gambles' doing isn't it?" Will said, preparing to leave. "I told you, Jeff, you can work with that madman if you want but don't expect any help from me. Or any sympathy when it all blows up in your face."

"Wait," Jeff said, grabbing Blake's arm. "Yes, it is Gambles but I'm worried about Laura. And you."

"What do you mean?"

"You obviously know something about Quinlan or you wouldn't have linked the name to Gambles," Jeff said.

Will couldn't help but be impressed. "Okay, so we might make a detective of you yet. Quinlan and Laura were married. He gave Laura a dog's life and then disappeared about six years ago. She divorced him. Never saw him again. Gambles dredged up his name, trying to cause trouble for Laura and me. So, what's new?"

"I heard a slightly different story, Will," Jeff said, sipping his coffee. "From a different source. I can't say who but the story they told me was of a huge stash of money being stolen and the two thieves vanishing. Laura was one of them and very much involved in Quinlan's business."

Will narrowed his eyes. "Who told you that?"

"I can't say but he didn't know Laura was back on the Wirral. He wants his money back. I'm worried about Laura, Will but I'm worried about you, too. What if Laura isn't telling you the truth? What if she's stringing you along?"

"Look, I know that Laura wasn't an angel in her youth, but she's changed. You only have to spend some time with her to know that she's a good person. But if she's in danger, I need to know who poses that threat."

Jeff looked pained. "Sorry, Will. A few hours ago, I was tied to a chair with a bag over my head. I don't want to end up back in that position."

"So, you'd rather see Laura in your place, would you?"

"No. Just tell her to be careful, that's all. Maybe she can point you in the direction of whoever might want to hurt her. Maybe she should have done that already." Jeff got up and Will grabbed his arm.

"If anything happens to her, Jeff, I swear…"

Jeff pulled his arm away. "Talk to Laura, Will. She needs to be honest with you."

Will watched him stalk out of the coffee shop and then took his phone from his pocket.

CHAPTER 26

There were police officers in the back garden behind Laura Vexley's flat. She clutched Charlie and watched them, her heart thumping against her ribs. Laura lived in a converted townhouse in Wallasey on the top floor. It was an old building with high ceilings and sash windows. The back garden of the flats was overgrown with feral shrubs and brambles, even a few saplings who had seen their chance and were making a headlong dash to full adult trees. Beyond that jungle, on the other side of a fence, was a proper garden. One Laura knew well. She spent a lot of time looking into it, especially before she met Will.

The garden was beautiful, with neat borders, a well-mown lawn and a patio dotted with planters full of flowers. The house that it belonged to was similarly immaculate and often Laura would watch the happy family who lived there with a spark of jealousy. But now she just felt panic.

It looked like slabs in the patio in the back of the house had been lifted and a hole dug. Laura covered her mouth with her hand. For a moment, she froze, uncertain what to do, then her phone vibrated. It was Will. She stared at the name on the screen for a second as it buzzed, then she threw the phone down onto the table and hurried into the bedroom.

Charlie watched, wagging his tail and skipping from paw to paw as she loaded the contents of her drawers into a suitcase. Opening her wardrobe, she dragged what she could out and crushed those into the case too. Toothbrush, toothpaste and some deodorant were swept out of the cabinet into a bag.

She looked down at the eager little puppy. "I'm sorry, Charlie, but you can't come with me." In the living room, she could still hear her phone buzzing away as Will tried to get in touch with her. But he mustn't. She just had to get away.

Lugging her case to the front door, she turned and looked out at the garden again. It was only ever a matter of time, she thought. She'd been fooling herself that she could have a normal life. Besides, Will would never forgive her.

Pushing Charlie back, she closed the door behind her. She could hear him yapping. Will would find him. He'd be okay. Right now, she needed to be as far away from here as possible. Laura froze. A creak of wood sounded below her. Someone was creeping up the stairs. She turned and stifled a scream, scrabbling at the lock to get back inside the flat. The steps grew heavier and more urgent then firm hands grasped her wrists.

*****

Kinnear and Manikas stood with Paul Percival in his kitchen, looking out across the back garden. "We really wanted a quick word with Brendan Dockley, Mr Percival."

"I haven't seen him since yesterday. He brought the shopping in and we had a chat about Florence and how much we missed her. Brendan feels so wretched about everything. I told him that it wouldn't bring Florence back."

Kinnear glanced at Manikas. "That's very understanding, Mr Percival."

"Oh, don't get me wrong," Percival muttered, shaking his head. "As soon as this is all over, I'm taking civil action against him. I'm going to ruin him for everything he's put me through. I haven't forgiven him."

"I think our priority is finding Florence, though," Manikas said. "Have you any idea where Mr Dockley might have gone?"

Percival shrugged. "I don't know. Maybe his parents," he said and then looked keenly at Kinnear. "Do you think it may be more than carelessness?"

"In what way?"

"I don't know. Why do you suddenly need to find Dockley? Do you think he might have planned Florence's disappearance?"

"We're just following lines of enquiry, Mr Percival. Often we just have to double check certain facts and details. All very routine," Kinnear said, hoping his poker face held.

"Only I was thinking along the same lines. I mean, if a random stranger had taken Florence, then fair enough but Leonard Hill? That's just too much of a coincidence. Dockley must have had some kind of arrangement with him."

"We haven't charged Mr Hill, yet, Mr Percival and it's dangerous to make connections that might not be there," Kinnear said. Manikas' phone rang and they all paused while he took the call.

"Can we use your garden gate to get to the park, Mr Percival?" Manikas said, when he'd ended the call. He glanced at Kinnear. "A body has been found at the side of the lake."

"Oh my God, is it Florence?" Percival whispered.

"An adult male," Manikas replied, looking into the garden. "Can we?"

"Certainly," Percival said. "I don't think it's locked. If Brendan turns up. I'll tell him you're looking for him."

"Thank you," Kinnear said. He followed Manikas out of the kitchen, through the conservatory and into the garden. As soon as they were outside and out of hearing, Kinnear blew out a long breath. "Is it just me or does that bloke seem more concerned about himself than about poor Florence?"

"I know what you mean," Manikas agreed. "Interesting that he'd come to the same conclusion as us though, right? He's not stupid."

"No," Kinnear said. Across the park, they could see flashing blue lights and uniformed officers setting up a cordon. "Come on, let's check this out and then go and see if Dockley is at his parents' house."

*****

Paul Percival watched the two policemen make their way out of the garden and smiled to himself. He was quite pleased with his performance, then. Especially the little bit at the end about letting Dockley know they were looking for him. Well, they were going to find him now, that was certain. He'd been quite nervous when they'd first arrived, a little bit disappointed, too. He'd hoped that Dockley wouldn't be found for a couple of days at least, so that any evidence would be degraded by the water. At least Dockley was dead and wouldn't be blabbing off to the police, so that was one thing.

"Still," he muttered to himself, "we are where we are." The coppers would be back soon and he had a few hours to get his story straight. To learn his lines.

*****

Blake stared at his phone. He'd been calling Laura on and off for over an hour with no success. That didn't mean there was a problem. Often she didn't respond because she was in the middle of work and the phone had been left in the car. She was an animal psychologist and fixed problem behaviours in pets. She always said that there was nothing worse than making a breakthrough with a problem dog only for the phone to ring and send the poor animal loopy. All the same, he was beginning to feel uncomfortable.

If what Jeff said was true, then Blake had a good idea where the threat came from. Laura had told him that Kyle Quinlan used to work for Harry Thorpe. Blake had met Thorpe before on a recent case and knew the man was crooked from the moment he set eyes on him. Thorpe had been the centre of a complaint against Merseyside police after a detective had gone too far and tried to frame him. If Quinlan had stolen money from anyone, it was likely to be Thorpe.

Florence Percival was out there somewhere, alive or dead, Blake didn't know, and she was relying on his team to find her. He couldn't just rush over the water to Wallasey and check up on Laura.

"Will? Are you with me?" Superintendent Martin said, startling Blake from his thoughts. "So where are we with this poor girl?"

"Sorry, sir," Blake said. "It's a troubling one. We've arrested Leonard Hill, a known paedophile who has a history with the family. He's been positively identified as being at the park when Florence Percival went missing and items belonging to the girl have been found at his house. Underwear with traces of Leonard Hill's semen on them and a lock of Florence's hair. Some tissues with Florence's blood on them too..."

"Seems like a slam-dunk, Will. What's the problem?"

"We haven't actually found Florence, sir and, yes, all the evidence points to Hill but he's adamant that he knows nothing about it. He says he can't tell us where she is because he doesn't know."

"One of those, eh? Well the only thing you can do is charge him and press on with the search. We should let the press know that we're charging him and get the public searching for Florence."

"Yes, sir," Blake said. "It's just..."

"Go on."

"I feel like we're being led by the nose on this

one."

"What's that meant to mean? If the evidence is there, what can we do?"

"That's what I mean. It was there, easy to find. In a jiffy bag. All neatly gift-wrapped for us. And Paul Percival... he's a piece of work, if ever I met one..."

"Come on, Will, don't do this to me. Please. You always look too deeply into these things, finding conspiracies where there aren't any. Sometimes people just aren't too bright. They don't know how hard we look for evidence..."

"But Hill has been convicted before..."

"There you go," Martin said. "Not very smart then. Let's get a press conference booked in and break the news. Keep it simple, Will. We made an arrest in record time, took a dangerous predator off the streets. All we need to do is find the girl."

"I meant more that Hill has learnt to be wary. Why would he just stuff a package of incriminating evidence under his mattress?"

"I long ago gave up trying to understand what went on in the minds of people like that, Will. Let's focus on bringing Florence Percival home," Martin said before returning to his paperwork.

"Right, sir," Blake muttered. His phoned buzzed. Martin lifted his scowling face from the desk. "It's Brendan Dockley, sir. He's just been found dead in the park. Maybe things aren't quite as straightforward as they seem."

CHAPTER 27

Once again, Birkenhead Park was full of officers and detectives. Blake stood by the lake with Malachy O'Hare, the Crime Scene Manager at his side. O'Hare looked as miserable as ever but that was just the way his face had set one day, Blake assumed. He wasn't miserable by nature.

"What is it with this place?" O'Hare said. "Do they have to go killing and kidnapping each other? Can't they just have a walk around, feed the ducks and maybe have a go on the swings?"

"I think that's generally what happens, Malachy," Blake said. "Any clue as to what happened to him?"

"Not really. The pathologist will have more of an idea but it's an odd one, I'll grant you that. A wound on the back of the head and he's all curled up like a baby. Rigor mortis has set in. He was bobbing in the water like a beachball. They're going to have fun straightening him out, for sure."

"How the hell would that happen?"

"I dunno, do I?" Malachy said, waggling his bushy white eyebrows. "But my guess is he didn't die here. If he was on his own, fell back and hit his head, he'd be sprawled out on the grass, right? If he'd been brained at the side of the lake, there'd be signs of a struggle. But there's nothing, just a few snapped twigs and some crushed grass. He looks to me like he's been bound up after he died."

"Could he have been injured and crawled in there? Maybe fell into the water?"

"Like I say, leave that to the pathologist. Mr Lah-de-dah Kenning can hold forth on such matters better than me but there's no sign he crawled."

"Brilliant," Blake sighed. "Anything on him?"

"Phone, knackered by the lake water. No wallet. That's it."

Blake looked across the park. "I've had enough of this," he muttered.

"What are you on about now?"

"Unless Dockley is just incredibly unlucky and met a mugger in the park, somebody killed him to shut him up. Hill couldn't have taken the kid without Dockley's help. But I think there's something else going on..."

"What're you going to do?" Malachy said.

"I'm going to give Paul Percival an earbashing for a start. That man should be a basket case, worried sick about that little girl, but he's more concerned about himself."

"Be careful, Will. Don't do anything stupid," Malachy said, but Blake had already set off across the park.

Blake wasn't quite sure what he was going to say but he was sick of pussyfooting around the likes of Paul Percival. If Leonard Hill was telling the truth then Paul had killed once already in his lifetime and if he could kill his little sister, why not his own daughter? And her nanny, especially if Dockley knew something about Florence and Paul.

The back gate was open, so Blake went through and banged on the conservatory door. He glanced around the garden, it looked orderly and tidy. Someone had been pushing a barrow across the patio, though, Blake could see faint tyre tracks.

Paul Percival appeared at the door. "Mr Blake..."

"Can I come in, please, Paul?" Blake said, barely waiting for Paul Percival to step back from the door.

"What is it? What's happened?"

"We've found a body in the lake. It's Brendan Dockley."

Percival put a hand to his mouth and sank into a chair. "Oh my God," he said. "How? What happened to him?"

"We don't know yet, but the crime scene investigators don't believe he died there. Rigor mortis has well and truly set in which means he died some time ago. Also, he's curled up suggesting he was tied up or put in a confined space shortly after death. When did you last see Mr Dockley?"

"Yesterday afternoon. He brought some shopping home and then went up to his room. I heard him go out about four o'clock and he didn't come back. Why are you grilling me like this?"

"Where did he say he was going?"

"He didn't. We had words. I was angry with him for losing Florence and I told him. I think he got upset." Percival put a hand to his mouth again. "Oh my God, I hope he didn't harm himself..."

"Unless he hit himself in the back of the head, and then hid himself under a bush in the lake, I'd say that's very unlikely. So what exactly did you say to Dockley?"

"I-I can't remember... something like, if he'd kept his eyes open and not been staring at his phone then Florence would still be with us..."

"Go on."

"I said I'd be suing him for negligence and he'd better get himself a good lawyer because I was going to ruin him."

"What did he say?"

"I don't know. He kept saying sorry. Saying it

wasn't his fault... what's your problem, Blake?"

"My problem? It's you, Paul. You've been nothing but calm since I met you. You're so self-absorbed. Even when your daughter is missing, you're more concerned about suing Dockley than finding her. If it was my child, I'd be out on the streets searching for her."

"Very laudable, Mr Blake and would that be effective?"

"Did you kill your sister, Paul? Did it get too much? Did you resent the attention she got from your parents?"

"What?" Paul went pale. "I-I... no. I didn't what's got into you? I'm going to phone your superiors..."

"I don't have superiors, Paul, and my colleagues share my suspicions. Come on, tell me what happened that night? Did you plan to get Leonard Hill drunk so that he'd take the blame for Undine's death? Where is your daughter Paul?"

Percival leapt to his feet. "I don't know!" he bellowed. "I don't know! You happy now you've seen me angry, Blake? Do I have to have some kind of nervous breakdown for your benefit? Get out of my house before I call your 'colleagues' to remove you."

"The truth will come out, Paul," Blake said, turning to leave. "It always does."

*****

Laura pressed herself against the dank brick-work of a side alley and sobbed for breath. Focusing on her breathing, she counted slowly trying to control it. Her heart thumped against her ribs and she shook.

As soon as the man had grabbed her wrists, Laura had gone into survival mode, throwing her head back hard. Stars had exploded in her skull, but the man had given a muffled oath and she was pretty sure she felt his front teeth give. But she didn't wait to recover; instead, she whirled around directed a sharp punch to where she guessed the man's face would be. She'd allowed herself a grim grunt of satisfaction as his nose flattened under her knuckles. One sharp kick to the left knee unbalanced him and she took the chance to jab him hard in the throat. Then snatching up her handbag, she scrambled down the stairs two at a time, not daring to look back. Her suitcase would have to stay there. She banged out of a back door. There was bound to be a car waiting out the front. How else would her attacker have got here and how would they have taken her away? If that's what they intended.

Now she looked down at her assailant's blood on her knuckles. He had seriously underestimated her, thank goodness. Her head throbbed and she gingerly pressed the back of her head with the tips of her fingers. She winced but there was no blood, so she didn't think she had cut herself. Slowly, she calmed down and began to assess the situation. Obviously, somebody had put two and two together at last and she was the answer. She knew she was in danger but hadn't realised things would develop so quickly. It was almost as though somebody had grassed her up. But someone would have to know the truth to do that. Unless they'd inadvertently passed on her name to the wrong person. Laura couldn't help thinking Josh Gambles was involved in this somehow.

But she could work all that out once she'd got away. Right now, she was still too close to her flat and her attacker would be getting to his feet and coming after her, for sure. Laura didn't know if the car at the front of the flats had other occupants. If more than one man came for her then she didn't stand a chance.

Pulling her bag onto her shoulder, she hurried from the side alley, trying to look as casual as possible whilst keeping up an urgent pace. She glanced back to see a dark BMW parked outside her flat. She wasn't certain but she thought another man sat in the passenger seat. Hurrying across the road, she slipped into another side street and headed for the nearest pub. From there, she could call a taxi and get away.

The Trafalgar pub was warm and welcoming.

Retired couples sat at tables and agonised over the menu. Laura envied them their simple dilemmas and worried that she might look odd or suspicious, hurrying in alone and out of breath. She dived into the toilets and checked her reflection for any traces of blood, bruises or scratches but she was clean. Her fist was a bit blue and grazed but she could keep that hidden.

Back out in the bar, she ordered a gin and tonic to steady her nerves and squeezed herself into a corner table. It was then she remembered she didn't have her phone. She'd left it on the bed quite deliberately. Will would probably be calling and what about poor Charlie? She sipped at her drink. She'd have to ask the young lad at the bar if he could call a cab for her. He looked friendly enough and she knew she could easily persuade him. Before she could move, though, a large, burly man with a shaven head, settled in the seat next to her and she froze in fear.

CHAPTER 28

There were things that Blake should have been doing, people he should have been interviewing. But his blow up with Paul Percival had made him more determined to find out the truth about the man. Blake was convinced he was hiding something. He knew he'd get a bollocking for hounding Percival like that but Blake didn't care. He'd phoned Vikki Chinn for the address and now found himself sitting outside the home of Davina Allisen, the woman Paul Percival was meant to be having a dirty weekend with whilst his daughter was being abducted. He should have rung ahead or given her some warning but she only lived in Heswall on the other side of the Wirral and Blake took it upon himself to just go.

As he drove through the town, he found himself wondering once again how a place could support so many coffee shops. This was a desirable area and even the smaller properties on the other side of Telegraph Road, which ran through Heswall, were expensive. The Allisen's house was on the river side of the road down a number of lanes which twisted and turned towards the shore. It was a huge, modern development with windows that looked out over the Dee Estuary and a gravelled drive that ran up from the narrow, hedge-flanked lane. The houses either side were kept at a polite distance by the property's couple of acres of garden. Blake turned into the drive, his tyres crunching on the shingle.

He rang the doorbell and somewhere inside, a dog yapped. Then it was silenced by a voice and finally, a woman appeared at the door. She was in her thirties, Blake judged, slim with long dark hair and fine features. He reminded Blake of Sam Percival but then maybe Paul had a 'type' that he liked.

"Mrs Allisen?" Blake said, flashing his warrant card. "Detective Chief Inspector Will Blake. I'm sorry to drop in on you unannounced but could I have a word?"

Davina Allisen glanced back into the house. "Is this about Florence?"

"Yes," Blake said. "Do you have a minute? It would help me enormously..."

"I don't know how I can help..."

"I believe you know Paul Percival," Blake said. "I believe you know where he was last weekend."

Mrs Allinsen went pale. "Okay, but we'll have to walk. My husband is inside, and he can't know."

She pulled the front door shut and stepped into a pair of Hunter Wellingtons that stood to the side of the front door. "Come on, we'll walk down the lane. I can always tell Nigel, my husband, that you're a surveyor for the electricity board or something. Not that he'll notice. Or care."

"Did he not notice your weekend break?" Blake said, striding after Davina Allisen as she strode off down the drive.

She gave a bitter smile. "No. But if Nigel found out I'd been seeing someone else, he'd be insanely jealous. Not because he loves me; he just couldn't bear to lose. Especially not to Paul Percival. You're that dishy policeman off the TV, aren't you?"

"Erm, yes. I mean, I was on Searchlight. It was a long time ago now."

"It was," Davina said, tracking her eyes across Blake's body. "We used to watch that at University just to see you. Imagine that, a whole house full of students all ogling you on telly, Inspector."

"As I said," Blake murmured, clearing his throat. "It was some time ago."

"You've still got it, though," Davina Allisen said, smirking at Blake's discomfort. "Even better in the flesh, so to speak. And to think, I can't brag online to my friends about this."

A skein of geese flew, honking to each other

over their heads. "So, you were with Paul Percival last weekend?"

"Yes," she said, with a grimace. "Nigel was away for the weekend and Paul talked me into going away too. I won't be doing it again, though."

"Why not?"

"He's an insufferable bore. All he did all weekend was talk about himself. He wasn't great in bed either..."

Blake looked out across the fields. Beyond them and the River Dee, the Welsh hills beckoned. Blake's father had loved walking and had taken him up and down those hills. It had been a long time since he'd been over there, what with work and his mother's dementia and disappearance but he felt a sudden pull and promised himself that he would dig out his boots and go. Soon. "So how long did you stay?"

"Until Monday. Nigel came back on Tuesday. He never knew I'd been away."

"While you were there, did Paul talk about his wife or his family?"

"He said his wife had mental health problems. He didn't really talk about Florence at all other than to say his nanny was looking after her."

"So what did he talk about all weekend?"

She shook her head. "What would you talk about, Inspector?" Davina said, lifting her head up to stare into his eyes.

Blake shrugged. "I dunno," he said, honestly. "The view, what we were going to do that day, my cat... maybe work..."

"I should have taken you," she said, giving him a flirtatious smile. "You'd have been infinitely more fun and better looking too. No, he just went on about the investment portfolio he used to have and the deals he used to close in London. He told me about the many times he put various people straight on points of finance, faced down muggers in Brixton and saved his company from ruin. Very tedious. He's been trying to get Nigel to invest with him, but we know Paul of old and did a bit of digging, ourselves."

"Really? You're old friends?"

"Acquaintances, really," Davina said. "We went to the same school. Paul was always a bit of a legend in his own lunchtime if you know what I mean? Full of himself. Nobody was a friend of Paul Percival not even that weirdo he hung around with. What was his name? Leonard, that's right."

"And yet Leonard Hill used to follow him slavishly, right?"

"Bravo, Inspector, you've been doing your research. Leonard the Loner, that's what we called him. He was a scholarship boy. Nothing wrong with that but Hill always gave me the creeps, but it turns out there was a good reason for that, eh?"

"That must have been quite a trauma for the school to go through..."

"Not really. None of us were really involved and we were only kids. I suppose now they'd have counsellors and psychologists hovering in the wings waiting to sweep us up and save our 'mental health.' It was just a source of juicy gossip for a while. Especially when Leonard tried to point the finger at Paul. That divided the school."

"Why's that?"

"Why do you think? Some kids thought Paul was more than capable of killing his sister. And poor old Tanya Ellman was accused of lying to cover for Paul. There was a graffiti craze in the school. You'd find 'Tanya Lied' scrawled on desks and on toilet walls all around the school. The poor girl had to move schools."

"And do you think she lied?"

Davina gave Blake a withering look. "Do you think I'd sleep with a man who'd murdered his sister? No, Inspector, I'm sure Leonard Hill was responsible for Undine Percival's death. Whether he deliberately meant to kill her, I don't know but I'm sure he caused it."

"You said you did some digging into Paul's past. What did you find out?"

Davina Allisen stared out across the fields. "What we always knew. He wasn't all that great with money. Or people."

"That was why he was after your money?"

"He's almost broke, Inspector. We hadn't seen him in years and he suddenly turned up at a cricket club party and started glad-handing everyone. He soon found out that Nigel was the man with the money and homed in on us."

"So, if he's such a boring loser, how come you agreed to go away for the weekend with him?"

"Paul Percival isn't bad-looking, he can be charming. Maybe I just wanted to see for myself what he was really like. I don't know. I'll tell you one thing, Inspector, it's all a front. He's like a cardboard cut-out and the creature that lurks behind that façade isn't very nice at all. Amongst the stories he regaled me with on our weekend, he did have one bitter rant about his work colleagues down in London."

"Really?"

"The world is against him, Inspector. Apparently, he'd been accused of inappropriate advances towards an intern. She took exception to them and reported Paul to her uncle, the CEO. Paul left London short of cash and with his professional reputation in tatters."

"It sounds like he's his own worst enemy,"

Blake said, suppressing a grin. "So, Paul Percival arrives home, ruined and broken..."

"His parents berate him but bail him out financially. According to Paul, his parents never took his side so he bought that house in the park to upset them."

"It did puzzle me that he chose to live so near to the scene of such a tragic event. It must drive a knife into his parent's heart every time they visited him."

Davina Allisen looked troubled for a second. "He scoffed at the way his parents doted on Florence. It was quite unpleasant to see. He bragged about them having to pay for the pleasure of seeing their granddaughter."

Blake thought back to what Samantha had said about using Florence as a bargaining chip. "Really?" he said, not giving anything away.

"That's what he said, Inspector. He's a nasty piece of work. Now, do I need to worry about Nigel finding out about my mistaken fling with Mr Percival?"

"Well, I can't pretend that it might not come out in court should Paul Percival need to provide some kind of alibi but..."

Davina's eyes widened. "Oh my God. Do you think he was involved with the kidnapping of his own daughter?"

"No," Blake said, wincing. "I don't know. It's unlikely but I'd hate to make a promise I couldn't keep."

"Right," she said. "So I'd better get my affairs in order, if you'll pardon the expression. Oh, don't worry, Inspector, I'm not contemplating anything fatal, just getting my ducks in a row in case I have to leave in a hurry. Who knows, if I'm a free agent, you could give me a call sometime."

Blake felt himself blushing. "Well, I couldn't. I mean, not that I... it wouldn't be... besides I have a friend already... a woman..."

Davina laughed and started to walk back down the lane towards her house. "Don't worry Inspector, you're too good for the likes of me. Your friend is a very lucky woman."

"No," Blake muttered, pulling out his phone as she left him and calling Laura. "I'm a lucky man." He waited for her to answer but it just went to speaker phone yet again. He called a different number and Vikki Chinn answered.

"Tanya Ellman, Paul Percival's alibi on the night his sister died? I can have a look, Will," she said. "Give me a few minutes. Why do you want to talk to her?"

"I don't know, Vikki. Just something nagging away at me that I need to lay to rest. I'm on my way in for the press conference. But I need to speak to her urgently."

CHAPTER 29

DC Andrew Kinnear hated breaking bad news to families but as he and Alex Manikas were searching for Brendan Dockley anyway and were actively involved with the case, it fell to them to drive over to Tuebrook to the Dockley household.

Now they sat in awkward silence in the small front room of Brendan's childhood home. Mrs Dockley filled her armchair, shredding an already soggy tissue. She had bright red hair and a kind face that was lined with worries. Mr Dockley ran his hands over his bare scalp. He had once been a wall of muscle but that had long since softened and given in to gravity. Probably aided by a few pints each evening, Kinnear thought.

"Who did it? Was he mugged? If I get my hands on those bastards..." Mr Dockley said to nobody in particular.

"We don't know yet, but rest assured we'll do everything to find out the truth," Kinnear said, shifting in his seat.

"I said he should never have taken that job with the Percivals. It was a bad idea from the start," Mrs Dockley said.

Kinnear glanced at Manikas. "Do you mind telling me why, Mrs Dockley?" he said, gently.

"They were a different kind of people. Living over the water in their posh house, with their posh accents and fancy ways," Mrs Dockley said. She looked up at Kinnear. "They were just different to us."

"Different to bloody everyone, if you ask me," Mr Dockley muttered darkly. "Friggin' vampires."

"What do you mean by that?" Kinnear said, keeping his voice soft so as not to antagonise or upset the grieving parents.

"I dunno," Dockley said. "They use people up don't they? We used to take Brendan to the Drama group in town. He'd come alive there, far away from here where he had a reputation for trouble. You know he had a bad incident with a stolen car? His best friend died. He always blamed himself."

"He did tell us that, yes," Kinnear said, nodding. "The Drama group must have been an escape for him."

Mr Dockley nodded. "I mean, I always thought it was a bit odd, like, but it made our Brendan happy. Those Percivals, though. They dominated the place, even though they were just members like Brendan. Took all the lead roles and bossed Mrs Fishwick who ran the group around.

They'd been going a long time…"

"It was a mixed age Drama group, then?" Manikas said.

"Yeah. They were good. They did professional shows in real theatres, like. Not just school stuff. Our Brendan was in a few pantomimes at the Empire and over at the Floral in new Brighton. Stuff with real celebrities, like."

Kinnear nodded in approval. "You said they used people up. What did you mean?"

"When they found out you had a trade, like a plumber or a joiner or something, they'd get you over to their house and have you working on it for next to nothing. A lot of us got wise to it. But there'd always be new blood coming through."

"And the way they spoke to you," Mrs Dockley said, staring at her tissues and shuddering with sadness.

"*If* they spoke to you. Most of the time, they'd just look right through you. Nah, they were bad news. You're right love, we should've stopped him going over there." Her husband sat on the arm of her chair and placed his hand over hers. They sat for a moment swallowing back their grief.

Mrs Dockley patted her husband's hand. "But he looked so happy at first, an acting role, they said it was…"

"An acting role?" Kinnear said, frowning.

"Yeah. He was meant to be doing some kind of acting in a promotional video for the Percivals or their son or something. Brendan wasn't very clear what it was," Mr Dockley said.

"But he ended up looking after their grand-kiddie. I mean, she was lovely and everything, he brought her over here a few times. But our Brendan? A childminder? And now look what's happened. I tell you, those Percivals have a lot to answer for."

*****

Something was wrong, that was certain. A suit-case lay open in front of Laura's front door and Charlie was yapping himself hoarse inside. Blake recognised some of the clothes that spilled out. Worse than that there was blood on the floor and some splattered on the walls. Blake made a call and then paused. He wasn't sure what had gone on here, but he felt sure there was some connec-tion with the mysterious vanishing Kyle Quin-lan. It went against the grain, but Blake had to ring DCI Matty Cavanagh.

Cavanagh was a thorn in Blake's side. A young, up-and-coming-at-you DCI, who dressed sharp and seemed adept at making friends and influen-cing people. His back-up was the almost cube-shaped DS Bobby Dirkin who looked like he'd been hit in the face with a shovel but had a mind as sharp as Cavanagh's trouser creases. In Blake's mind they were like a kind of scouse Jeeves and Wooster, with Dirkin pulling Cavanagh's fat out of the fire innumerable times. Cavanagh was a scouser to the core as well, never missing an opportunity to wind Blake up about his Woolly Wirral roots. Cavanagh had ruffled Laura's feathers by looking into the Quinlan disappearance and just falling short of accusing her of murder. So he wasn't Blake's favourite person but he was in charge of the investigation and there had to be a link.

"Right, Blakey? You okay?" Cavanagh said. "You found that missing kiddy yet, or are you asking for some help?"

"Just... shut up and listen," Blake hissed. "I got some information today, about Kyle Quinlan. Apparently, he stole a large amount of money from someone nasty on the Wirral. My money is on Harry Thorpe, given that Quinlan used to work for him."

"Right. So far, so theoretical and nothing we hadn't considered before. Carry on."

Blake gritted his teeth. He hated saying the next words. "My contact thinks that Thorpe has got it into his head that Laura was somehow involved and is after her. I'm standing outside her flat, there's a suitcase on the floor, and blood, too. The dog's inside going mental."

"Wait, you're outside Laura's flat?" Cavanagh said.

"Yeah, why?"

"I'm just round the corner. At the house she used to like watching from her window, had its patio dug up in the middle of the night. Something was taken but we aren't sure what. Funny coincidence, that. Should I come to you, or you to me?"

"Get CSI round here and I'll try and get into the flat," Blake snapped and ended the call.

*****

The atmosphere in the Incident Room was tense as Superintendent Martin strode between desks muttering Blake's name as though he might find him hiding underneath one. "Where the bloody hell are you?" he held a phone in one hand.

"Sir," Kath Cryer said. "Do you want me to stand in for him?"

Martin scowled at her and for a second, Kath wondered if she'd said the right thing. "It's not like Will. If he had a problem, he would have let us know. Thanks, Kath. Yes, let's get on with it." They headed down to the press conference and Kath suppressed a smile. This was good experience and if she did it well, she might just impress Martin. Never a bad thing if you're planning on promotion.

There was confusion amongst the reporters as they looked from Martin to Kath. Cameras flashed and whirred.

Martin held up his hands. "I'm afraid DCI Blake has been detained with the investigation. I hope you'll forgive us for not being celebrities, but this is DI Kath Cryer who is also working on the case."

The assembled journalists chuckled and Kath tried not to smirk at the jibe about Searchlight. She knew it rankled with the Superintendent as much as any mention of it annoyed Blake but for different reasons. She felt a little disloyal towards Blake but launched into the statement.

"Today, we are charging a Wirral man for the abduction of Florence Percival after DNA evidence and personal effects of Florence's were found at his house. As yet, we have not found Florence, but we won't rest until we do. In addition, a body that was found in Birkenhead Park has been identified as Brendan Dockley, Florence's nanny. As yet we have not established the cause of death, but we are treating it as suspicious..."

Hands shot up and questions followed, quick-fire and multi-part but nothing that Kath couldn't handle. It went in a flash and Kath kept her best poker face but inside she felt like she was winning Who Wants to be a Millionaire.

"Nicely done, Kath," Martin said. "It's a relief not to be in a press conference that ends in drama for once."

"Thank you, sir," Kath said. "I'm just glad we nailed Hill."

"As for Blake. If you speak to him before I do, tell him I need a word, urgently. If he can fit me in."

CHAPTER 30

Laura's landlord was a scruffy-looking man in a stained grey sweatshirt and matching jogging bottoms. He had a halo of nicotine blond hair frizzed around his head and a week's stubble on his chin. After some extensive questioning, Blake and Cavanagh had established that he lived in the bottom floor flat but waking him had been another story all together. Now the man stood scratching his beer belly, thoughtfully.

"I generally have a no-pets rule," he said scowling at the front door.

"If you let us in, we'll take it away and find out where Miss Vexley has gone," Cavanagh said, the detectives united for a moment against this smelly, obtuse man.

"Okay, okay, no need fly off the handle. Have you got a warrant?"

"No but the dog is going to crap all over the floor in there if it hasn't already and if we go now, you'll have to deal with it," Blake said.

The man's eyes widened and he fumbled with the keys. A cannonball of white and tan exploded from inside, almost knocking Cavanagh and the landlord over. Barking and yapping it almost ran up Blake's leg and somehow, he ended up holding Charlie as he licked, furiously at his face.

"Right," Cavanagh said as two officers in white coveralls appeared at the top of the stairs. "This is a crime scene now, so, off you pop."

"Yer what?" the Landlord began.

"You heard me, I hope we don't find too much of your DNA here. Could be incriminating. We'll let you know when we're done." Cavanagh turned and winked at Blake, who held a wriggling Charlie at arm's length. The young detective's grin slipped as Charlie's excitement got the better of him and an arc of urine cut through the air towards him.

"Bloody hell, Will, watch where you're pointing that thing!"

Charlie stopped and Blake cradled him in his arms. "Sorry, Matty. He's a bit of a force of nature."

"It looks like she was getting ready to leave," Cavanagh said, peering into the bedroom and the empty wardrobe with its gaping doors.

"Jeez, Matty," Blake said, looking out of the window. "She must have seen your team working on the patio across the back there and panicked…"

"I hate to say it, Will but that kind of implies she knew what was under the paving slabs in what was her old house."

Blake wrestled with the logic of the statement, trying to find an excuse or some kind of way out. "Unless she just thought that you'd put two and two together..."

"Oh, come on, Will. You and I might not always see eye-to-eye but you're a good copper. If this wasn't Laura, what would you say?"

"I don't know, Matty. I wouldn't jump to conclusions."

"Okay. Suit yourself but I'm telling you, she knew something about that garden."

"What was under the patio?" Blake asked, hoping against hope.

"Not a body, if that's what you're thinking. Nah. Judging by the hole they dug, whatever was under there was removed but it was in a rectangular box, like a flight case or that suitcase size, maximum. Could be the money you were saying was missing."

"Could be," Blake said.

"Have you got any of Laura's DNA?"

"Oh, yeah, Matty, sure. I carry a locket with some of her saliva in it, just for sentimental reasons. Jeez."

"We've got to establish if that blood on the landing belongs to her or not. It's very possible she's been taken, if what your contact told us is true. I'm worried about her, too, you know."

"Are you two going to contaminate my crime scene all night or can you bugger off, so I get some work done?" The Crime Scene Investigator snapped from beneath her mask. "And keep that dog still!" Charlie wriggled in Blake's grasp, threatening to leap onto the Investigator and lick her to death.

"I'll get you her toothbrush from my house," Blake said. "But I'm going to have a word with Thorpe first." He turned and strode out of the flat, still carrying Charlie.

"Walk on the bloody stepping plates!" The CSI called after him.

"Will! Will! Don't do anything stupid, Will!" Cavanagh called after him, but Blake wasn't listening.

*****

The day had gone from bad to worse to even worse for Laura. Sitting in the Trafalgar pub, she had contemplated screaming and running from the man but as he leaned forward, she glimpsed a pistol under his jacket.

"I'm not here to hurt you," he said.

"Oh no?" Laura said, her voice shaking. "I suppose your friend just wanted to give me a hug when he grabbed me from behind…"

"He wasn't my friend, I swear. Anyway, you got away from him easily enough, didn't you? You made quite a mess of him."

Laura narrowed her eyes. "You went up there? What about the man in the car?"

The man shrugged his huge shoulders. "He was having a nap, when I entered the building. Let's just say that both those men have gone home rubbing sore heads and wondering what happened to them. I'm here to take you to my boss." He held up his hands. "Don't worry. We won't harm you. We just need to talk to you."

"Who are you?"

"Just a rival business to the one that seems to want to hurt you. Now at the very least that should be in our favour, right? My enemy's enemy is my friend. Yeah? Now, my name is Nick. I have a car in the carpark. If you don't want to accompany me, that's fine. You can take your chances on your own and I think you'll do okay for a while."

"For a while?"

"Those men will come back, Laura with their friends, and soon," Nick said. He glanced around. "If they aren't here already."

Laura glanced over at the lad behind the

bar, catching his eye as he lowered the phone. "Okay," she said. "Let's go."

Nick stood up. Laura was tall but Nick towered over her. He was taller than Will and wider. His shaved head glistened in the dim light of the pub. They walked out into the cold night and Nick paused in the shadows. "Just wait here."

Laura shivered and pressed herself into the corner of the porch that covered the door. Traffic rumbled around them and a plane flew overhead. Nick had vanished and suddenly, she felt alone. She wondered whether the lad at the bar was really phoning someone about her or if she had imagined it. Maybe she should just go to Will but what would he think? And how much could she tell him? When Cavanagh had revealed that she had been married to Kyle Quinlan, she couldn't bear the look of betrayal in Will's eye.

A car rolled up and Laura caught her breath, releasing it as she saw Nick in the driving seat. He leaned over and opened the passenger door. "You can sit in the back if you want."

"No," she said. "Front is fine. Actually, I'll drive if it's all the same to you."

Nick thought for a second, then a smile spread across his face. "Sure, if it makes you feel safer, no problem, as long as you look after the car and follow my directions."

He slid over awkwardly, obviously wary of actually getting out of the car when she was so near the driver's side. "You'll forgive me, but I'd look a right idiot having to go back to my boss to explain that not only did I fail to persuade you to come but you stole the car." He paused for a moment. "Actually, he'd probably quite like that. Come on then. Out the carpark and turn right."

*****

It was only when Blake got to the car that he realised he was carrying a small Jack Russell puppy. He paused. Was it safe to put it in the back of his car? What if he stopped suddenly? "You'll have to sit in the footwell but don't crap in there," he muttered to Charlie. The dog just kept trying to lick his face. "Great."

It was late but he knew his first port of call would be Jeff. He needed to be sure that it was Harry Thorpe he'd spoken to. He remembered that Jeff was house sitting in Bebington for a friend of a friend and, not for the first time, wondered where he got his stuffy luck from. If that had been Will, he'd have found himself in the most expensive and yet the most dilapidated bedsit in some horrible corner of town. Maybe it was because he was more of a people person than Will. He actually knew more than three people. Will hardly knew anyone outside of his work.

The house was an innocuous semi-detached in

a quiet road not far from Port Sunlight station. Blake knocked on the door, Charlie under his arm. Nothing stirred at first, so Blake knocked again. A curtain rippled and he could see his brother peering nervously out. A moment later, the front door opened and Jeff let Will in.

"He won't chew anything will he?" Jeff said looking at the dog.

"He'll chew your balls off if you don't tell me who took Laura today," Blake snapped. "I'm not in the mood for playing games, Jeff. She's been snatched. There's blood outside her flat and a suitcase…"

"She was leaving?"

"I don't know but I'm going to find her. So tell me. Was it Harry Thorpe you spoke to?"

"I can't say, Will. He'll…"

"I don't have time, Jeff, was it Thorpe?"

Jeff looked at Will and then at the puppy which wagged its tail eagerly and gave a high-pitched yelp that obviously frayed Jeff's nerves. "Okay, okay!" He said. "It was Thorpe. But I don't know where he was…"

"Don't worry, I think I know where to find him."

CHAPTER 31

Kath Cryer sat in the interview room. It was very late, and her wrist ached under its splint. She should have gone home to Theo, her partner, hours ago. Leonard Hill looked equally drained. His brief sat, dispassionate and silent having advised him to say nothing.

"So you've been charged, Leonard. You may as well come clean and tell us where Florence is," Kath said. "That poor little girl, all on her own somewhere, frightened and cold. Is she cold, Leonard?"

"I don't know," Leonard said, his voice flat and tired. "Because I've never met her."

"Come on, Leonard, look at us. We're like two prize-fighters who won't throw in the towel, up against the ropes. We're both exhausted. Let's finish this. Where is she? Help me out, here."

"I wish I could help you," Leonard said. "Honestly, I do. If there was some way I could point you to her, I would but I don't know because I don't even know what the girl looks like."

"We know she must be somewhere between the park and your house. It's unlikely that you had any chance to put her anywhere else. There just wasn't the time before you got back for your sick little romp with Geri Sharpe…"

Leonard blushed and looked down at the table. Then he looked up. "Talk to Tanya Ellman."

"Who is she and why would that do any good?"

"Read your notes, I've already told Mr Blake all about it. Talk to Tanya Ellman. Then go and talk to Geri Sharpe again. That's all I'm going to say on the matter."

"Where's Florence, Leonard?"

"No comment."

*****

It was very late by the time Blake pulled up outside Harry Thorpe's house. He lived in a converted farm in Thurstaston on the Dee side of the Wirral. Rows of converted barns and workshops surrounded a large, gravelled courtyard. He imagined that at one time, it had been a busy place with chickens scratching in the yard, cattle lowing under open sheds and maybe a couple of tractors parked alongside the barns. Now there was no sign of any livestock and the tractors had been replaced with sleek Mercedes and BMWs. The security lights clicked on the moment he drove into the yard, but Blake wasn't trying to sneak into Harry Thorpe's house.

He pulled up his car and slammed his door noisily. He looked back to see Charlie curled up asleep in the passenger footwell. The place was silent and Blake assumed everyone was in bed. He wished he was home himself, with Laura by his side. The main farmhouse stood in one corner of the yard. Blake hammered on the shiny black front door and rang the bell a few times.

Eventually, a man with a plaster over his nose and two black eyes answered the door. He was wearing a hoodie and sweatpants and had obviously just got out of bed. "What d'you want?"

"What happened to you? You didn't meet a woman you didn't agree with, did you?"

The man flinched at the comment but kept his cool. "I said, what do you want?"

"I need to talk to Harry," Blake said, flashing his warrant card. "Go and get him."

"He's asleep…"

"I'm not in the mood to argue. Just go and get him or I'll arrest you for obstruction." Blake was talking rubbish, but he was counting on the bruised goon not realising that. The man hovered indecisively at the door for a second then nodded Blake in.

"I'll see if he's awake, but he won't be happy at all. Wait here."

Harry Thorpe took a while to come downstairs, Blake looked round at the wooden panelling, cut flowers and gentle opulence of the hallway. It was all a facade, like Paul Percival's impression of a successful businessman. Why did people wrap themselves in an illusion of respectability if not to trap and ensnare the gullible or greedy?

The staircase creaked with heavy footsteps and Thorpe appeared in a dressing gown and slippers. "This better be bloody urgent, Blake. I was just dozing off."

"Where's Laura Vexley?"

"Who?"

"Come on, Harry, don't play games. Where is she? I know somebody went to her flat to pick her up. Maybe this joker here. I want her back."

"Even if I did send someone to get her, d'you think I'd admit that to you? Go home, Blake, you're over-tired. Aren't you meant to be looking for a little girl or something? Thought I saw that on the news... Show Mr Blake the door..."

The bruised man stepped forward but Blake fixed him with a gaze. "I wouldn't unless you want me to reset that nose of yours." The man hesitated. "Look Thorpe. Just let me have her. I'll walk away and not trouble you."

Thorpe looked keenly at Blake. "Off the record? Okay, I did go to get her. I sent this chump and his pal, but she had back up. She got away. I don't know where she is. And I don't know who they are, but your girlfriend has got some powerful allies and I don't mean Merseyside Police."

"And why were you after her?"

"I think you know that. Tell your little brother he's a blabber mouth and I won't be so lenient if our paths cross again. I'm too soft, that's my trouble." Thorpe turned and started shuffling upstairs. "Now if you'll forgive me, Blake, I need my beauty sleep. So do you. You look like shit. Goodnight. Sleep tight."

Blake turned to the bruised man. "Did she do that?"

He nodded, ruefully. "Bloody head butted me backwards, then proper punched me in the face. Caught me off guard. But the guy with her, he was a tank. Put my mate in the car out cold. He didn't know what hit him."

"Maybe you need to find another line of work," Blake said.

"Yours doesn't seem to be agreeing with you, very much, either," the man said, gesturing to the front door.

Blake nodded. "You might have a point."

CHAPTER 32

Ignoring your phone was meant to be good for your mental health but Blake knew that it was a bit like sticking your head in the sand. The deeper your head is buried, the easier it is to get your arse kicked. There were several text messages from his colleagues and two from Superintendent Martin. The last one had block capitals. An arse-kicking was definitely on the horizon.

Blake had hardly slept. He'd dozed on and off between wondering what had become of Laura. At one point he woke to find Charlie nuzzled against him and Serafina sleeping on his legs. Thoughts, worries and anxiety chased each other around his head like rats in a maze, losing each other, then finding each other and magnifying in his mind. Florence Percival still hadn't been found and now he fretted about Laura, too.

Why hadn't Laura been straight with him? He could have accepted that she had a past that wasn't quite on the straight and narrow. Nobody is perfect and we're moulded by our life history and those around us. But if she knew that there was a stash of money under that patio, why didn't she just say? Or abandon it? Why wait and watch it?

Lies and deceit surrounded Blake in his work and, now, it seemed, in his personal life, too. Had she targeted him deliberately, thinking he might keep her safe while she waited for the right moment to dig up the money and run? But Quinlan had vanished six years ago. Why wait all this time? It didn't make sense. And where was she now? Would she just vanish like his mother had? Disappear without trace like Kyle Quinlan, never to be found?

And what about Florence? That little girl could be trapped in a dark room somewhere, wondering where her parents were and what was happening. Or she could be lying cold and dead, abandoned and lost. It didn't bear thinking about.

He sat up in bed, sending Serafina rolling to one side with a rumbling growl. Charlie whimpered and snuggled further into Blake's warm pillow. Dragging his laptop from the bedside table, he tried to concentrate on the Percival case. Laura could look after herself. The little girl couldn't. He needed to talk to Tanya Ellman about Paul Percival's alibi the night his sister died. Blake couldn't help thinking that somehow, the death of Undine Percival, all those years ago and Florence's disappearance were somehow linked, he felt sure of it, even if everyone else thought the case was straightforward. And Leonard Hill's 'girlfriend,' Geri Sharpe, interested Blake too.

The fact that she'd taken up with a character like Hill surprised him. Reading Kath's report, it was clear that Geri Sharpe was effectively selling sex and Hill's money would have been as good as anyone's but their liaison still puzzled him. Her insistence on meeting at the park, that day, when they lived so close to each other meant something, he knew it.

And the look on Hill's face when Blake had shown him the texts asking where he was, which implied that he had spent longer getting from the park to his house. The man did seem genuinely shocked when Blake showed them to him. Blake typed in Geri Sharpe's name and was rewarded with a Facebook profile. Geri Sharpe either hadn't heard of protecting her privacy online or she didn't care.

Her Facebook Page was a mishmash of inspirational memes and selfies of her in various states of inebriation and undress. Geri on the beach, small and painfully thin, Blake thought. Geri making a 'V' sign with some mates and an inordinate number of balloons at a party. Geri with her kids blowing out birthday candles, at Chester Zoo, and Alton Towers. The birthdate on her Facebook profile put her in her late thirties. He scrolled through a number of 'warning' posts showing various men. They were either mugshot type photographs or hastily snapped images of them in playgrounds or shops. Each one said something along the lines of: This man is a dangerous predator and is in your area. Share this and protect your children now.' One post had Geri tagged in it. It showed a lank-haired man trying to cover his face while a gang jostled him along the street. The post read: 'Another nonce bites the dust. Nice one Geri Sharpe.' It came from a page called 'TorPaedo – Hunter Killers, 'sinking' pervs so kids can be safe.' He looked at the administrators of the page and one name leapt out at him: Ian Vale. The man who had been hanging around Leonard Hill's house. Maybe if Blake got a chance, he'd go and visit Geri Sharpe tomorrow, too. First, he had to face the wrath of the Superintendent.

"No, first, I've got to find someone to look after you," Blake muttered looking at the sleeping Charlie.

*****

It didn't surprise Blake that Ian Youde, his neighbour, was up and about already. It was quite possible he hadn't been to bed. The man lived a solitary life, tending to his garden and his collection of World War Two memorabilia. As Blake walked up the road to Youde's house, Charlie squirming in his arms, his eyes were drawn to the blackened skeleton of the house opposite. It was Youde who had pulled Blake from that burning building, wearing an old gas mask. Since then, Blake had found they got on well.

He knocked on Ian's shining black front door. The man kept every aspect of his house immaculate; windows clean, frames wiped and paths swept. Even the garden was regimented in neat lines and square borders. The lawn was cut to a cropped half inch, green and striped. At first Blake had interpreted this as a flaw in the man but he'd come to admire Ian Youde's self-discipline.

Youde opened the door. He had a forbidding appearance to those who didn't know him; small suspicious eyes and a tight letter box mouth. His skin was nut brown from years of working outdoors and it made his thin, cropped white hair seem even whiter. Even though it was seven in the morning, he wore paint spattered blue overalls. "Morning, Will," he said, his eyebrows fluttering briefly in surprise at Charlie. "Who's this?"

"Hi Ian," Blake said, trying to sound casual and hide the fact that a request for a favour was coming soon. "This is Charlie. He's not mine. Laura's looking after him for a friend. Only Laura's gone missing and I've got to find her. I know you don't like animals but..."

A frown creased Ian Youde's tanned forehead. "I said I hated cats, fuckin' messy buggers if you ask me. I used to have a Jack Russell. I was gutted when he passed away. Couldn't bear to get another. You want me to look after him, don't you?"

Blake nodded wincing with pained gratitude. "I wouldn't normally but..."

"Is Laura okay?"

"I don't know, Ian. I need to find out. But I've got to find this little girl, first."

"I read about that in the papers. Can't imagine what it's like losing a kid like that," Youde said, holding out his arms. "Give the little fella here. I'll look after him. If he digs up my borders or shits on my lawn, I'll have him for breakfast, though..."

Blake grinned and handed over the whimpering Charlie. Blake marvelled at the gentleness with which Youde handled the puppy and it wagged its tail and started licking Youde's chin almost immediately. "Now stop that fussing, Charlie boy," he said. Youde looked up at Blake. "It's a motto of mine: never let a terrier lick your face. It's stood me in good stead over the years. Go on, Will, you get off. Find that girl."

"Thanks, Ian, Will do," Blake said. *Which one, though? Laura or Florence?*

*****

Superintendent Martin wasn't a shouter or a bawler. Blake would have preferred that, but Martin was a lecturer, which was worse because it could go on for what seemed like days. It made Blake feel like a naughty schoolboy being told off by a teacher, too. Martin listed all the reasons why Blake should have been in touch the day before. Listed the people he'd let down. Explained in detail how much anxiety he'd piled on his team and also how well Cryer had coped being thrown in at the deep end with the press conference.

"It's unprofessional, Will," Martin said. "The press may love a celebrity copper who makes up his own rules, but it doesn't wash here. I'm that close to considering disciplinary procedures against you."

"I'm sorry, sir, but Laura has gone missing and..."

"And DCI Cavanagh is looking into that, okay?" Martin let out a deep sigh. "I know you're worried, Will but we'll find her. You have to prepare yourself for the possibility that she might be more involved with this Quinlan affair than you thought. Whatever it is!"

"I know, sir..."

"Now, Cryer has made good headway on this Percival case, give her a bit of a run at it, let her show what she can do. She's ambitious and if we can find the girl quickly, then that would be a Godsend."

"Yes, sir," Blake muttered. But he had his concerns about Kath Cryer and he had a few loose ends he wanted to tie up himself.

CHAPTER 33

Matty Cavanagh sat with his feet up on the desk, gently pushing his swivel chair from side to side. He had a pair of black Chelsea boots on, but he wasn't sure about them. If he was honest, he liked a lace-up boot better than a slip-on. The Chelsea boots made him feel like an extra from Star Trek. Bobby Dirkin sat opposite him on the other side of the desk. And Blake leaned against the wall, looking out of the window.

Cavanagh never really understood Blake. The man had so much going for him, good looks, intelligence but he always looked like he'd just blown all his savings on the Grand National and lost. Of course, he understood that Blake was worried about Laura, right now, but that didn't explain all the other times.

"So, what we got, Bobby?" Matty said, tapping his pen against the desk.

"Thorpe won't cooperate," Dirkin said. "Says he doesn't know anything about any missing money. Says he knew Quinlan, but that he disappeared years back. He remembers Laura but only in passing."

"Lying bastard," Blake muttered. "That isn't

quite what he told me, off the record. Still, wouldn't expect him to say anything different under the circumstances."

"Yeah," Cavanagh muttered. "So it seems it wasn't him who lifted the case from under the patio at Laura's old house."

"Could've been, boss," Dirkin said. Sometimes, he reminded Cavanagh of an old prize fighter, his face squashed and wrinkled by years of punishment. Or maybe one of those dogs what were they called? Shar Pei. Yeah that was it. He looked like a Shar Pei. Only one that could take you apart in a matter of seconds. Cavanagh knew that Dirkin was tough. Dirkin continued. "We don't know that Thorpe hadn't got his money back and then went after Laura realising that it was her living there when the money went missing."

"It'll be a while before we get any feedback from forensics on the blood but that was certainly Laura's suitcase on the floor. Where was she going? Why didn't she call me?"

"Don't beat yourself up, Will," Matty said, feeling himself going red. He didn't like all this emotional stuff, he much preferred a bit of banter and a chat about the footy. "She probably didn't want to get you involved..."

"But I am involved, whatever she thought," Blake said.

"A house-to-house revealed that Laura was seen running from the side of the property and hiding in a side street. So it looks like she got away," Dirkin said. Matty gave a brief smile. He was a clever sod, throwing in a bit of practical consolation there, rather than any touchy-feely crap.

"Did anyone see where she went after that?"

"Not really but, given that she'd left her phone in the flat, I guessed that she'd probably head for a pub," Dirkin said.

Matty looked puzzled. "Why the hell would she go to a pub? Did she fancy a bevvy to steady her nerves?"

"Nice one, Bobby," Blake said, nodding in appreciation. "Plenty of people around, so nobody could grab her and she could ask to borrow a phone or get the bar staff to call a taxi for her without arousing too much suspicion."

"Ah, right," Matty said, feeling a little crestfallen that he hadn't figured that out. "Still, she might just as easily jumped on a passing bus or something."

"I checked the timetables, Matty," Dirkin said. "None went past there at that time. Plus, a guy in the Trafalgar pub said he saw a woman who looked like Laura come in looking upset. She had skinned knuckles."

"Could be her after the scuffle."

Dirkin nodded. "I thought that too. She left with a big man. A really big man, the guy behind the bar said. He called him a gorilla, but I doubt he'd say that to his face." Bobby allowed himself a short, crumpled smile. "They drove off in a black BMW. The lad had the sense to take the registration number."

"So we can trace that," Matty said, sitting up.

"Already have, boss. It's a rental car. But we should be able to establish who rented it and follow that trail."

"I wonder where they were taking her," Blake said.

"That was the thing, sir," Dirkin said. "The lad was certain it was Laura driving. She wasn't being *taken* anywhere."

*****

Blake's mind was in turmoil as he left Matty Cavanagh's office. It was hard to deny that, from all the evidence, Laura was mixed up in something criminal and didn't appear to be an innocent victim of circumstance. But it also occurred to Blake that there were two groups involved here. Thorpe's people trying to capture her and another team who Laura knew and maybe trusted. He shook his head and tried to set that idea aside. Even if he thought Cavanagh was a bit of a lightweight, you wouldn't find a more logical and thorough copper than Bobby Dirkin. That man was worth his weight in gold. There was nothing Blake could do and his priority was a little girl who was still missing.

Kath Cryer sat smiling to herself at her desk. Blake couldn't help feeling a spark of irritation as he approached her. It wasn't her fault that she had to take his place at the press conference and, if he was honest, he'd gladly never do another press conference again. But her self-satisfaction grated with his own feeling that he'd failed in his duty in some way. Why he couldn't just be glad that she'd done a good job, he didn't quite understand, but there was a barrier between Blake and Kath at the moment and it was something to do with this case.

"Any news?" Kath said, laying a hand on Will's arm.

Blake shook his head. "Nothing. Has Leonard Hill said anything more about Florence's location yet?"

"Nope," Kath sighed. "The twisting bastard just keeps saying we need to talk to Tanya Ellman."

"The girl who provided Paul Percival with an alibi when they investigated his sister's murder?"

"Yeah. I think he's trying to tangle Percival up in the murder of his own daughter, too. Which would be perfect wouldn't it?"

"How do you mean?"

"Well, think about it. Hill kills Undine Percival and tries to blame Paul Percival. The case goes to court but Hill ends up getting the blame, if not getting convicted for the actual murder when he wanted Paul to go to prison. Years later, he finds out Percival is a successful businessman with a little girl of his own and decides to punish him by doing the same thing again…"

"Except, if he wanted to frame Paul, why pick a day when Percival was away? And why keep a jiffy bag full of incriminating evidence under his mattress? Plus Paul Percival is far from successful. He's broke. No there's something else going on here…"

"Oh, come on, Will. Paul Percival may be hard up, but you wouldn't think it to look at him, would you? Big house in the park there, fancy car, trips away. Leonard Hill sexually assaulted Florence and took the evidence as trophies," Kath said, her voice rising a little. "He hid them under the mattress just while Geri Sharpe was in the house. He was going to find a better hiding place, but we arrived. It's obvious."

"We need to check Tanya Ellman," Blake said, feeling the colour rise in his cheeks. "And while we're at it, I'd like to talk to Geri Sharpe again about her involvement with the Tor-Paedo vigilante group. I found it mentioned on her Face-book timeline."

Kathy pursed her lips. "Okay," she muttered. "I'll get onto it."

"Okay, Kathy. I'll come along. I want to have a chat with her myself. See if you can phone both of them up and we can pop round."

CHAPTER 34

The years hadn't been kind to Tanya Ellman. Or maybe it was just the last couple of days, Blake thought. She had a round, doughy face that was frozen in a look of constant disapproval and was framed by lank brown hair. She constantly pulled a huge, pale blue cardigan around her large frame. She worked in one of the department stores in Liverpool and had agreed, reluctantly, to come in and chat rather than have police officers coming to her place of work.

"I don't know how I can help you. It was all a long time ago," she said, as they sat in an interview room.

Blake nodded. "I know, but the Florence Percival case seems tangled up with it, Ms Ellman…"

"Leonard Hill was the prime suspect," Kath chipped in.

Blake glared at her but carried on. "We just want to get a bit of an idea about the Undine case as obviously, the same personalities are involved with our search for Florence Percival."

"I mean, if he's done it once, he might well have killed again," Kath said, fixing Tanya with a steely gaze, "and nobody would want that on their conscience, would they?"

"Thanks Kath," Blake said, giving her another look. She was a blabber mouth sometimes but right now, she seemed to be dead set on steering the interview, even if it was an informal one. Blake turned to Tanya. "So, if it's okay, could you, in your own time and your own words just run through the events of the night Undine Percival died?"

Tanya Ellman blinked and tangled her fingers around each other. Blake noticed that her nails were bitten to the quick. "It was a long time ago. I don't like thinking about it," she said. Her eyes glistened with tears. "Do you really think he's done it again?"

Blake held up a hand and silenced Kath before she could talk. "It's a possibility but we're exploring all avenues. We just want to find out the truth, Tanya, that's all."

"Okay, but I was just a kid. Only sixteen. It wasn't my fault. I didn't think much of myself then," she took a breath and gave a tearful laugh. "I don't suppose I do, now. I wasn't what you'd call 'a looker.' 'A bit of a plain Jane,' that's what dad always called me." She pulled the cardigan around herself even tighter. "So, when Paul Percival showed an interest in me, I was bowled over."

"How long before Undine's death was this?"

"A few months. He was such a gentleman, even at that age. It's amazing how easily you can be taken in."

"How d'you mean?" Kath said.

"That night…" Tanya started and then she held her breath as though trying to muster her courage. "What you have to understand is that up until then, he'd been lovely. I was so young and inexperienced. I'd never been out with a boy let alone done anything else. It wasn't my fault."

"If you want to take a break, Tanya, we'd quite understand. I know this must be difficult. I know you've suffered because of that night and your part in the case."

She looked up at him. "You do?"

"The graffiti in the classrooms claiming you'd lied? Having to move school. None of that was your fault, was it?"

Tanya Ellman looked down at her hands. "Maybe it was," she said. "Maybe I deserved it for what I did. Maybe it was true."

"What?" Kath said.

"The night Undine Percival died, I was expecting Paul to take me out. He'd promised we'd go into town and see the Christmas lights. I was just a kid, really. So excited. And then he didn't turn up until later. Much later. He said that Leonard Hill had done something terrible. He was really upset, crying and trembling. He told me that Leonard had hurt his sister, maybe even killed her and that Leonard was going to blame it on him. I worshipped the ground he walked on. I'd have done anything for him then. And Leonard was so creepy, I believed him. So... I... I lied in court."

"You said in court that Paul Percival had been with you all evening when in reality, he'd only been with you for less than an hour. Which begs the question, what was Paul doing before he came to you?"

"I know what he was doing, Inspector, he was murdering his sister and framing Leonard Hill for it. When I sat in court and heard the evidence, I began to realise that it was Paul who had got Leonard drunk, Paul who led them both down to the lake in the dark, Paul who pushed Undine into the water."

"And how did you know that?" Kath said, making Blake wince.

"I just knew. You know that expression, 'the scales fell from my eyes?' It was like that. I sat in the court and watched Paul's face as he followed the proceedings, and I just knew he had engineered the whole thing and his father helped cover it up."

"Really?" Blake said. "Would you care to explain?"

"Before I was interviewed by the police, Paul's dad came to see me. Roland Percival. He got me to learn my times off by heart. The time Paul arrived, the time of a favourite TV programme I was watching before he called. The time Paul left. Everything. It was like learning a script for a play. I'm not sure Roland knew what his son had done, just that Leonard Hill was trying to implicate him, so he made sure his son had a cast-iron alibi."

Blake glanced at Kath. "And did you see Paul again after the case had closed and Hill had been found not-guilty?"

Tanya heaved a huge sigh. "I did a couple of times. Each time, he would hug me and kiss me and beg me not to tell anyone that I'd lied. The last time I saw him was different, though."

"In what way?"

"He was colder towards me. He said he was finishing with me because I reminded him of that terrible night too much. I-I accused him of setting me up and said I'd go to the police. That was when he became threatening. He said they wouldn't believe me and even if they did, I'd be an accessory to murder. He said he'd creep into my bedroom and kill me, make it look like suicide. By the time he left me, I was a wreck. I couldn't breath for the anxiety. I've never recovered, really."

"So, why tell us this, now?" Kath said, leaning forward so fast that Tanya flinched back in her chair. Blake scowled at Cryer but she ignored him.

"Because of what you said, that he may have struck again. I wasn't going to say anything. Just bottle it all up, like I do every day. But you're right. If Paul Percival has killed his poor little daughter, then he needs bringing to justice. I'm not important. He's got away with murder for too long!"

"But- but I meant Leonard Hill," Kath said, blinking at Tanya.

Tanya Ellman gave a short, slightly hysterical laugh. "Oh, I see. Leonard Hill is a creepy pervert but he's not a murderer. No, when he threatened me, Paul Percival said that killing came easily to him. And I believe that it does."

*****

The silence in the car was almost total apart from the swish of traffic and the regular thump of the windscreen wipers. A steady drizzle had set in and it barely looked like daylight outside. Kath made a pantomime of keeping her eyes on the road while Blake flicked through his phone, hoping for a text or a call from Laura or about Laura; anything that would tell him she was safe. At last he put his phone in his pocket and looked out at the cars in the other lanes.

"So do you want to tell me what's going on, Kath?"

"I dunno what you mean, sir," Kath said, craning her neck to look in her wing mirror. A car beeped somewhere behind them.

"Ever since we started this case, you seem to have been on a mission to prove that Leonard Hill is guilty."

"That's the job, isn't it, sir?"

"No," Blake said. "The job is to get to the truth of what happened. It's up to the courts to establish guilt or innocence. We just find out what is going on."

"But he's such a creep and I bet when his computer comes back, it'll be full of horrific child porn. You just know it will..."

"And if that's the case, then he will face charges for it, but it doesn't mean he murdered Undine Percival or abducted Florence."

Kath honked her horn at the car in front that had stalled at the lights. "Come on, numb nuts!" she yelled.

"Steady, Kath," Blake said.

"It's not right, sir. Not fair. People like Hill wandering around free to abuse and groom kiddies while the victims just... just... "

"What's going on, Kath? Is this case close to

home or something?"

"I'm not a victim of child abuse, if that's what you're thinking," Kath said, swerving around the car in front and putting her foot down. "Not directly, anyway."

"What do you mean?"

"Mr Freeman," she said. "He was a youth worker when I was a kid. He ran a club for teenagers at Bebington Memorial Hall near where I lived. He seemed like a lovely man. Had a family, cute, groovy wife who used to come along sometimes and help. Me and my sister, Isabelle used to go along and it was fun. To begin with."

"So what happened?"

"I got bored or got a boyfriend who thought it wasn't cool to go to the Youthie, as we called it. So I stopped going but Isabelle went on her own. She'd come back later and later from the place. She went off her food, wouldn't talk about what she'd done there. She wasn't sleeping very well, either. Then she stopped going to the Youthie. And Mr Freeman started visiting our house."

"Jeez, Kath, I'm sorry..."

"Looking back, we were all so naïve; my mum and dad, me, we never suspected a thing. It just seemed like he was concerned for her. 'One of her regulars,' he called her. God how stupid were we?"

"Nobody expects that to happen to a member of their family, though, do they Kath? You can't blame yourself or your parents."

"I know, Will, but you do blame yourself. My sister was never the same again. She can't keep a relationship together, she can't hold a job down. She has constant flashbacks and nightmares. And then she uses anything she can get her hands on to dull the pain. When she finally plucked up the courage to tell us what had been going on, Mr Freeman had fled, leaving his groovy wife and kids to pick up the pieces."

"Did they ever catch him?"

"No. When I joined up, I searched for him but he'd gone abroad. So an evil fucker like that wrecked God knows how many people's lives and then just vanished. It's not right. And I'll be honest, I look at Leonard Hill and see Mr Freeman. I'd hang 'em all."

"That's awful, Kath. I never knew. I wish I could say something that would change your mind, but I don't think I could, or should. I would ask you though, what if Freeman had done that and someone else got the blame? Someone is still escaping justice aren't they?"

"As far as I'm concerned, Freeman did murder my happy, bright, confident sister but, yeah, I take your point. Having said that, if I can send Hill down for something, then I'll be a happy girl."

"If he's committed a crime, Kath, we will. But not at the expense of someone else's justice. Let's see what Geri Sharpe has to say."

CHAPTER 35

Chaos ruled in the Sharpe household when Blake and Kath arrived at her house in Noctorum. They could hear the shrieking from inside the car. At first, Blake jumped out of the car, thinking an assault was in progress but then he heard Geri's voice bellowing, "put that bloody Lego away and get back upstairs. If you're not well enough to go to school, you can't play Lego!"

Blake turned and was relieved to see Kath grin at him. "Looks like we came at a bad time, Will."

"Or a good one, if you want to catch someone off their guard," Will said.

"Are you the Truancy Man?" A voice said behind them.

Blake turned and saw an old man in slippers and wearing a fawn cardigan with leather buttons standing at the end of his drive. "No," Blake said. "Why do you ask?"

"Them kids, they hardly ever go to school, do they? I just thought you might be from the education or something. If you're not that, you must be bizzies. You look like bizzies to me."

Blake smiled. "Well, nice talking to you."

"About time you lot came. All the comings and goings at that house. Blokes from all over. Bloomin' disgusting. Even couples, sometimes. All ages. She'll have 'em all, you know. Saw an old couple just the other week. That's got to be illegal."

"Last time I looked it wasn't," Blake said. "I guess it depends what's going on in there. Anyway, have a good day."

"I've got CCTV if you need it," the old man said as Blake turned away. "All the comings and goings. I'm sure it's a knocking shop. Imagine those kids being in there, too."

"Thank you, Mr...?"

"Ormand," the man said. "Vic Ormand. Just give me a shout if you need any CCTV, my camera doesn't reach into the house, but it picks up people parking in the front. Bloody disgusting."

Blake returned to the matter of Geri Sharpe. The screaming had stopped. "Do you think it's safe to go in?"

"We could give it a go," Kath said.

Geri Sharpe was in a sour mood. The house was littered with toys and building bricks and a nursery rhyme blared away in the background. "This really isn't a great time, to be honest, my son isn't well and had to stay at home. Could we do it tomorrow or something?"

"It really won't take long," Blake said. "We're searching for a missing little girl and time isn't on our side."

Feet thundered through the ceiling above them and Geri leaned over to the bottom of the stairs. "If you aren't in that bed in three seconds, Dominic, I'm phoning a taxi to take you to school! One, two…" The thundering stopped. She turned back to them. "Sorry. He's got ADHD, they don't always get it right at that school. Puts him off going for weeks, sometimes. Come in."

They picked their way through the toys and sat down on a sofa. Blake glanced around. "Nice place you have," he said, and genuinely meant it. The house felt homely and lived in. he contrasted it with Leonard Hill's oatmeal bland décor.

"Thanks but I don't suppose you came round to critique my soft furnishings," Geri said and then giggled. "That sounds a bit naughty doesn't it?"

Blake gave the briefest of smiles. "Kath has already talked to you about your involvement with Leonard Hill, but I just wanted to get a little more background. How did you meet him?"

"Oh, you know, one of them apps, swipe right, swipe left," Geri said. "To be honest, he was no looker, but I thought, you know, he might have a nice personality. Or a bit of money to spend." She winked.

Kath glanced at Blake.

"Are you alright Kath?" Blake said.

"Yeah, sorry, carry on," she said, not taking her eyes off Geri.

"So, were you aware of his background history when you met him?"

"Background history? What d'you mean?"

"His convictions for having images of children and his involvement in a murder case when he was younger?"

"God, no! I don't do personality checks on all my gentlemen, that'd be mental but if I'd known, I'd have steered clear."

"Would you?"

"Too right. Don't want nonces like that coming near me."

"So, you'd say you'd avoid anyone with a record like that?"

"Yeah, deffo. Why are you asking me all these weird questions?"

"It's just that I was doing a bit of background research before coming to talk to you, Geri, and I stumbled across your Facebook page."

Geri shrugged. "Yeah, so I go to a few parties, enjoy a bevvy every now and then. That's no crime, is it?"

"No. Do you know a man called Ian Vale?"

"Never heard of him, should I?"

"Yeah, he runs the Tor-paedo Facebook group. There are photographs of you confronting a number of men about them trying to groom you online when they thought you were a fourteen-year-old girl..."

Geri's mouth clammed shut.

"So, it isn't the case that you don't go near people like Leonard Hill, is it? You actively 'seek and destroy' I think the term was on the Face-book page. Feel free to correct me, any time."

"Okay. I have helped Ian out sometimes. We use a fuzzy web-cam and lots of makeup to disguise me but, yeah, I don't mind catching perverts out. If you lot did your job properly, maybe we wouldn't have to."

"So was Leonard Hill just another target? Is that it?"

Geri shifted in her seat. "No," she said. "I didn't know anything about him. He was just a punter."

"You just told me you didn't know anything about Ian Vale and it turns out you did, Geri. Are you lying now, or telling the truth? Only it's get-ting hard to tell."

"I'm telling you, I hardly knew him."

"So, how did you meet him again?" Kath said,

suddenly. Blake looked over at her, trying to get her not to interrupt.

"I told you, one of them apps, swipe right, swipe left," Geri said. "To be honest, he was no looker, but I thought, you know, he might have a nice personality. Or a bit of money to spend."

"Word for word," Kath said.

Geri held up her hands. "What?"

"That's the third time you've answered that question with exactly the same words. It's like you've learnt them from a script."

"I dunno what you're going on about," Geri said.

"Did someone put you up to framing Leonard Hill?"

"No," Geri said, standing up. "This is stupid. I haven't done nothing wrong. You've got that paedo in jail where he belongs. All you have to do is throw away the key. Now, if you don't mind, my son's up there and he's too quiet to not be up to something. I want you to leave."

Blake held up his hands. "As you wish, Geri but if it turns out you've been obstructing our enquiries in any way, then we'll be straight back with a search warrant. You attend to your son. We'll see ourselves out."

Back on the pavement, Kath looked troubled. "She's not telling us something. That answer was memorised. Like from a script."

"That sound familiar, Kath?"

"Tanya Ellman said that Roland Percival got her to learn her statement off by heart. But why would the Percivals want to frame Hill? What do they hope to gain from it?"

"I can think of a whole host of reasons. Maybe just getting him out of your area is reward enough. It's more complex than that, though." Blake stared across the road at the bungalow opposite. "Maybe we should have a word with Mr Ormand and see if he'll lend us his CCTV footage."

Kath's phone rang and she listened to the call, frowning. "That was Kinnear," she said. "They've found Florence Percival."

*****

Laura stared out of the window across the Dee Estuary at the Wirral. The grey sky hung low and a veil of misty drizzle drifted across the slate sea, slowly obscuring the peninsula. Will was there somewhere, knocking on doors, demanding answers and probably wondering where she was. She hoped he was okay and not too worried but knew he would be beside himself. This had all happened at a terrible time; just when Will was getting back on his feet and deciding to live life again, after discovering that his mother was, in fact, dead. This was a kick in the teeth.

It had worried her the night before, when Nick had directed her onto the motorway and then towards North Wales. They hadn't travelled too far but far enough to feel distanced from the events of the day. They'd arrived at a large house up in the hills on the opposite side of the River Dee. Laura had a hazy memory of it being a hotel once but now it seemed privately owned. Very private. Laura noticed the high stone walls topped with razor wire as they passed through the electric gates.

"We'll spend the night here," Nick had said. "Don't worry, you'll have your own room. It's all very luxurious."

He'd led her into the house which smelt of polish and potpourri but underneath, there was an undertone of damp as though the place hadn't been lived in for a while. She followed him up a wide, carpeted staircase with heavy wooden banisters. The whole place teetered between country hotel and haunted house, as if it couldn't decide whether to be creepy or welcoming.

The room Nick had showed her was amazing, with a four-poster bed, an en-suite bathroom with an enormous bath and its own dressing room. Laura was exhausted, though, and sank onto the side of the bed almost immediately. "The boss'll see you in the morning. You just rest for now. You've had a busy day," Nick said and left. He paused at the door and popped his head back round. "Good work on that numbskull back at your flat, by the way. There aren't many women could inflict that much damage on a guy like that." He'd left and Laura hadn't even bothered to undress. She just curled up on the bed and fell into a deep, dreamless sleep.

She had awoken to the sound of water being run and silver clinking on china. She looked up to see a small, Filipino woman in a black dress, settling a tea tray on the bedside table.

"Bath is nearly ready for you," she said with a smile. "Eat and drink first."

But Laura had pulled herself up out of bed and gone over to the window to look out and get a good idea of where she was. The tide was low and much of the estuary was brown and green. To her left, the sea and wind farms took over and to her right, the marshes were more apparent. She could see the white rows of houses and shops that made up Parkgate and the green of the fields but they were slowly swallowed up by the grey rain.

She picked up the teapot and poured herself a cup, heaping three sugars in for energy. Not that she felt that tired; she had slept soundly but felt she should keep alert. The sound of the bath running stopped and the woman came out of the bathroom.

"Where am I?" Laura said.

The woman shrugged. "I don't know. I was brought here too. Tomorrow, I'll be somewhere else. I think we're in Wales. It's a good view."

"Thanks," Laura said. Not a lot of help, then. She buttered the toast that sat next to the tea and bit into it. She hadn't realised how hungry she was and wolfed the toast down. Soon, she had demolished the entire rack.

When she came out of the bath, she found a new set of clothes on the bed. They were practical rather than flattering, jeans, a T-shirt, socks and underwear but they were clean and fitted her perfectly. She was about to try and have a snoop around when there was a knock at the door. It was time to meet the boss.

CHAPTER 36

By the time Kath and Blake arrived at the row of innocuous garages in Higher Tranmere, the place was flooded with media. Officers had managed to cordon the area off, but it was clear that they were the last on the scene. The garages sat at the end of a terrace of Edwardian houses, a concrete yard faced by a row of square prefabricated garages. A scrum of journalists had cornered someone at the far end of the yard but whoever it was didn't seem to be in any hurry to leave. As Blake drew nearer, he realised it was Ian Vale at the centre of the commotion.

"Like I say, I was searching the area as a likely spot for Hill to have hidden the little girl and sure enough, I heard her calling out from inside there." He pointed over to one of the garages. The pull-down door had been lowered and officers stood on guard. "So I smashed the lock with a brick and got her out. She was in a right state. Must have been there for days, poor little kid…"

Blake saw an ambulance pulling away, presumably carrying the child off to hospital. "This is a right cat's arse," Blake muttered to Cryer. "We need to get these people out of the way now and pick Vale up for questioning."

One of the journalists caught sight of Blake and hurried over. Kath slipped away, to organise some of the uniformed officers into clearing the yard. Blake groaned inwardly as the young woman dashed over to him.

"Detective Blake, have you got any comment on this development?"

Blake held up his hands. "We haven't even identified the little girl in the garage as Florence Percival, yet. As soon as we've established her identity, made sure she's okay, and spoken to Mr Vale, then we can comment. Now, if you'd like to clear the area, this is a possible crime scene, after all…"

"So you know Mr Vale, then?" the journalist said, her eyes gleaming with excitement. "Are you aware he's the leader of the vigilante group Tor-Paedo? What do you think of their methods? Do they help or hinder your investigations?"

"I am aware of Mr Vale and of the group. I'm not going to make any comment until I know exactly what is going on here. Now, if you could move out of the garage yard, that would be helpful…"

"You finally got here, Blakey?" Vale jeered across the yard. "It's a good job there are decent citizens like me ready to do your job for you, isn't it?"

"Mr Vale," Blake said, smiling and striding over to him. "Always grateful to conscientious citizens and I'm so glad you're able to come and help us further with our enquiries."

Vale's face fell. "What?"

"I just need you to come with me and make a statement," Blake said, keeping his smile fixed. "You even get to ride in a police car. We'll do the lights for you if you want. Shall we go?"

"Am I being arrested?" Vale said, glancing around at the journalists. "There's gratitude for you. I thought you liked help from members of the public. That's what you used to say on Searchlight, anyway…"

"We aren't arresting you, but we do need to take a statement," Blake said. "And the best place to do that would be over at the station. I need to get the facts from you as soon as possible, while it's fresh in your memory."

"What if I don't want to?"

Blake shook his head. "If you have some other place you have to be then we can arrange a time to meet…"

"I've got a dental appointment," Vale said. "In half an hour."

"Really? So you were just squeezing a bit of amateur sleuthing in before you went for your check up?"

"Nothing wrong with that, is there?"

"Which dentist?" Kath said, wearily.

"What?"

"Which dentist?" she said again.

"O'Reilly in Prenton..."

Kath rolled her eyes. "You got a car?"

"No... no... I..."

"Then you've missed your appointment, sunshine. Come on. Tell you what, you can have a chat with us and then we'll drive you down to the dentists and explain what a hero you are. They'll probably give you a free scale and polish on the strength of that."

Blake watched in mute awe as Vale followed Kath meekly to the car. The journalists turned to him. "So, Detective Blake. Is this case closed?"

"Is it true that members of the family are under suspicion?"

"Can you comment on this latest discovery?"

Blake just raised his hands and shooed the journalists back off the yard without comment. Then, leaving a couple of uniformed officers, he went back to the garage and got a constable to raise the door.

He recognised the Constable as Mark Robertson, an experienced officer who had a keen eye and a level head. "What do you reckon, Mark?"

Blake said, staring into the bare garage.

Constable Robertson peered into the space. "Looks empty, sir. Apart from the shelving at the back. Without being gross, if a little girl had been trapped in there for a few days, there would be an unholy mess. There's no food or water."

"My thoughts exactly. Were you here first?"

Robertson nodded. "I was," he said.

"The little girl. What condition was she in?"

"A little dazed and tearful. But otherwise fine. Come to think of it, sir, she didn't look like she'd spent three or four days locked in there. Her clothes were clean."

"CSI on their way?"

Mark nodded. "Any minute, I reckon."

"I bet you a tenner they don't find any trace of Florence Percival in that garage. I'm going to have a chat with Mr Vale."

*****

Tasha Cook watched in amazement as Florence Percival stood obediently in the side ward while a doctor and a nurse took swabs and changed her clothes, folding and bagging them carefully. She'd hardly said a word since Ian Vale had found her. Tasha had teased a name out of the solemn little girl and made her smile a couple of times but that was it. Florence had remained sphinxlike throughout. Tasha watched as the items were passed carefully like holy relics to a Crime Scene Investigator and then her brow creased when she saw the bag containing a pair of knickers. She pulled out her phone and called Blake. The phone went to voicemail, so she left a quick message, her attention drawn by a commotion down the corridor. Sam Percival raced towards her. "Where is she? Where's Flossy?"

Tasha held up her hand. "She's fine, Mrs Percival. The doctors are just taking some samples and swabs. She won't be a minute…"

Sam's red-rimmed eyes widened. "Swabs? Oh my God. My poor little girl…"

"She's fine, Sam," Tasha said, putting a gentle hand on her shoulder. "There's no apparent evidence of any kind of physical harm. We'll know more after the doctors have finished but she seems okay. She's just very quiet. Did you bring spare clothes?"

Sam sniffled up a sob and nodded. "Yes, I had to buy some. I couldn't go near Paul and that house. I hope they fit…" Her face crumpled again. "How could anyone do this to my little girl?"

"She's safe now. It's okay for you to take her home but we will need to interview her with a specialist officer tomorrow. You can be there, of course. Will you be going back to Birkenhead with her?"

Sam shook her head. "That place isn't home. I'll go to my mum and dad's. I never want to set foot in that house in Birkenhead Park again. We're going to start over, me and Flossy. Somewhere else."

"And what about Paul?" Tasha asked.

"Believe me, I want to be as far away as possible when Paul realises we've gone. I'm not sure what he'd do."

"Sam! Sam! Thank God!" Paul Percival's voice rang down the corridor as he hurried towards them. He put his arms out to hug Sam, but she pushed him away.

"Get away from me," she hissed.

"But Sam, I got here as soon as I could. Isn't it great news? Flossy's safe. We can bring her home."

"No," Sam said. "We're not going home. I'm taking her to my mum and dad's..."

Tasha watched as the muscles on Paul Percival's face struggled to keep his expression neutral. "I don't think that would be wise, do you? It's not very private there. All the neighbours gawking at you."

"We can live with that. At least we'll be safe," Sam said. "Now I want you to leave."

Paul folded his arms. "I have just as much right to be here as you. I demand to see my daughter."

"With the greatest respect," Tasha said, raising a hand, "I think Florence has been through enough for one day and doesn't need to see her parents having a stand-up row. Now, Sam, you need to go in there and help your daughter get changed. Mr Percival, you can go in but we need to keep things calm for Florence. She's been through a lot."

Paul Percival glared through the window at his wife as she helped Florence get her T-shirt on. "So have I," he muttered. "That woman is insane, do you know that?"

"We have no official evidence of that, Mr Percival. Just your say so…"

"The clinic's view doesn't count for anything, then?" Percival said, coldly. "Have you spoken to Dr Gillespie?"

"One of our officers and a social worker spoke to a therapist who has worked closely with Sam for some time. To be frank, Mr Percival, she was puzzled as to why Sam hadn't left six months ago."

Percival glared at Tasha. "That child is mine. Not hers." He turned and stalked away. Tasha watched with a sickly, uneasy feeling as he disappeared down the corridor.

*****

There were times when Kinnear puzzled over

285

his role in the force. If ever CCTV needed looking through, it felt like he was the go-to man. He wondered what it was that made senior officers look at him and think, 'watching television!' He sneaked another biscuit off the plate that Marge, the receptionist from downstairs had rescued from a meeting room. Often, she would appear at Kinnear's desk with offerings from various top level meetings. A big plate with a few sad, left behind, ham sandwiches and a bit of wilted salad on the side would appear. Or she'd bring some wedges of cake or, on a good day, a few Danish pastries from an early morning meeting. Usually it was biscuits. Quite why Marge brought them to Kinnear was another of life's mysteries. The last thing anyone would think if they looked at him was, 'needs more biscuits.'

He crunched, absent-mindedly as he looked through the speeded-up CCTV footage that Blake had brought back. It was a series of cars pulling up at a house across the road from the owner of the camera. Kinnear thought it a bit odd that the man had it set so high. It caught the image of his driveway and his car but it mainly seemed focused on Geri Sharpe's house. Kinnear thought that maybe it was like a Freudian slip, a comment that revealed the unconscious desires or feelings of the commentator. Maybe Mr Ormand angled his camera so high because secretly, he was obsessed with Geri Sharpe and envious of those men who were brave enough to knock on her door.

Car after car zoomed to the kerb, doors opened and men in baseball caps or without hats, bald men and hairy men, tall and short, fat and thin, all went to the front door. Kinnear saw a pattern of men, too, regulars who called every Tuesday. Not all would be clients, of course. Some would be family members or friends. There were quite a few older men shuffling to the door, looking around warily as though they might be caught visiting. Watching this speeded up procession became somewhat tedious and Kinnear found himself humming the Benny Hill theme under his breath. More cars pulled up. Kinnear began to imagine the high-speed shenanigans going on off screen and smirked to himself. Then he stopped. He rewound the film. A car pulled up and someone got out. Someone he didn't expect at all.

*****

Matty Cavanagh sat at his desk as he normally did, feet up, swivelling back and forth on his chair. It drove Blake demented at the best of times. But right now, Blake wanted to tell him to sit up and pay attention. He was meant to be searching for Laura. How did he get away with it? If someone told him that Cavanagh played video games all day on his work computer, Blake would have half believed them. Only half believed because Cavanagh did get results and senior management seemed to like him. Blake couldn't shake the feeling that DS Bobby Dirkin did all the heavy lifting, though.

"So, my mate down at the car hire office reckons that the top end cars like the BMWs have GPS tags on them," Dirkin said, handing Blake a piece of paper. "He checked for us and it looks like your girlfriend's car is parked in a country house in North Wales somewhere between Mostyn and Pen-y-ffordd."

"Pennyforth, Bobby," Cavanagh said, emphasising the 'TH' sound at the end of the word. "That double 'd' in Welsh is a 'th.'"

Blake looked at the slip of paper with an address and postcode on it. "So, what are we waiting for?"

"You know as well as I that we can't just go charging over there, banging on the door, Will," Cavanagh said, pulling a pained face.

"Last time she was seen, Laura was alive and well, driving a car with a passenger. We've no reason to believe she's been abducted," Dirkin said.

"The blood outside her front door belonged to Terry Ford, an ex-bouncer, he's been done for a few drug offences, affray, we know he works for Thorpe," Cavanagh said. "I don't think we can take it any further, can we Bobby?"

"No, boss," Dirkin said. "And we can't tell you the address, either, Will. I mean, what if you were to get that address and go over there?" Dirkin shook his head.

Blake pursed his lips and looked at the address again. "Thanks, lads," he said and turned, almost running into Kinnear.

"Sorry, but I've got something you really need to see…"

Blake clutched the paper that Dirkin had given him, in his fist. "Can it wait?"

"No, sir, I don't think it can," Kinnear said.

CHAPTER 37

He was just as she remembered him. Tall, good-looking, with a mane of raven black hair. He'd grown a beard and had been working out too, it appeared, but apart from that it was the same old Kyle Quinlan.

"Hi Laura, did you miss me?"

Laura hesitated, wondering whether to try and run. "Not really," she said at last. She turned to Nick. "Okay, you can take me home now."

"You aren't going anywhere, Laura," Kyle said. "Not yet anyway."

Laura folded her arms. "You think we've got anything to discuss? You and I are finished, Kyle."

"I never assumed anything else, after what you did to me," Kyle said. His voice was mild, even jovial but there was an undertone of accusation in it.

"After the dog's life I got, Kyle Quinlan, I reckon I deserved some compensation. You thought I'd just let you get away with that? All those beatings?" She turned to Nick. "Did he tell you about how he knocked me about? Even put me in hospital once."

Quinlan winced. "I know what I did, Laura and I'm not proud of it, but I can't undo the past. You can't say that you didn't lay a finger on me. I've still got a metal plate in my cheek to prove it. Every time I go through customs, it's a little reminder of you."

Laura snorted. "Sweet."

"When you stole that money from me, Thorpe wanted my head on a pole, which is exactly what you thought would happen, right?"

"Maybe," Laura muttered. "No more than you deserved."

"But it was the best thing that ever happened to me. I ran for it. I left the country. I'd stashed away a few grand of my own, so I went to America. I've been working for a big outfit down in New Mexico. It was tough and I took a lot of knocks, nearly died a few times too. But it changed me. Made me stronger."

"Am I meant to be impressed by this speech?"

Quinlan shook his head. "You know, at one point, I found myself kneeling in the desert with a gun to the back of my head and I thought, 'this is it. I'm done.' And I swore that if I got out of that fix, I'd come back home and stop running."

"So you took the money from where I hid it."

"Half the money, Laura," Quinlan said, grinning. "You already took half for yourself, didn't you?"

Laura felt her face reddening. "What if I did? Like I said, it's less than I'm owed for the shit I had to put up with. All the money in the world wouldn't compensate for that."

Quinlan grinned. "Perhaps. And the cat's out the bag now, isn't it? I have the other half of the money and Thorpe is scouring the Wirral and Liverpool looking for you. You can't go back."

"Well, thanks for that, too. If you'd just left things as they were, I'd be perfectly happy, now..."

"And do you have a right to be perfectly happy? Shacked up with your big brave policeman to protect you? Things were unravelling the moment Josh Gambles opened his big mouth about me and set the police on you. Oh, yeah, I know all about that. I have my eyes and ears peeled. But do you think that's going to go away? Gambles will keep agitating. He's obsessed with your boyfriend. He won't rest until he's destroyed both of you."

"We can handle Gambles," Laura said but she couldn't keep the quaver of uncertainty out of her voice.

"I'm sure you'll do your best to ignore him and get on with your life, but he'll keep on intruding. Making accusations. He has quite a following now, after his atrocities. You'd be amazed how many sick fucks there are out there just ready to do his bidding. Each one of them will be digging. And what they'll find is the truth."

"They won't find anything. You took it."

"But eventually, somebody will decide that it's worth doing a bit of forensic accounting to answer the puzzle of why Laura Quinlan..."

"Vexley."

"Okay, why Laura Vexley, part time worker and volunteer at a cat's home can live on next to no wages. It's all going to come tumbling down around your ears and then imagine the look on Will Blake's face, Laura. What is he going to think?"

"That's not fair."

"I tell you what isn't fair; leading a man into thinking you're one thing when you're not. That's not fair. Will Blake thinks you're a wronged woman, someone who has had a chequered life but has come out a better person..."

"And I haven't?"

"No. You're tough, independent, yes, but you'd never fit in with his life. You're from the wrong side. Always will be."

"No. I'm not."

Quinlan held up his hands. "Fair enough. Then

I'm going to make you an offer, Laura, for old times' sake. And you'd better think hard before you decide."

*****

Kinnear's hand trembled slightly with excitement as he clicked the mouse to start the CCTV footage. "I was just looking through and it's all middle-aged blokes coming and going, if you pardon the pun…"

"Okay, okay, Kinnear. Just calm yourself and tell me what you've found." Blake just wanted to jump in the car and drive over to Wales. He could be there in an hour or so and he'd know if Laura was safe, then. Maybe he'd get some answers, too.

"Wait for it… there!" A dark saloon slipped up to the kerb outside Geri's house and an old couple got out. Kinnear froze the shot.

"Jeez," Blake said. "What are Xanthe and Roland Percival doing visiting Geri Sharpe?"

"I know. Weird, right?"

"No," Blake said, stuffing the slip of paper with the address on it into his pocket. "It all makes sense. Ian Vale is giving his statement downstairs. I'll have a word with him and then pay a visit to the Percivals and find out exactly what they've been up to. I suspect nothing good."

CHAPTER 38

Ian Vale sprawled in his seat, sipping a coffee, a stupid grin spread across his stubbly face. Kath sat opposite him, leafing through a file. Blake came into the room and sat down across the table from him. "Sorry to keep you waiting, Mr Vale," he said. He just wanted to wipe the smile off Vale's face. "I had to check a few details. I hope you don't mind."

Ian Vale held up his free hand. "Happy to help, you know me."

"So can you just go through the events leading up to when you found Florence Percival in the garage?"

"Yeah, like I told the journalists, I was searching the area as a likely spot for Hill to have hidden the little girl and sure enough, I heard her calling out from inside. So I smashed the lock with a brick and got her out. She was in a right state. Must have been there for days, poor little kid..."

Blake looked over at Kath, who nodded. "Yeah, it sounds familiar, sir," she said turning to Vale and closing her file slowly. "Just tell me again how you came to find Florence Percival."

Ian Vale's smile flickered. "Well, like... I said... I was searching the area as a likely spot for Hill to have hidden the little girl and sure enough, I heard her calling out from inside there..."

"So you smashed the lock with a brick and got her out. She was in a right state. Must have been there for days, poor little kid..." Kath said. "Spooky..."

"What is?"

"How big was the brick you broke the lock with?" Blake said. "Was it a half brick or a complete one?"

"I-I dunno," Vale said. "What's going on here? Don't you believe me or something? Wait, it was a half brick. Yeah, a half brick."

"So what happened then?"

"I told you, she was in a right..."

"State, yeah, you've said that. What did she look like? Was she dirty? Mucky face? What made you think she'd been in the garage for days?"

"Well, she's been missing for days, hasn't she?"

"But, if you were locked in that garage for four days, what would you have to do? At the very least? Think about it."

Ian Vale stared down at the tabletop, his face a picture of concentration. "I suppose I'd have to go to the bog at some point..."

"Did you see any evidence that Florence had been? Any at all? You'd have to drink? Did Florence look dehydrated at all?"

"I dunno," Ian Vale said. "She must have been..."

"What were her first words when you opened the garage door?" Kath asked.

"She asked for her mum," Ian said. "But she didn't say much, to be honest. She was scared, poor kid."

"Do you know Roland Percival?"

Ian's eyes darted about the room. "No. Is he Florence's dad or something?" It was a feeble lie.

"He's Florence's grandfather. A bit of a thespian..."

Vale looked alarmed. "A what?"

"Likes acting. Helps at an amateur dramatics group over in Liverpool. What about Geri Sharpe?"

Vale shrugged. "Maybe. What's all this about?"

"Just answer the question. Do you know her or not?"

"Yeah, I know her. She's done a bit with the Tor-Paedo group..."

"Ah," Blake said, glancing at Kath. "The Tor-Paedo group."

"What's that meant to mean?"

Kath opened the file in front of her. "You were convicted of assault last year, weren't you? Assault on someone called Norman Carter…"

"Yeah, well he was a fucking nonce wasn't he? Deserved it."

"And you were criticised by the police for compromising an investigation against a prolific child molester the year before, weren't you?"

"So? We moved him on."

"So you'd say that your methods aren't really that orthodox. Many of these online vigilante groups only confront their targets and wait for the police. You delivered summary justice."

Vale shrugged. "They just get a slap on the wrist, don't they? Doesn't seem right. I'd hang 'em."

Blake raised an eyebrow and looked at Kath Cryer who blushed. "Okay, Ian, I'm going to ask you one more time and I want you to think very carefully about your answer because it's important. Do you know Roland Percival?"

"No," Vale said. "I told you. I've never heard of him."

"Okay," Blake said. "We'll leave it there. Arrest him for conspiracy to abduct a child. We'll interview him under caution when his brief arrives. You do have a solicitor, don't you, Mr Vale?"

*****

The case was bigger than she remembered, and Laura wondered how she'd managed to move it and bury it under the patio. It still smelt of the dank earth. The money lay inside, wrapped in plastic, row upon row of fifties. The other half of the haul.

"It's all there," Kyle Quinlan said, squatting beside it. He and Nick had dragged it from a cupboard and dumped it in front of her. "Must have been a logistical nightmare laundering it."

"It wasn't easy," Laura said. Banking the first half had been tricky and she'd lost a lot investing in barely legal businesses that folded.

"It'll be even harder this time because the authorities are suspicious, now," Quinlan said. "And so is Harry Thorpe. But I've got contacts here and abroad who can quickly get this money cleared for you."

She looked down at the cash. Once upon a time, she would have hugged Quinlan, grabbed a handful and thrown it in the air. Now, it didn't seem as appealing. It was part of a past she wanted to leave behind. "What are you suggesting, Kyle?"

"We can use it to build something big. You and I in business together as partners again."

"A criminal business?"

"That's what I do. It's who we are, Laura. We're

criminals but that's not a bad thing. It just means we don't take any shit. We're just braver than ordinary people."

"But I like being ordinary, Kyle. I like living in a small flat and going to work and coming home and having pets. I don't want to be a criminal."

"You already are," he said. "Anyway, you can spend the proceeds of the business any way you want. We can channel funds into a cat sanctuary or a donkey hospital. I don't care. It might even be a smart move."

"Thorpe would love us setting up in competition with him."

Kyle grinned. "Thorpe wouldn't be here to object one way or the other, would he?"

"You see? You talk about snuffing someone out as though they weren't a person with a life and feelings, and a family. I've never thought like that."

"Thorpe would kill you in a heartbeat if he had the chance and not even worry about it, you know that, right?"

"So, this is your offer? To join you in your criminal world. Are you mad? No, Kyle, take your money and disappear again. Things have changed and I'm not the same person anymore."

"That's a shame, Laura. Really it is because I'm not going to disappear again. I'm back for good."

"What are you talking about?"

"I've got plenty of money and I've already made contacts in this part of the world. I'm going to set up in business in this area. With or without you."

"And what about me?"

Kyle Quinlan leaned back in his chair and spread his arms. "I made you my offer. I think that was more than generous. But I can see that you've moved on, Laura. When you set me up and took Harry Thorpe's money, I had to run. Like I said, though, it was the making of me. If that hadn't happened, then I'd still be standing at his right shoulder, roughing up losers or maybe even doing a prison stretch for him. So I guess I kind of owe you."

"And how do you intend to show this warped sense of gratitude?"

Quinlan pursed his lips and steepled his fingers. "I'm going to give you a head start."

"What?"

"Here's a backpack," Quinlan said, pulling the bag from under the desk and slapping it down in front of him. "You can fill it with as much cash as you can and then go. Leave here and go as far away as possible."

"You want me to leave? A moment ago, you wanted me to be with you."

"If you won't be with me then you won't be with anyone. I could kill you right now but I'm giving you the same chance you gave me. Fill the bag and go."

"And what if I refuse?"

Kyle Quinlan sighed and opened a drawer. He pulled out a handgun, placing it heavily on the desktop. "I'll shoot you here and then go after that dozy boyfriend of yours. He won't know what's hit him. Of course, if you stay away from him, he'll be fine. So what's it to be?"

"Doesn't look like I have much choice, does it?" Laura said, snatching the bag from the desk. "You haven't changed one bit, Kyle Quinlan."

Quinlan just shrugged. "I'm giving you the same kind of chance you gave me. By the way, when I said I'm giving you a head start, I meant it. You've got twenty-four hours to get away from here, then Nick is going to come looking for you. You won't have Harry Thorpe to worry about for much longer, but I want you to know what it's like to be hunted. We'll be watching Blake, too. If he starts searching for you, we'll be right behind him. He'll lead us straight to you."

"You bastard," Laura hissed.

"What can I say? I'm just a jealous guy. The clock's ticking, Laura. Better grab as much of that cash as you can. What's left will be invested in my new enterprise on the Wirral."

CHAPTER 39

Roland Percival looked perplexed when Blake and Kath Cryer turned up at his door. He ushered them into the plush living room. "I didn't expect to see you again, Inspector, you've arrested that hideous Leonard Hill and Flossy is safe. I thought we were done with it…"

"Just a few loose ends to tie up, Mr Percival."

Percival cleared his throat. "Of course, yes, forgive me. Old age, you know. I'm sure I'm going senile. Maybe it's all this stress."

"Perhaps, Mr Percival. Your words strike me as odd, if you'll forgive me."

"You've lost me, Blake. What do you mean, my words are odd?"

"I mean, most people would refer to Florence being safe first and foremost. We reveal so much in our off-the-cuff remarks, don't you think?"

"I haven't a clue what you mean, Blake."

"Do you think Paul was with Tanya Ellman the night your daughter was murdered, Mr Percival?" Blake said, hoping to catch Percival off guard.

"What? Yes. Of course he was. She said so in

court, didn't she?"

"Yes, but we've had an interesting conversation with her that suggests that he wasn't with her until much later in the evening. And that you helped her learn her lines for court. Why did you do that if you thought your son was innocent?"

"It was all a long time ago," Percival said. "I don't really remember."

"You do know we're treating Brendan Dockley's death as murder, don't you?" Blake said, deliberately jumping from topic to topic to wrongfoot the man. "Does your son have a temper, Mr Percival?"

The blood drained from Percival's face. "Murder. Really? I-is Paul involved?"

"Is that a possibility?"

"No... I-I don't think so...oh no. It's all our fault. We should never have..."

"Inspector Blake, I didn't know you were here," Xanthe Percival said, entering the room. She glared at Roland. "You should have told me, darling."

"They are suggesting that Paul murdered poor Brendan..."

Xanthe Percival's face twitched a little at the news. "That's dreadful. I don't think Paul is capable of harming anyone, though, Inspector. How did Brendan die?"

"A blow to the back of the head, we suspect. His body was dumped in the lake in the lower park."

Again, the woman twitched at the mention of the lake. "And why do you suspect my son was responsible?"

"I never said that. I merely asked if your son had a temper. It was your husband who asked me if Paul was involved with Mr Dockley's death." Blake turned to Roland. "You started to say something about it being all your fault, Mr Percival. Can you explain what you mean?"

"My husband is prone to being a little melodramatic. We found Brendan the post. If it weren't for us, he'd be over in Liverpool still, instead of dead. I imagine that's what you meant, wasn't it, dear?"

Percival nodded silently, but he had a haunted look about him.

"A couple of other things, if you could help clear them up. Brendan's parents were convinced that the job you offered Brendan was an acting role. He told them he was playing a part and then suddenly it became a nannying post for which he wasn't qualified in any way. Can you explain that?"

Roland glanced at Xanthe who glared back. "I don't know what they thought the job was, but we were always clear that it would involve childcare," she said. "Obviously, what went on in

Brendan's head would be a mystery to me. Now if there's nothing else, Inspector..."

"There is one other thing I hoped you could clear up," Blake said, not standing up. "I wondered if you could explain what you were doing at Geri Sharpe's house last month."

"I don't know who you're talking about," Xanthe Percival said. "I think you've asked enough questions..."

Blake rubbed his forehead. "We have CCTV footage of you entering Geri Sharpe's house on three occasions last month, Mrs Percival. Both of you. Geri Sharpe is the woman who was having a sexual relationship with Leonard Hill and the woman he'd arranged to meet him at the park on the day that Florence disappeared. She's part of the Tor-Paedo vigilante group run by Ian Vale. I don't think I've even started to ask enough questions. Do you want to help me out?"

Xanthe Percival's mouth opened, and she sank onto the sofa. Roland Percival's shoulders slumped. "I'm so tired of this."

"Roland, don't you dare," Xanthe hissed.

"Oh, what's the point, Xanthe? Do you think these people are stupid? Like you think everyone else is stupid? D'you think their... their... forensics won't track us down? I told you it would never work and look, I was right."

"She was never taken, was she?" Blake said. "Brendan was just play acting in the park that morning. A little drama to catch everyone's attention and distract everyone. In fact Brendan had dropped Florence off with you that weekend. Everyone had their lines, you made sure of that, didn't you Mr Percival?"

Roland Percival glared at his wife who sat fuming, crushed up at one end of the sofa, her arms folded. "We never got over the murder of our daughter, Blake. Imagine how you'd feel if your child's killer walked free. You'd do anything to get justice. And the fact that he's in and out of prison for committing all kinds of atrocities doesn't make it any easier. Then Ian Vale approached us, asking if we were aware that Leonard Hill was back in the area."

"Was it his idea to set Hill up?"

"Leonard Hill has never paid for what he did to my daughter," Xanthe said, trembling with rage. "All we had to do was incriminate him, keep Flossy hidden here and then Ian could 'find' her in the garage and Hill would have been behind bars where he belonged."

"It was an elaborate plan, Mrs Percival. They usually fail. As your husband says, we're not stupid. So, did you pay Geri Sharpe to bring you a used condom after one of her sessions with Leonard Hill? And you actually rubbed that into a pair of Florence's knickers?"

Roland Percival put his head in his hands. "Oh, God."

"It was a moment's work. Distasteful, unpleasant, but I wore Marigold gloves," Xanthe Percival said, holding her chin up. "Nothing compared to the depravity he envisaged for my daughter. As for payment. We might have covered her expenses but she was glad to do it, once she knew what kind of a man Hill was."

"So she took the Jiffy bag with the knickers, a lock of Florence's hair which you took when she had her hair cut recently and the tissues, presumably used to staunch a cut knee or something and she put that under Hill's mattress."

"Yes. We wanted her to scatter the things around the house, but it seems like she panicked and stuffed them in the guest room while Hill was in the toilet," Roland said. "Ridiculous to think it could have worked."

Blake nodded. "If it's any consolation, it was your care for Florence that gave you away."

Xanthe looked confused. "What do you mean?"

"Unless Florence was wearing two pairs of knickers when she was abducted, there was no way she would have a nice clean fresh pair. Also, you hadn't considered what the inside of that garage would look like if a small child had been kept in there for four days. I mean, Imagine the filth for a start."

Xanthe's mouth tightened and Blake thought he could hear her teeth crack.

"The text messages were a stroke of genius, though," he continued. "She must have sent them when he was in the bathroom too and then looked at them on Hill's phone so that they didn't show as new. That made it look like he had time to harm Florence. Even if he'd seen the messages, the worst he would do was delete them."

"It was too elaborate and unnecessary," Roland said, wearily. "But Xanthe has held that grudge for twenty years. She wouldn't let it go."

"The trouble with you is you've no backbone," Xanthe spat. "Hill deserved it. How can you just accept that the killer of your own flesh and blood is walking free?"

"Because I was never convinced, in my heart of hearts, that Hill did kill Undine, and neither were you, Xanthe," Roland sighed, shaking his head. "We've lied to ourselves all these years. Otherwise we'd have gone to the police with our suspicions about Paul and Undine."

"So you covered up for Paul and put pressure on Tanya Ellman even though you suspected your son was guilty of drowning your daughter?"

Roland Percival looked tormented. "And what was I to do? Lose both children? Paul was all I had left. All my hopes and aspirations wrapped up in that one boy. Besides I wasn't certain he'd had a hand in Undine's death."

"It was Leonard Hill," Xanthe sobbed.

"It was only when Flossy came on the scene that we realised what a dangerous person our own son was. Xanthe, you've seen how Paul treats Samantha, how he looks at Flossy with that cold detachment. The same way he used to look at Undine."

Tears spilled down Xanthe Percival's cheeks and she trembled with rage. "That's ridiculous... no..."

"You built up a hatred of Leonard Hill to smother our fear of our own son," Roland said. He sighed and looked out of the window. "So, Mr Blake. What happens now?"

Blake paused, trying to gather his thoughts. "We'll have to arrest you and take you down to the station," he said. "We'll take statements, gather more evidence. It'll be up to the Crown Prosecution Service and maybe the courts to decide what happens then."

"And what about Paul?" Roland said. "Do you think he killed Brendan?"

Blake shrugged. "Do you?"

Roland stared at Blake, concerned etched across his wrinkled face. "Inspector, if I were you, I'd find my son quickly and bring him in. When he finds out about this, he'll be a danger to us all."

CHAPTER 40

Paul Percival crouched behind a low wall and watched as Tasha Cook escorted Sam Percival and Florence into Sam's parents' house. Mr Hughes, clutching a small Yorkie in his big meaty hands had to step back to let them in. Paul clenched his teeth and he could feel the blood pulsing around his temples. "Bastards," he hissed. *His* wife, *his* daughter being taken away from him without any consultation or discussion. Even Tasha Cook had swapped sides. She was meant to be *his* Family Liaison Officer when this all kicked off. The door clicked shut, leaving Paul crouched in the dark, empty street.

Paul couldn't forget the look in Cook's eyes at the hospital, when she told him to go home. A thinly veiled distain. It was Sam who had poisoned everyone's mind against him. She'd stolen his daughter from him and told them lies about him. It wouldn't surprise him if she hadn't planned it all in the first place.

Paul caught his breath. He stood up and had to steady himself against the wall for a moment as the full realisation hit him. She had planned all this. Dockley must have been working with her all the time. He could easily have hidden

Flossy and waited for Samantha to escape from the clinic and come and get her. Sam knew Paul well enough to realise that he'd catch on and interrogate Dockley. Maybe she'd even factored in that Paul might get violent if Dockley provoked him enough. That would weigh against him in a family court, if they were battling for custody, wouldn't it? It was all so clear now. "The conniving bitch," Paul muttered under his breath. To think, he'd taken her away from all this squalor and set her up in a beautiful house, given her a gorgeous daughter and she threw it all back in his face. No, it was worse than that, she'd actively plotted against him. The evidence was there.

Watching the upstairs windows flick on in the house, Paul considered his options. Right then, he felt like stuffing a petrol-soaked rag through the letter box and setting the whole house on fire. But he did what he'd done when Dockley had died, he stifled the rage and panic and let ice fill his veins. Sam wasn't going anywhere. Tasha Cook would come out soon and Paul didn't want to be seen hanging round here. He would be back in the morning and deal with Sam then.

*****

Blake stood outside the old house, rain slicking his hair to his scalp and trickling down his neck. He hadn't expected to find Laura here. Once he'd got the slip of paper from Dirkin and Cavanagh, he wanted nothing more than to jump into his car and race over to North Wales to catch her but duty had stopped him. He cursed himself. Kath could have confronted the Percival's with the truth and he could have been over here but, no, he had to do everything himself.

The house was dark and locked with no sign of anyone inside. He'd had a job getting through the perimeter wall and had to leave his car parked down on the road. After a bit of snooping around in the shadows, tripping over and cursing, Blake had found a gap in the defences and squeezed through.

He had searched around the outside of the house, using his phone as a torch and found fresh food scraps and packaging in the bin. There was an old case, covered in dirt and he wondered if that had come from under the patio behind Laura's old house. Nobody moved around inside and there were no cars parked on the gravel drive.

It occurred to Blake that Laura may be inside, unconscious or worse. Pressing his face against the glass, he peered through the windows, but could see nothing more than the shadowy out-lines of the furniture. Even though the house stood on the side of a bleak hill, in its own grounds, Blake glanced around to see if anyone was watching him and then jabbed his elbow through the front door window. The old glass tinkled to the floor inside and he let himself in.

The cold house smelt damp, but a hint of cooking lingered in the air. Some cut flowers stood proud and fresh in a vase by the door. Someone had been here very recently. He stepped into the nearest room and switched the light on, dazzling himself for a moment. A long, polished mahogany dining table surrounded by matching chairs filled this room. Place mats lay in front of each chair but no cutlery. The room looked forlorn and empty. Blake switched the light off and went back into the hall. His phone began to buzz. It was a number he didn't recognise but he answered, standing in the darkness once more.

"Will? It's me. Laura."

"My God, Laura, where have you been? Are you okay? I was worried sick. The blood outside your door and the case. What's going on?"

"Will, just listen. I'm okay and I'm safe…"

"Great. Where are you? I'll come and get you…"

"No. I'm sorry, I can't explain but I'm going to have to go away for a while."

"What? Laura, what are you on about? Listen, if you're in trouble, we can work it out. I can help."

"No, Will, you can't. I just need to get away for a while and let things cool down…"

"What things? What's going on? Was it to do with the digging at the back of your old house? Is it something to do with Kyle Quinlan? I'm at the house in North Wales, I tracked you down..."

Laura gave a short, sad laugh. "Ever the policeman, Will. The less you know, the better. That way you won't come searching for me and stir things up."

"Honestly, Laura, Cavanagh doesn't have a clue what was in that hole. And he certainly hasn't linked it to you..."

"And it's best it stays that way. Keep Cavanagh in blissful ignorance. But if I stay that won't happen."

"I'll keep looking for you. I won't rest..."

"Just stop, Will. Listen. I love you. I loved what we had but if I stay, it'll never work. That's all I can say. It's better that I just leave. Maybe one day, I can come back. This isn't your fault, Will but it's also something you can't fix. So please don't try."

"It's Thorpe, isn't it? He's after you because of the money Kyle Quinlan stole," Blake said. "I know all about it, Laura... and I don't care. You aren't the same person, you've changed."

There was a pause and Blake thought he heard Laura sniffling up tears. "It wasn't Kyle who stole that money from Thorpe. It was me. Kyle was transporting it and I beat him up and stole it. He left rather than admit what had happened. But those chickens have come home to roost. I'm sorry. I can't stay. Don't try and find me."

"Laura! Laura wait…" Blake stared at the phone and then tried to dial the number back, but it was dead.

*****

There was too much noise in the custody suite reception as Leonard Hill tried to count his change. He was certain that he'd had five pounds forty-seven in loose change and now he could only see five forty. A drunk young man in a baseball cap kept singing and it put Leonard off. His other belongings had been intact but he was damned if he was going to let them steal money off him. Just along the counter from him, an old homeless man leaned his head on the cold surface. "I'm not guilty, I'm not guilty," he said, over and over again. A uniformed officer was trying to get some sense out of the old man. Leonard gave the young singer a sidelong glance and shook his head, returning to his money.

"Are you ready to sign for your belongings, Mr Hill?" the woman behind the counter said.

"No. There's some missing." There'd been no apology, no explanation. Just a 'more facts have come to light. You can go home. We'll be in touch.' Leonard had asked them about the DNA evidence in his house and how it had got there but they just said that they 'weren't at liberty to disclose any more information at this time.'

"What's missing?" the woman behind the counter said.

"Seven pence. Someone's stolen it... ah, no, wait.. here it is..."

He was at liberty and about time, too. He knew who was responsible for this, that bloody Geri Sharpe. She'd led him on and then stitched him up good and proper. Clearly, they'd spoken to her. But she was just a puppet and he knew who was pulling the strings.

"When do I get my laptop back?" he asked.

The woman shrugged. "I don't know, Mr Hill," she said, frostily. "You'll need to speak to the investigating officer about that."

The drunk singer started up again, the off-key notes drilling into his head. Leonard gritted his teeth. It would be hard to relax as long as the police had his laptop. He was good with computers and he'd buried his photos and videos deep but they weren't impossible to find.

"I need it for work, you see," he lied. He was exhausted but knew what would welcome him when he got home. After being searched thoroughly and things turned over, cupboards and drawers left open, his house would be a mess outside and in. Everything would be in the wrong place. The whole house would feel like it had been picked up and shaken. At least tidying up would keep him occupied while he worked out what he was going to do about Geri Sharpe.

That's what he'd thought, anyway. But then someone called his name and he turned to see Detective Inspector Kath Cryer strutting towards him. In his opinion, she was too big a woman to be wearing those heels. Her feet looked like pig's trotters squashed into the shoes. He'd be glad to see the back of her.

"Well, I didn't expect you, detective," Hill said, trying to sound brave but his voice shook. "Come to say goodbye?"

"No," Cryer said, giving a pained smile. Her eyes looked dead and flat.

"So what can I do for you?"

"What do you think, Leonard?"

"I'm rubbish at guessing games, I don't know."

"We've just had an email from the tech people who were having a look at your laptop, Leonard. We've got some images that are quite… unpleasant. Would you mind coming back to the interview room and explaining how they ended up on your computer?"

"Do I have to?"

Cryer shook her head. "No, I can arrest you here and now for having indecent images of children on your laptop if you want."

"No," he said in a low voice. "No, I don't want that." Hill looked at the floor. Tears blurred his vision. It was over and he'd been caught again and the only person he could blame this time was himself.

CHAPTER 41

The red spots on Martin's cheeks were a rare sign. It meant that he'd gone from 'annoyed' to 'about to tear a new hole in you verbally' but was restraining himself. Blake wondered if the Superintendent was going to have some kind of stroke.

"So, let me get this straight," Martin said, massaging the bridge of his nose, pushing his glasses onto his furrowed forehead... "It wasn't Leonard Hill who kidnapped Florence Percival but her own grandparents..."

"And a couple from an online vigilante group," Blake said, trying not to relish Martin's discomfort. "They did it to frame Hill, who Roland and Xanthe Percival mistakenly believed had killed their daughter twenty years ago."

"Mistakenly," Martin said.

"Roland Percival confessed to helping Tanya Ellman fabricate an alibi for Paul Percival. It looks to me like Paul murdered his own sister but we have no concrete evidence."

Martin pulled his reading glasses off. "No concrete evidence. It's never simple with you, is it, Will? We've got a press conference lined up this morning and I was all ready to step out there and tell them that we'd found the girl, arrested the paedophile and patted a conscientious member of the public on the head. But no. Instead I come in this morning to find we're charging the entire Percival family and the local hero who found the girl!"

Blake scratched the back of his head like he was trying to solve a conundrum for the Superintendent. "Yes, it's not really that straightforward. I suspect Paul Percival also killed Brendan Dockley, whether deliberately or in some kind of scuffle, I'm not sure."

"Any evidence?"

"Dockley's jumper was embedded with all kinds of food detritus…"

"Food?"

"Yeah, like you'd find at the bottom of most domestic freezers, breadcrumbs, frozen peas that kind of thing. The pathologist believes Dockley's body spent some time in a freezer, which suggests he could have been killed at Paul Percival's house and dumped in a freezer. It's ground for a warrant, at least. I'm pretty sure we'll find matching food fragments in Percival's freezer and maybe some other traces of Dockley."

Martin sighed. "I suppose it's just going to be another one of those days. At least the girl is safe. That's all they need to know. We can keep other names under wraps for now."

"Can I make a suggestion, sir? How about giving Kath Cryer another round in front of the cameras. I mean you're always saying that my old TV persona clouds the issue, and she was present at the last one."

Martin stared at Blake suspiciously. "I thought you'd be eager to get back in front of the cameras, Will."

"No sir. As I keep telling you, I've had more than my fill of limelight. If Kath's presence at the news conference keeps things low key, then I'm all for it."

"I see. Fair enough. Get Kath in and I'll go through the details with her," Martin said, leaning back. A weight seemed to have lifted from his shoulders.

"I'll crack on, then," Blake said. "I'm pretty sure Ian Vale will crumble once he realises that the Percivals have dropped him in it."

*****

Ian Vale arrived at the interview rooms with Geri Sharpe more penitent than Blake could have hoped for. There was none of his previous swagger as he sat hunched at the interview table. "I want to come clean," he said. "I did help the Percivals to frame Leonard Hill but it wasn't my idea."

"So how did you even come to be speaking to the Percivals in the first place?"

"I knew about Leonard Hill," Vale said. "A mate of mine reckoned he'd caught him trying to pick up his daughter after school. He recognised him as a local fella and warned him off. But I reckoned we could catch him out. So I did a bit of research and the Undine Percival case had been all over the papers twenty years ago. It soon came up online."

"That still doesn't explain why you approached the Percivals if you had no intention of framing Hill," Blake said.

"I went to see them to get some background," Vale said. He reddened a little. "I thought they might fund our Facebook group, too. It costs money tracking these paedos down. They're clever. You need some decent kit."

"I can't imagine your request for funds went down too well," Blake said. "I mean, the Percivals don't look like the most hi-tech couple…"

"You'd be wrong, though," Vale said. "Once I showed them what we did, they were mad keen. It was that Xanthe who had the idea. She saw Geri confronting that other paedo on the Facebook page and asked who she was. Then she asked how far she'd go to put a pervert like Hill in prison."

"Those were her exact words?"

Vale nodded. "Yeah. I was a bit shocked, to be honest. I mean, a respectable old lady like that…"

"So what did you get out of this?"

"One less paedo on the streets?" Vale said, with a shrug. "I was hoping if we went along with it, the Percivals might stump up a bit more cash for the cause, you know. People like Leonard Hill are a menace. They're always up to no good, aren't they? It's no skin off my nose if he's banged up for something he didn't do. Anyway, he got away with killing that poor little disabled kid, didn't he?"

"No, Mr Vale, he was found guilty of manslaughter," Blake said. "So, what was your role?"

"All I had to do was introduce Geri and the Percivals and then 'find' Florence at the end of it all. It was simple, really. Except it didn't work." He looked a bit crestfallen. "It was all a bit complicated, really, wasn't it?"

"I'd have said so. What was Roland Percival's take on things?"

Vale scratched his chin. "I'd say he was less enthusiastic. I remember him saying something about letting sleeping dogs lie or something."

"What d'you think he meant by that?"

"I'm not sure but they'd mentioned their son, Paul. For some reason, Roland didn't want him to be in on it. He seemed a bit scared of him. They both did."

*****

Geri Sharpe chewed at her nails and wouldn't meet Kath's gaze across the table. Vikki Chinn sat next to her, giving Sharpe time to compose herself. "It's all right for him," she said. "All he did was pretend to find Florence at the end of it all. He didn't have to shag bloody Leonard Hill, did he? It's me that'll get in trouble."

"I'm sure Ian will be held just as responsible as you…"

"And those bloody stuck-up Percivals. It was their stupid idea!"

"Let's focus on what you know and see if we can't get to the truth," Vikki said. "So, when did you first know of the plan to frame Leonard Hill?"

"Ian told me…"

"Ian Vale?"

"Yeah, who else? He told me that there was this paedo who'd murdered a disabled kid twenty years ago and got away with it. I said he should be in prison and Ian said it was funny I should say that because that's what Tor-Paedo were going to do. Put him in prison."

"And what did you think of that?"

"I thought, yeah, let's do it. I didn't realise then that I'd have to shag the filthy bastard, did I? That only came up later when Xanthe and Roland came round to my house with Ian."

"What did they say?"

Geri Sharpe winced and pulled a face. "they said I had to get a sample. Of his... you know..."

"His semen," Kath Cryer said, watching her squirm.

"Yeah. Ian had been hunting Hill online and found him easily enough. He was in loads of groups and on all the sites, too. So I gave him the nod..."

"The nod?" Vikki said.

"Yeah, you know, the come on. I asked if he fancied a good time. And he said yeah."

"Romantic," Kath muttered. "So how did you get the sample?"

"How d'you think? I nicked a condom after we'd finished. He didn't even notice it was gone. I don't think he could believe his luck. Ian took the condom to Xanthe and Roland who smeared the knickers." Geri pulled a face. "That's so fucked up isn't it?""

"Just going back, why did you arrange to meet him at the park? Surely that's the last place he'd want to go with his history."

"Ian said that we needed to place him there a few times, so people remembered he'd been there when Florence went missing from nearby. To be honest, I think he was so focused on the sex that he hardly thought about it."

"So you met Hill a few times more?"

"Yeah," Geri said, shivering. "Ian said I had to so he wasn't suspicious. It's all right for him, he wasn't the one getting poked by Hill. I've been with some mingers in my time, but Leonard Hill was just horrible. His breath stunk and his cold, clammy skin made me sick. I daren't even think of what he'd done before."

Vikki pulled a face, but Kath shrugged. "But you went back for more. All for the cause of putting Hill in prison. Very noble, Geri. How much did you charge the Percivals?"

Geri lifted her head up. "I'm not ashamed of that, they gave me five grand as a gift. Anyway. I was the one doing all the dirty work."

"It nearly worked. So what happened on the day Florence went missing?"

"I didn't go to the park. I dropped the kids off and went straight to his house. When he rang, I made up some story about the kids and said I'd meet him at the house. He got there about ten to nine or thereabouts and we went inside."

"And then?"

"I had the jiffy bag with the knickers, the bloody tissues and the hair. Once we'd done the deed, he always legged it to the toilet, so I had the chance to hide the things around the house but I had to do the texts asking where he was, too, so that took a bit more time and he came out of the bog early. So I panicked and just stuffed them under his mattress. Then I left. I didn't have anything more to do with Leonard Hill."

"When I came to talk to you, Geri," Kath said, "you said the same thing almost word for word..."

"That was Roland Percival. He gave me lines to learn. He said it was just like being in a play. You just had to remember your lines when the police asked you any questions. He said that concentrating on the lines would make me less nervous. Will I go to prison for this?"

Kath shrugged. "Dunno, Geri. It's not up to me. But next time, maybe leave the crime fighting up to the police, eh?"

CHAPTER 42

Sam Percival hadn't been too concerned when she first got off the train at James Street Station in Liverpool. It had just seemed like another morning. Sleepy-eyed commuters shuffled out of the huge lifts. Flossy sat in her pushchair and kicked her feet a few times, grazing people's legs. Sam tried to stop her but most of Flossy's victims just gave an indulgent smile.

It had been her idea to go over to Liverpool and talk to Detective Blake about what had happened. Tasha Cook, the family liaison officer, had offered to work with her at her mum and dad's house but Sam wanted to get out. Besides, she wanted to get some new clothes for herself and Florence before Paul realised that she was serious about leaving and cancelled her credit card.

It was only when she stepped out into the cold November light and felt the wind blowing up from the Pier Head that she stopped and glanced around her. Generally, Sam didn't subscribe to the idea of 'instinct' or 'gut feelings' but recent experiences had sharpened her awareness of her surroundings. Maybe it was the feeling of being trapped when she was in the clinic or hiding in a stolen car on the way down from Scotland. Whatever it was that made her hypervigilant, she couldn't escape the feeling that someone was watching her and she weaved through the crowds hurrying to work. And then she saw him.

Paul Percival stood glaring at her with red-rimmed eyes. She'd never seen him looking so dishevelled. His hair stuck out at all angles, and a few days' stubble greyed his chin and neck. His shirt and jacket looked crumpled. But it was the sheer malice in his eyes that disturbed her.

Ramming the pushchair through the crowds, Sam hurried on up the street. She ignored the shouts and complaints as she passed, and kept looking behind her. Her heart thumped against her ribs and she lost track of where she was going. All she wanted was to get away from the grim-faced man following her. Every time she glanced back, he was there, some distance away, slowly weaving his way towards her. Oblivious to what was happening, Florence squealed with excitement as Sam pushed faster. She wasn't sure where she was now, or where the Police HQ had gone. All she knew was that she was being chased.

Up ahead of her, Sam saw a sign for Liverpool Central Station and swerved the buggy into the shopping precinct that lead to the station gate. Pulling out her phone and the card Blake had given her at their last interview, Sam stabbed

Blake's number into the screen. Her fingers trembled and she cursed as she fluffed the number. She didn't have time for this. Paul was gaining on her.

*****

DC Andrew Kinnear glanced sidelong at the plate of biscuits that sat on his desk in the Major Incident room. Once again, Madge from the front desk had brought them up, leftovers from another meeting somewhere. Madge thought of Andrew straight away. "Why do middle-aged women always target me with biscuits?" he muttered. "And who the hell leaves a jammy dodger on its own on a plate of Nice biscuits?"

"Andrew," Blake said, striding into the office. Kinnear jumped, spraying crumbs across his desk.

"You okay?" he said.

"Yes, sir," Andrew croaked and took a swig of tea from his mug. "Just went down the wrong way."

"Nice."

Kinnear looked puzzled. "Sir?"

"Nice biscuits. They aren't really nice at all are they?"

Kinnear nodded, looking down at the plate. There were always more of the rectangular, sugar-coated ones with 'NICE' stamped into them left behind. "They're okay, I guess, sir," Kinnear said. "You couldn't stamp 'okay' across them though, could you? Not a great marketing ploy."

Blake took one and wolfed it down. "It's all they are, though, really. They're just okay." They stared at the plate in silence for a second or two. "You have to feel a bit sorry for them."

"The biscuits doomed to be left behind," Kinnear said.

Blake shook himself and slipped another biscuit from the plate. "They're nice when you're hungry, though."

Before Kinnear could answer, Blake's phone rang.

"Blake. Sam? What's wrong? Slow down. Stay calm. Where are you? Right, just find the nearest member of staff and tell them what's... Sam? Sam?" He slammed the phone down. "Get some officers down to Central Station, right away, Kinnear, then follow me there. Sam Percival's in danger."

*****

Central Station was just ten minutes' walk from Police HQ in Canning Place but as Blake ran, dodging around people, it seemed to get no nearer. Cars blared their horns as he sprinted across the road, narrowly dodging a bus. When he finally got to the entrance of the station, a police car was pulling up, lights flashing. Blake whipped out his warrant card.

"There's a woman down there being chased by her husband. He's a murder suspect and may be violent."

They ran through the shopping area to the ticket barrier where a member of Mersey Rail staff waved them through. A pushchair lay abandoned on its side at the top of the escalator. Blake took the escalator two steps at a time, just hoping he didn't lose balance and plummet down the steep flight of metal steps. At the bottom, he barrelled round onto the platform towards the screams that echoed in the tunnel.

A crowd gathered at the end of the platform. People were shouting, and some held their phones up, recording everything. Blake pushed his way forward as the officers followed him, telling people to move back up to the ticket area.

Paul Percival stood pressed against the wall at the end of the platform, on the edge where the tunnel opened into the boarding area. He had a knife near Sam's face. Florence huddled behind his legs, her eyes squeezed shut as though she was trying to block out what was going on. Clearly, he'd gone for Sam but passengers waiting for a train had challenged him and now there was a stand-off. Three burly men in bomber jackets and a Mersey Rail guard hovered just out of arms' reach of Paul, uncertain what to do next.

"Paul, are you okay?" Blake said, indicating to the men that they should fall back.

Paul sneered at Blake. "What? You care about me all of a sudden? Instead of this... this piece of work? Ha!"

"Your daughter was safe, Paul, that's all that matters. But she doesn't look too happy right now. You don't look very happy, either."

"I'm not," Paul said, spittle flecking his lips. "The ingratitude. That's what really grates on me. I dragged her out of the gutter. Gave her a child and a perfect house but, no, she wants more."

Sam whimpered and he tightened his grip on her neck.

"That must be annoying, Paul but you can re-build your life, can't you? You don't need her, do you?"

Paul froze for a second as he thought about what Blake had said. "No but she's betrayed me. She's going to take my child away from me. I have rights too, you know!"

"Of course you do, Paul," Blake said, keeping his voice level. "How about letting Flossy come over here to me?"

"No," Paul snapped, bringing the blade close to Sam's throat. "She's staying here. She's mine."

A breath of cold air ruffled Blake's hair. "A train's coming Paul. At least do me the favour of moving away from the tunnel entrance. You're too close, there. It's not safe."

"I don't owe you any favours, Blake," Paul hissed. "You've had it in for me from the moment we met. Berating me for not being upset enough about the disappearance of my daughter."

The breeze grew stronger and a distant rumble heralded the imminent arrival of the train. "Paul come away from the edge, please."

"Maybe I want to be here. Maybe I'll end it all and take this bitch with me," Paul yelled, tears of rage streaming down his cheeks. "Maybe I've killed before, Blake! What difference is one more going to make?"

Sam's eyes widened in horror and she lurched forward away from Paul as the roar of the train filled the tunnel. The world slowed down. Blake watched helplessly as Paul pivoted on one leg and Flossy suddenly sprang forward, pushing her dad to one side to get to her mum. Sam, grabbed Flossy and wrapped herself around her, rolling to safety across the platform. Paul's eyes widened as he almost cartwheeled off the platform into the path of the train that exploded into the tunnel with a shriek of brakes. A meaty thud accompanied the mist of red blood that spattered the front of the train and platform. Then Paul vanished under the train and it howled by, screeching to a halt a second later. Screams of horror replaced the sound of the brakes and, for a second, Blake tried to process what had just happened. He looked down and saw Sam huddled on the floor, hugging Florence who shuddered in her arms.

CHAPTER 43

The prison visiting room seemed restless today, as though everyone in there was agitated and argumentative. Maybe it was just the way Josh Gambles sat opposite Jeffrey Blake, twitching his leg and glancing around all the time. He didn't seem very interested in Jeff's news about Laura.

"I thought you'd be pleased with yourself," Jeff said. "After all, that's what all this was about, right? Splitting Will and Laura up. Making my brother's life a misery."

Gambles hissed impatiently. "Perhaps," he said. "The trouble with you, Jeffrey is you don't see the bigger picture."

"I'm sorry, I don't follow you."

"No, Jeffrey, you don't do you? I shouldn't blame you. I have my ear to the ground. Knowledge that you don't possess."

"Go on then," Jeff said. After being kidnapped by Harry Thorpe and coming so close to losing his life or being tortured, Jeff was a bit tired of Gambles' melodramatics. "Impress me with your superior knowledge."

"Something spooked Laura," Gambles said.

"Yes, probably me revealing her whereabouts to a *psycho* like Thorpe." Jeff had used the word deliberately, knowing that Gambles hated it.

"No. Something bigger. You see, I calculated that Laura would be alarmed at Thorpe knowing she was back in town, but he was small-time, really. The kind of person your brother could have dealt with easily. But for her to vanish like that suggests a bigger evil…"

"You just spoke of Harry Thorpe in the past tense," Jeff said, leaning forward and lowering his voice. "What bigger evil?"

"I think we'll be using the past tense about a lot of people soon, Jeffrey, if Kyle Quinlan is back in town."

*****

Blake sat in his kitchen and sipped at a mug of tea and stared morosely at Serafina and Charlie who lay huddled together in a dog basket that Ian Youde had bought. The cat glared back at Blake, just daring him to try and stroke Charlie. Ian Youde sat in a wooden rocking chair blowing into his own mug and appraising Blake.

"The little girl is safe, that's the main thing, Will," he said.

Blake nodded. "It was horrible, though, Ian. Percival just disappeared. I keep seeing his angry face, those furious eyes glaring at me and then bang. Gone..."

"Give it time, mate. Give it time. Will the force give you any counselling?"

Blake looked up at Youde. The man never ceased to surprise him. He seemed so tough and workmanlike on the outside, the kind of person who would dismiss any kind of therapy out of hand. And yet it seemed Blake had misjudged him again.

"Yeah," Blake said. "I dare say I could see someone if I needed to..."

"Worth having a chat if it's on your mind all the time. Just saying."

"Right. Maybe I will. I want to find Laura, before I do anything else, though."

"Any idea where she's gone?" Youde said, his letterbox mouth barely moving. For a moment, Blake wondered how on earth the man ate. Did he cut it up into strips and post it through?

"No," Blake said at last. "I went to the house, but the hire car had gone. Dropped back at the rental place by a big guy called Nick Duplicitous."

"That's never a real name."

"I'd have queried it but the young man at the car hire office seemed to have no problems with it. The man had all the relevant documents, too.

Maybe he just couldn't read his name properly."

"Kids these days," Ian muttered. "So what're you gonna do?"

"I don't know, Ian. She said she didn't want me to go looking for her. Laura wouldn't be happy if she thought I was chasing her."

"So you're gonna look for her then," Ian said with a grin.

"Jeez, Ian, who're you, my Mum? You know me so well. Yeah, of course. I might take some time off, see what I can turn up. Can't just leave it can I?"

They both paused for a moment to savour their tea and stare at the strange sight of the most oppositional cat in the world licking the ear of a Jack Russell puppy. "Maybe she's tenderising his ear before she eats it," Blake said.

Ian grinned. "I guess she'll miss Charlie, when he goes back to his owner."

"I don't think Charlie's going anywhere, mate."

Ian Youde's narrow, suspicious eyes widened for once. "What?"

"I never believed her for one minute. All that stuff about a friend called Chelsea. It was obvious to me that Charlie was Laura's all along."

Ian nodded. "That kind of makes sense. I mean, someone called Chelsea would be more likely to have a chihuahua or a pug called Chardonnay. Not a Jack called Charlie."

"Chardonnay?" Blake gave Youde a pained look. "Where did that come from? No, I think she left him for me to look after while she was away. Which will be a pain in the arse without a bit of day care..." Blake looked at Ian expectantly.

"Okay, okay," Youde said, cracking a rare smile. "I can take him out for a walk during the day." He paused. "You don't sound too cut up about Laura leaving, if you don't mind me saying so, Will..."

Blake shrugged. "If this had happened a few months ago, I think I'd be in pieces, but Laura taught me to face up to life and meet it head on. I wish she'd taken her own advice. Besides, Ian, I'm going to find her and bring her home. She shouldn't have to run away from anyone or anything. If she's done anything wrong, then she should face up to whatever she's done."

"Ever the copper, Will," Youde said, grinning. "Ever the copper."

ABOUT THE AUTHOR

Jon Mayhew lives on the Wirral with his family and has done all his life. A teacher for many years, he enjoys traditional music and plays regularly in ceilidh bands and sessions. Jon is also an award-winning author. His dark children's books are published by Bloomsbury.

Find out more at www.jemayhew.blogspot.com

Find JE Mayhew on Facebook and twitter.

Made in the USA
Las Vegas, NV
06 April 2021